ESCAPE *!*

DAVID EMIL HENDERSON

Also by David Emil Henderson:
MONTANA MIDNIGHT

Also From Pine Tree Arts:
SO BRAVE...SO QUIET...SO LONG!
An Anthology of Patriots
By Larry T. Bailey
(Proceeds to Rotary International)

Later version of this novel:
ESCAPE !

DEADLY DIVIDENDS

A NOVEL
DAVID EMIL HENDERSON

Pine Tree Arts
Penn Valley CA USA

Pine Tree Arts, P.O. Box 129
Penn Valley, California 95946
pinetreearts@gmail.com
Pine Tree Arts is the creative division of
Pine Tree Press of Penn Valley, California, USA.
pinetreepress@comcast.net

The characters, places, events, products, companies and policies, and all things in this book are fictitious or are used fictitiously. Any similarity to real events, companies, places, policies, products, or persons living or dead, is coincidental and not intended by the author.

Cover design and author photo: Pine Tree Arts
Print edition ISBN: 978-0-615-43714-9

*A later edition of this novel
is titled 'ESCAPE !'*

0 1 2 3 4 5 4 3 2 1 0

This book is for Darlene

Introduction

An Unreported Mystery

THE END OF THE COLD WAR supposedly allowed the United States to reallocate vast military assets to civilian purposes — the so-called "peace dividend."

Thirty miles north of Chicago, many suburbanites waited with great expectations after the 1993 closing of the century-old Fort Sheridan army base.

That base had been operating since 1887 on 632 magnificent acres adjoining Lake Michigan — property ripe for upscale commercial development, lakefront parks, all sorts of good things.

Yet, in all the years since 1993, the "dividend" dream has not fully materialized.

Why not?

This report begins two years after the base closure.

June 7, 1995; Approx. 8:45 A.M.

Chapter 1

THE ARCHITECT has faced other disputes with construction men, usually minor disagreements resolved with reason and compromise. Today, they were wanting to kill him.

There were three husky foremen, grimy with sweat, eyes shining with malice. Behind them, on densely vegetated land overlooking Lake Michigan, a brigade of heavy equipment was chewing the ground raw with tracks and trenches.

In voices as guttural as their machinery, the foremen demanded to know who the devil this architect was and what the hell kind of authority he had over them.

His name — Grey Harper — meant nothing to them. He was new, arriving from California to take charge. He wore a knitted tie over a checked shirt and a white hardhat. His eyes remained hidden behind aviator sunglasses.

Harper's clean hands made fewer motions than the others, and his voice stayed calm despite their caustic threats.

He repeated his orders to switch off the ignitions, to stop all work. He stood as solid as a statue in front of them.

The foremen finally turned away in disgust, scuffing the dirt with their work boots. Then they separated, striding toward different areas of the site, waving down the earthmovers and backhoes. The staccato bark of the engines died away. Within minutes, all activity had stopped.

Hiking toward the roadway, Grey Harper whipped off his hardhat, exposing dark hair sprinkled with silver. Approaching him was a black limousine, braving an atmosphere filled with dust. It pitched to a halt a few feet away.

From the back seat emerged a dark and wiry man in a tailored suit. He spoke angrily and jabbed a forefinger repeatedly against the architect's chest. Harper responded with a few quiet words and moved along to a silver Mercedes convertible. Within seconds, his car was skimming through a U-turn, disappearing into the speckled light and shadows of a forested lane.

The man from the limousine turned his attention to the construction site. Perched on bluffs overlooking Lake Michigan north of Chicago, it had been part of Fort Sheridan, one of the army's finest reservations. The base had survived a century of war, only to succumb to the specter of peace. This portion had been set for sixty million dollars of residential luxury — until the architect had stopped it all.

One disgruntled foreman tramped up to the sedan. "Mr. Munro, what about this? You gonna allow this shutdown?"

Munro frowned. "It seems I have no choice."

"God-damn it, we got twenty-eight men and sixteen..."

"I'll deal with it," Munro said. "Just take a breather."

"The hell you say. A breather? Until when?"

Munro squinted. "When I find out, I'll get back to you."

"Hell. Somebody oughta just shoot that son-of-a-bitch!"

Munro ignored the man and got into the limo. It rolled away, soon followed by a noisy fleet of vans and pickups.

After days of man-made thunder and quaking, the trees and fields re-settled into a primitive peace.

Chapter 2

THE WOMAN parking the jade green Volvo alongside the curb was in her mid-thirties, wearing a powder blue cashmere sweater and black silk skirt.

As her high-heeled pump pressed against the parking brake, her stockinged leg stretched into that sleek shape so often admired by theatre parking attendants as they watched her slide out of the driver's seat. Those stares usually annoyed her. On this quiet Lake Bluff street, shadowed by elm trees, there was no one watching. Elissa Bennett Pope drew the hem of her skirt up her thighs and smoothed her nylons before shutting off the ignition.

Striding toward the cottage, she sensed a pleasant bounciness in her mass of brunette hair. She felt better than she had in years — vibrant, sexy, and *pleased*, finally, with her various accomplishments.

Elissa Pope was a residential property manager, a real estate broker, a summer stock theatrical performer; and a divorcée. Her income was derived mainly from finding vacant houses for transient families of company executives. Grey Harper had been her first architect. He also had been the first male house hunter — in the several years since she and Patrick Pope had parted — who was both attractive and unattached.

It had taken a whole day to fabricate an innocent reason for this visit. Now, with fingernail poised at the door chime, Elissa experienced an odd sensation — a ripple of uncertainty. She swallowed a breath to calm herself and was about to tap the bell button when the door snapped open.

"*Oh!*" She stepped back, drawing a hand to her chest.

Elissa had remembered Grey Harper as a tall and angular man with a California tan, water-blue eyes surrounded by crinkles whenever he smiled, a man who spoke in a masculine voice and possessed a wry sense of humor.

This man at the door was not the Grey Harper she remembered.

"Mrs. Pope," he said flatly.

"Mr. *Harper?*"

"What are you doing here, Mrs. Pope?"

The unexpected frost in his eyes, and the sharpness of his question, disturbed her. She had to take another breath before answering.

"I... we had an appointment, Mr. Harper... about the insurance clause in your rental agreement. Remember?"

"Sorry," he said dryly. "This is not a good time."

Elissa reflected on her glowing expectations just moments ago. And now she felt like a damned fool.

"Very well," she murmured. "Perhaps another day." She turned to go.

"Wait."

Elissa hesitated.

"It happens I do need to see you," Harper said. "Come in." He stepped aside for her.

Without moving, Elissa reexamined her client. His face was tense, his hair unruly. Behind rimless reading glasses, his eyes were stern.

She suggested, "If it's not a good time..."

He said, "It may be the only time."

Elissa was drawn into the house.

The living room was dim, its windows and drapes closed. Harper motioned her to a chair. He remained standing, watching as she crossed her legs and smoothed the thin silk of her skirt. His eyes were invisible now behind reflections on his eyeglasses.

"Mrs. Pope," he said. "Have you told anyone that I rented this cottage from you?"

The question surprised her. "Well — yes."

"Whom?"

"Donald Rogers. He's the attorney for the owner, Mrs. Arthur Barrington. As I explained to you, this cottage is part of the Barrington estate."

"Yes, I know. A converted carriage house."

"That's right."

"Anyone else?"

"I don't know... I might've mentioned it to a few people in my office. Why?"

"Has anyone asked you about me?"

"Mr. Harper, I simply don't understand why you're asking these questions."

Exhaling, he moved to a chair facing her and sat heavily. After a moment, he said, "I think it would be best for you to answer my questions — without knowing the reasons. I have a problem that doesn't concern you." He leaned forward. "Let's keep it that way."

Elissa said nothing. She felt chilled.

Harper repeated, "Has anyone asked you about me?"

"No."

"Who has access to the keys for this cottage?"

"I keep a set in my office — in a locked cabinet drawer."

"What about the lawyer you mentioned?"

"Donald Rogers? I don't know. He might have keys. I suppose he would."

"When was the last time you saw the keys in your office?"

"Oh, God." Elissa shook her head. "I can't keep answering these ridiculous questions without knowing the reason."

"Mrs. Pope..."

"*Mr. Harper!* I am personally responsible for this cottage. I'm conscientious about its tenants. If you are involved in something — I don't know how to say this — if there's anything *sinister* going on... I'd prefer that you live elsewhere."

Elissa waited for a response, breathless. Despite heat in her face and a knot in her chest, she was determined.

In the dimness, Harper's lean frame seemed to rise like a ghost, approaching her with a calm menace.

Her heart thudded.

He said, "I didn't mean to frighten you."

"Then you've failed," she said.

"Someone entered this cottage last night," Harper said quietly. "Uninvited."

"Good grief. Were you harmed?"

"No — not physically."

"Did you see him?"

"No... Not a trace."

"Was anything taken?"

"No. I inspected the entire house. Nothing was taken."

"Do you know how he got in?"

"Again, no... The downstairs was locked tight, and nothing was forced or even scratched. The upstairs bedroom windows were open, but a visitor would have had to climb a ladder and leap across cartons of my construction documents in order to go anywhere. There are no disturbances, no marks of a ladder or footprints outside."

"Did you *hear* anything?"

Harper paused. "Unfamiliar houses make odd sounds at night. I heard nothing more sinister than that."

Elissa shuddered. Reviewing what Harper had just told her, she asked, "How do you know anyone was here?"

"I know."

"But — you saw no one, you don't think you heard anything, nothing was taken. You found no damage. What did your phantom *do*, Mr. Harper?"

"He left a gift."

"A gift?"

"A dead rat."

Elissa was astonished. "Has it occurred to you that a rat could have sneaked in all by itself?"

"Not with a hunting knife stuck through it, pinning it to a bathroom wall."

It took a moment for the image to register.

"Oh my God!"

Chapter 3

AT THE DOOR was a young man in tan slacks and navy blazer, red-striped tie knotted like a rope, a face carved from pine, shoulders shaped like an iron anvil.

"Officer John Baker," the young man said, showing a badge to Grey Harper.

Elissa Pope stood in the dimness of the living room a few paces behind the architect. She watched his attention shift toward an electric-blue Thunderbird parked a few inches behind her Volvo. A spidery web of antennas decorated the roof. Harper asked, "Do you have some other identification?"

"Sure."

Elissa leaned against a wall, folding her arms beneath her bosom, crossing her ankles. Watching Harper inspect the officer's credentials, she wondered if she'd be able to decipher their authenticity. She wondered why Harper would try. Then Harper stepped aside, motioning Baker to enter.

The policeman, carrying a satchel, halted when he saw her. His eyes traveled from the glossy black of her heels to the soft turtleneck of her sweater. "Hello, there," he said.

Lowering the satchel to the floor, the man stuffed big hands into tight pockets and rocked on his heels.

"Mrs. Pope, meet Officer Baker," Harper said to her.

Elissa nodded. "Thank you for coming."

"Sure," Baker said. He switched his attention to Harper. "You complained about a break-in — and a dead rat?"

"It's upstairs," said Harper. "In the bathroom." He waved at the stairway.

"Hold on." Baker extracted a notebook from his jacket, clicked a ballpoint. "Full name, please."

Harper flipped a hand. "It's Franklin Graham Harper," he said wearily.

Baker jotted. "And is this your permanent address, Mr. Harper?"

"No. I'm renting for a few months. I live in California."

Baker looked up. "Just visiting?"

"Business," Harper said.

"I'll need your permanent address, please."

"Is this necessary?"

Baker grinned. "Afraid so."

Sighing, Harper said, "I live at One-Fifty-Seven Spindrift Road in Carmel."

"Ah, Carmel," Baker said. "Isn't that where they have that famous golf course — where they held the old Bing Crosby tournaments?"

"Pebble Beach," Harper said. "The tournament is sponsored by AT&T, and it's actually several courses."

"Yeah," Baker said, writing. "And I heard the Japs bought it all." He turned to Elissa. "Mrs. Pope, what's your relationship to Mr. Harper?"

Elissa stiffened, galled by the officer's use of the term
Japs and sensing extreme rudeness in the word *relationship*.
She said, "Mr. Harper is my client. I rented this cottage to
him."

"Oh, then this is your place?"

"No, I'm an agent," Elissa said.

"I see... May I have your full name and address, please?"

Harper became indignant. "Mrs. Pope is not involved in
this. Can we get on with it?" He motioned again at the
stairs.

Baker stared at Harper. "I got a job to do, fella. Cool it."

Elissa said, quickly, "Elissa Bennett Pope. I live at
Twenty-nineteen Western Avenue in Lake Forest, apartment
three-D."

"Thank you, ma'am," Baker said, writing. "Now, then,
Mr. Harper, why would anyone want to stick a dead rat on
your wall?"

"I have no idea."

"Just a prank, maybe? Delinquents? Vandals?"

"In this neighborhood? I doubt it," Harper said.

"How about enemies, Mr. Harper? Is that possible?"

Harper frowned. "That's possible. Yes."

"Any enemy in particular you can think of?"

Harper paused, then said, "Yesterday, I shut down a major construction job at Fort Sheridan. The workers were
outraged and they made some threats. That's understandable, because they have families to be fed and mortgages to
be paid. I didn't take them seriously."

Scribbling notes, Baker did not look up as he asked,
"What was your reason for this shutdown, Mr. Harper?"

"I had safety concerns. I needed some expert advice."

"Oh? What sort of concerns?"

"I..." Harper shook his head. "It's mostly technical — a long story."

Baker raised his eyes to Harper's. "I'm not in any hurry. Let's have it."

"That land has been under federal control since 1887, and its ravines have been used for dumping a lot of waste, some of it toxic. There was no regulatory oversight until the State of Illinois started litigation in 1979. There's never been a test for radon; so I collected samples and sent them in. It seems there is radiation from some source. I can't allow the work until we know if there are serious hazards."

"So, you told the workers about this radiation?"

"No."

Baker lifted his pen. "You didn't?"

"No." Harper removed his eyeglasses. "I didn't want to cause unnecessary fears among them. If it's radon, it's harmless in the open air. But they might not have understood or believed that. All I said to them was that the plans were faulty and needed reworking."

A minor smile flicked across Baker's mouth. He asked, "Did you tell *anyone* about these hazards?"

"Yes, of course. I told Keith Munro, the area operations manager for Pacific Empire Corporation, the developers."

"Pacific Empire? Is that Japanese?"

"No. It's a privately held company in San Francisco."

Baker stared keenly at Harper. "You told none of the construction workers — only this Munro guy — about this radon. Did you tell anybody else? *Anybody?*"

"I've just told you," Harper said.

"What about your Pacific Empire outfit?"

"I left that to Keith Munro," Harper said. "I'm sure they'll call me to discuss details. But it's two hours earlier on the West Coast, and I doubt that I'm their first priority. They run major projects all over the world."

Baker sniffed. "And so, this rat... You think it's some kind of threat, maybe? From the construction crew?"

"You're the cop. You tell me."

Baker turned to Elissa. "Mrs. Pope, what do you think?"

"I don't know."

"Have you seen the rat?"

"Definitely not. I didn't want to." She shivered. "Still don't."

The officer clapped his notebook shut. "You said the rat's in a bathroom upstairs?"

"Yes," said Harper, turning. "I'll show you."

"Stay put," Baker ordered. "I wouldn't want you disturbing any *evidence*." He grinned, grabbed his satchel, turned to the staircase and started up.

Harper and Pope sat down, facing each other. After several minutes of silence, Elissa said, "I'm sorry."

"No," Harper said. "You were correct to insist on calling the police."

"I mean, I'm sorry that such a hideous thing happened to you — to anyone. Do you think the construction workers did it?"

"Well," Harper said easily, "that rat was an Easter bunny compared to some things they called me. And it's not a horse's head."

Elissa rolled her eyes. "Good Lord, must you remind me of that old Mafia movie? That was a real head. Poor thing."

They could hear Baker's movements on the floor above. Harper seemed more concerned as he listened. The sound eventually shifted toward the staircase. From the top, Baker called down, "Mr. Harper, come on up here, please."

"Find the *evidence?*"

"Just get up here now — you too, Mrs. Pope."

Harper ascended the stairs with Elissa following.

Baker greeted them with hands on hips, a gleam in his eyes. "Well, Harper," he said, "the answer you want is *N-O!* There's no kind of rat up here."

"For God's sake! Are you blind? It's in here..." Harper strode past the bedroom, into the bathroom — and stared at a blank wall.

Elissa followed Baker into the master bathroom. It was one of the cottage's best features, white and spacious, with a whirlpool bath and separate shower, a marble-topped vanity and solid brass fixtures. But Harper's puzzled face looked totally lost in it.

Baker said, "I did find something else, though. Maybe you could explain this?" He stepped to the toilet, used one hand to hoist the tank lid, the other to motion inside. "Can you tell me what *that* is doing in there?"

Frowning, Harper peered into the tank.

"That," Baker said, "is a nine-millimeter Beretta automatic with an illegal silencer, sealed inside a plastic bag. Is it just one of your architect's tools? *Hmm?*"

"It isn't mine," Harper said quietly. "I have no idea how it got there."

"Interesting," Baker said. He lifted the bag at one corner, shook it lightly and examined it. "Can't tell if it has prints."

"I've never inspected the tank," Harper said. "I've lived here less than a week."

"Uh-huh." Baker dropped the bag in his satchel, closed it, then raised his notebook and pen. "The man from your outfit — Munro — when was the last time you saw him?"

Harper raised his brows. "What's does that have to do with this?"

"Answer the question."

"Yesterday afternoon. When I told him about the radiation problem."

"And what was his reaction?"

"He was angry, of course." Harper shrugged. "The project was a milestone in his career, and now it's in jeopardy."

"Did he blame you? Did you and he have some big fight over it?"

"Not really. His anger wasn't directed at me. He isn't a shoot-the-messenger kind of guy... Again, what does that have to do with any of this?"

Baker lowered his notebook. "Munro was shot dead last night."

Elissa's hand went to her mouth. "Oh, no!" She had never met Keith Munro but was stunned by news of his murder — any murder — within the North Shore's peaceful villages. "Good Lord, where did it happen? Does anyone know who did it?"

The officer glanced at her, then back to Harper. "What can *you* tell me about it, Mr. Harper?"

"I'm shocked," Harper said, his voice lowered. "Are you certain it was Keith Munro?"

Baker grinned. "The body was found at Fort Sheridan not far from your project. On the ninety acres still owned by the government. He was drilled with four of your nine-millimeter rounds, Mr. Harper."

"This is insane." Harper's hands rose and fell at his sides.

"Let's go," Baker said, nodding toward the stairs. "You, too, Mrs. Pope."

Harper tossed his hands wide. "I've told you! Mrs. Pope has nothing to do with any of this!"

"She's at least a potential witness," Baker said. "Mrs. Pope, did you not just observe the discovery of a possible murder weapon in that toilet tank?"

Elissa, mouth ajar, found nothing to say. She nodded vaguely and followed the men to the stairs.

At the top, Harper paused beside Baker and saw the officer pull back the flap of his blazer, exposing a holstered handgun. Baker's hand moved to the weapon.

That's when Harper surprised both visitors.

He kicked the back of Baker's knees. The officer plunged headlong down the stairs and crashed at the bottom, his pine-like face splintering as it hit the tile.

Chapter 4

HER SCREAM, contained within the closed cottage, went unheard on the surrounding estate. Elissa stood stiffly on the stair landing, hands clenched to the railing, her sweater quivering from her gasps for air.

"Don't you touch me!" she warned, her voice thick.

"I won't," Harper promised.

"Why did you do that?" She pointed shaking fingers at the unconscious heap.

"Would you believe an accident?"

"Not on your life!" she snapped, eyes flashing.

"Well, that's exactly what it's all about — my life and yours, Mrs. Pope, because that's an extremely dangerous man down there."

"What are you talking about? That's a cop!"

"Maybe not. He knew right where to go. What if he's the fellow who broke in last night?"

"*What if?*" Elissa Pope stared at him, her lips trembling.

He said, "I'll explain later. Right now, can I trust you not to run off — to just hold still and keep calm?"

"Mr. Harper — I am too frightened to move."

He nodded. "I understand. Now, if you'll excuse me, I need to do something with that Officer Baker down there."

"You won't kill him... "

"God, no. I just hope he isn't already dead." Harper went past Elissa, down the stairs, and bent over Baker.

Elissa thought of the phone in the bedroom. She could reach it in a few steps and dial 911 before Harper could stop her. But she saw him remove the officer's handgun and tuck it under his belt. The sight of the weapon froze her.

"He seems okay," Harper said from below, finding Baker's handcuffs and snapping them onto the officer's wrists. "I'll need to lock him somewhere before he comes around. Can you lend a hand?"

She struggled for a response... "Do you expect me to become an accomplice?"

"If you prefer, I can point the gun at you. You could say I forced you."

Elissa had nearly stopped trembling. Now she was shaking, aghast at the concept of a gun pointed at her face. She gripped the railing and started slowly down the stairs.

Fingering his jaw, Harper gazed around, evidently deciding where to put Baker. "Let's see — maybe we could use the closet in the study..."

"It has no lock," Elissa muttered.

"That's right. You know this cottage very well."

"I've shown it many times."

"Do you know where there's a hammer and some nails?"

"There's a toolbox on the shelf in the entry closet." She made a tiny gesture.

"Good. Please get it for me."

"The shelf is high, Mr. Harper. I'm only five-five. Can't you get it?"

"No," Harper said. "I can't turn my back to this man — or to you. Use one of the chairs."

Elissa, succumbing, dragged a chair to the closet. She had to raise her skirt in order to step onto the chair, exposing her thighs.

When she handed over the toolbox, Harper smiled and said, "Thank you."

"For the toolbox, or the flash of leg?"

"Well, both," he admitted.

"Don't mention it."

"I wouldn't have," he said, brows raised. "But you asked."

She rolled her eyes in disdain.

Harper went to her side. "Mrs. Pope, I know how upset you are. But I want *you* to know — I did not shoot Keith Munro."

Without looking at him, she said, "I'd really like to believe that."

"I'll try to prove it. But first we need to stash Officer Baker. I'll drag his feet. Your job is to watch out for his head."

She glanced at the officer. "His face is bleeding."

"I know. We'll just have to manage."

Through effort, they did manage. They dragged Baker into the study, cleared the closet, pushed him inside. Harper said, "By the way, notice the white stuff on his shoes."

Elissa saw some powdery dabs. "What is it?"

"Later." Harper nailed the door shut and tested it. "Well," he said. "That won't hold him forever. We'll need to move quickly, Mrs. Pope."

"Where are *we* going, Mr. Harper?"

He said, "At our last meeting, I gathered you live alone."

"That's right. But I won't allow you there."

"I wouldn't dream of it. Besides, Baker has your address. We need someplace else that's safe. Any suggestions?"

"The police station," she said.

"Please, Mrs. Pope, not yet. We must have a temporary hideout, a place to collect our wits." He added sternly, "Remember, our lives could depend on this."

Anxiously, Elissa said, "Why can't you just let me go?"

He touched a hand to her shoulder. "Mrs. Pope, please understand you are in serious danger — not from me, but from men we don't know. I'm trying to help you. But you need to trust me, until we understand what's happening."

His touch had bothered her, but the steadiness in his gaze, the sincerity in his voice, seemed authentic.

Elissa sighed. "All right, Mr. Harper." She thought a moment. "I have charge of a vacant home in Lake Forest. I could take you there — but I'd have to stop at my office for the keys."

"Fine. We'll take my car. Have you driven a Mercedes Five Hundred SL?"

"No."

"Be my guest." He gave her the keys.

"What about my car?"

"We'll come back at the first opportunity." He motioned toward the door.

Elissa asked, "Aren't you taking anything?"

"The boxes of documents are no longer needed, and my personal items are in the trunk. I had packed up this morning. I had been about to leave, in fact, when you showed up." He paused. "I should've kept going. Then I wouldn't have a mystery man nailed inside that closet."

Elissa glared at him. "You're blaming me? You're the one who sent him catapulting down the stairs!"

Harper's brows went up. He said, "Do I detect a wave of anger? That's a good sign."

"A sign?"

"That you're not so awfully afraid anymore."

"Mr. Harper, not only am I still awfully afraid and actually *terrified* — I will stay awfully terrified until you get far away from me and my life returns to *normal*."

He frowned. "Well, if it's any comfort, I'm not getting a happy buzz out of this, either."

"I certainly would hope not."

"Listen..." Harper leaned forward. "What I did... I concede that was a dreadful impulse. But if I hadn't sent that man down those stairs at that moment — he and his handcuffs would have prevented any further opportunity. He was armed with deadly force. Surprise was our only option."

"*Our* option? Since when have *I* got anything to do with your impulses!"

"Yes, well... perhaps you hadn't noticed how he looked so smug when I said I hadn't told anyone else about the radiation. It was just between *us three*. And I wasn't the one who hid a gun in the toilet tank. I'm also somewhat confident I didn't shoot Keith Munro." He stared at her.

Silence. Then Elissa said, "I'm so far at sea, I can't think. But I will absolutely swear on Bibles I never saw, heard, or *smelled* anything of any sort whatsoever. Can we go now?"

Chapter 5

THE MERCEDES had impressive power and stability. Its five-liter, 322-horsepower V-8 engine produced a stimulating antidote to Elissa's anxieties. She could almost feel her self-confidence returning.

"Okay," she said, steering blithely along a shaded lane, "what about that white stuff?"

"Hmm?"

"Those little white spots on Officer Baker's shoes — remember? You showed them to me."

"Of course," Harper said. "Let me ask you — do you believe my story about the dead rat?"

Elissa briefly thought about it. "Well, I didn't see it. I don't know what to believe now, to be honest... "

"Can you think of any reason I'd contrive such a story?"

"No. But then, I don't know anything about you." Elissa drove across a shallow pothole. The car barely flinched.

"Well, you do know I'm an architect," Harper said.

"I know you *say* you're an architect."

Harper exhaled. "Well, I forgot to bring my license."

"But... I guess I believe it," Elissa said. "So?"

"Fine. And you know something about the housing development I am... or *was* handling at old Fort Sheridan."

"I know a *lot* about it," Elissa said. "It's been a hot North Shore controversy. Lots of people have favored a public preserve on that property."

"They might get their wish. You heard me tell Officer Baker that I had found radiation there. It's probably radon."

Elissa glanced at Harper. He was looking straight down the road. She said, "Okay. You said you stopped the work because of it. Can radon be that dangerous?"

"It can be. Radon is a product of underground radioactive decay. Normally, the gas dissipates into the air and causes no evident harm. But a building can trap it. And because it's colorless and odorless, it can reach hazardous levels indoors without being detected. It causes lung cancer."

"Uh-huh... So, your entire project has to be scrapped?"

Harper angled his head and crossed his arms. "Not necessarily — but it certainly has to be reconsidered. Every structure would have to be sealed against radon penetration and efficiently vented, adding considerable expense. Even then, even if we made it perfectly safe, most people wouldn't want to risk it. They certainly wouldn't spend a lot of money to live there."

"Unless they didn't know about it," Elissa suggested.

"That's right," Harper said.

"And so, to shut you up, somebody's tinkering with dead rats and guns in toilet tanks and... Good grief — why don't they just shoot you!"

Having said that, Elissa cringed. "God. What am I saying? What am I thinking?"

Musing over her remarks, Harper said, "Well, shooting me might not have been the end of it. As Baker indicated, they also need to find out who else knows about this."

A shudder surged through Elissa's body. It was far more rattling than hitting a pothole. "Good grief, *I* know about it! You've told me the whole blasted story!"

Harper patted her shoulder. "Yes. Unfortunately, Baker knows that you know. And he managed to get your full name and address."

Elissa quickly pulled the car to the side of the lane.

"What are you doing?" Harper asked.

"You drive, Harper. I'm too shook up. Again."

"Well... Let's sit a minute."

She shut off the engine. "I won't jump out, if that's what bothers you. I certainly won't try bonking your head with a shoe while you're driving."

Facing him, Elissa found his gaze fastened on her eyes. She recognized the effect on him. Her eyes were large and somewhat alluring, even in fear and doubt. Those eyes had helped her land lead roles on summer stages. "Okay," she said again. "What about that white stuff?"

Harper blinked. "Oh, yes. Do you remember that Baker carried a satchel with him and insisted on going upstairs alone? Clearly, he intended to remove the rat and knife from the wall without being observed. The wall in that bathroom is made of sheetrock, a fairly soft material. The knife made a clean puncture, easily patched. The patching material commonly used is a spackling compound. It dries quickly, and it's white — an almost perfect match for the walls. You'd have to look closely to see the patch."

"It was spackling stuff on his shoes," Elissa surmised.

"It was. I have seen lots of it. It always dribbles off when you wipe a blade across to smooth it. Baker cleaned up thoroughly, but he didn't notice his shoes."

Elissa was dubious. "That's pretty far-fetched, Mr. Harper. How could he have done all that so quickly? He wasn't upstairs very long at all."

"A thin patch takes seconds to apply and dries in minutes. I'll bet if we drove back, we'd find the proof in his satchel. Or he tossed the critter out the window. Do you want to go back?"

"Lord, no!" After a few rapid heartbeats, Elissa turned to Harper and asked, "By the way, what did you mean when you said he knew right where to go?"

"If you recall, you conducted my first tour of the cottage and showed me *everything* — well, except the tool box."

"Good grief. The one thing I overlooked." She sighed.

"It's not important. But the next day, on my way up to the bathroom, I opened the first door — the bedroom. I'd forgotten the bathroom is, oddly, farthest from the stairs. But as I heard Baker's movements... have you ever had the eerie feeling of hairs standing up at the back of your neck?"

Elissa's eyes closed. "It so happens, I know that feeling. But I don't want to talk about it."

Harper nodded. "Well, Baker went straight to the second door entirely on his own — and I got that odd feeling. So when he pegged me for murder and went for his gun..."

"Yes, I get it. But can you explain *why* he did all that?"

Harper said, "I can only assume the rat was intended to scare me into running like a fugitive, or maybe provoke me into calling the police. In that case, Baker would respond, prowl the house with my consent, and learn everything he needed to know about everything I knew."

"And he could find the gun."

"First plant, then find."

"Why?"

"Well, Mrs. Pope, to frame me for Keith Munro's murder, or intimidate me in any number of ways."

"I mean, why bother? The question remains, much as it bothers me — why not shoot you and be done with it?"

Harper gave her a sympathetic glance. "Mrs. Pope, you were there. You were a complication. They needed to know what you knew. Remember how Baker called you a witness?"

"A witness. Oh God." Elissa — eyes huge — gazed into the sky. "Who the hell are *they?*"

"I have no idea."

Her hands shook. The implications — being stuck in a witness protection program or being dead — were awesome.

Harper said, "You still want me to drive?"

"Please." Her voice was brittle.

"Okay." Harper motioned. "You get out first."

Elissa's expression was plaintive. "You don't trust me?"

"Do you trust me?" he asked.

She felt helpless. "God, I don't know," she said. "Maybe."

***

FROM THE EAVES of Harper's cottage, a flock of sparrows sprang into the air, startled by a tremendous racket underneath them. In the study, the closet door bulged, then shattered apart as Officer Baker burst through with his anvil shoulders. His face was red with blood and anger. His eyes wildly scanned his surroundings. He shouted, "Harper! I'm comin' to get you! I'm going to pound you into meatloaf!"

There was no sound around him.

After a moment, Baker began to cool down. He was still handcuffed in back, and he decided he'd better take care of that first.

Baker had spent part of his boyhood studying the tricks of Houdini and other escape artists. This would be simple.

Kneeling on the floor, he arched his back until his fingers could reach his right ankle. He felt under his sock and, yes, the spare key was still taped there. Harper, an amateur, hadn't even considered looking for it.

Although the cuffs had bruised his wrists, and his shoulders ached from battering the closet door, his fingers became nimble as he worked the tubular key into position. While doing that, he decided his angry impulse to kill Grey Harper was probably not professional. He didn't need the anger to set things right.

The cuffs snapped open and Baker was free. Now in full control, he'd go to his car and use its secure Motorola cell phone to activate his local backup team. No more playful parlor tricks. In tweaking information out of people, you could take magician methods only so far. This time, he and his team would strike fast and hard, and they would keep everything contained the old-fashioned way.

Given any leeway, he would take some personal pleasure in tormenting Harper and the woman until they gave him everything he wanted.

Otherwise, he'd simply trash them and move on.

Chapter 6

THEY PARKED a block from Elissa's office on Scranton Avenue and entered through the back. In Harper's left hand was an attaché case. Inside the attaché was Baker's handgun.

Elissa, introducing Harper to her secretary, was disturbed that he kept his eyes concealed behind his aviator sunglasses. The secretary couldn't see that he was watching Elissa's every move.

Harper stood aside while Elissa scanned her phone messages and sorted her mail. Finally acknowledging Harper's impatience, she went to a cabinet and unlocked a drawer. Rummaging, she found a set of keys and dropped them into her handbag. As she was about to close the drawer, Harper put a hand on her wrist and said, "Wait."

She nodded at him and said quietly, "Yes, I know, I checked. I have the keys for the house I'm taking you to — but the spare set for your cottage is gone."

"No," he said, mildly. "They're here." He held them out to her. Attached to the ring was a tag bearing the address of Elissa's office.

"Where did you find them?" Elissa asked, astonished.

"In Officer Baker's pocket."

Elissa leaned against the cabinet for support. She said, "How the hell did that happen? Why didn't you tell me?"

"I waited to see if you'd try to cover up, pretending the spare set was still in your drawer."

"You're a suspicious bastard, Harper."

"Sorry. But *you* had urged me to call the police, and then Baker arrived with keys in his pocket from *your* office. And *you're* the one who rented the cottage to me."

"Oh my God," Elissa said. "You think I'm part of a conspiracy against you?"

"No, I'm satisfied. You're in the clear." He nodded at the secretary. "But what about her?"

"I..." Elissa's gaze shifted to the woman. Glorietta Weinberg had been at Elissa's office for about two years and had keys to everything, including the cabinet.

But Glorietta was honest and very loyal, kind-hearted, approaching sixty years old, the mother of two grown children, wife of a local merchant. Elissa sighed. "I really can't picture her snatching a grape if she were starving — much less a set of client's keys."

Harper nodded. "Who else knows about the keys?"

"Either of my associates — Jeannie Dunlop and Lawrence Higgins..." Then: "And, of course, Donald Rogers."

Knitting his brow, Harper said, "Mrs. Barrington's lawyer — but you said he has his own keys for the cottage."

"I said he might. If he does, he surely wouldn't allow his own set to be used in a break-in..." She hesitated. "But... "

Harper stared at her. "Yes?"

"No. I'd rule him out. He's been a strong advocate of land preservation at Fort Sheridan. I can't imagine how he could be aligned with commercial developers."

"Then what about your associates?"

"I... Sorry, I just can't see any connection." Elissa bit her lower lip and frowned. "But what the heck do I know? I'm gullible enough to trust almost anybody — maybe even you."

***

Leaving Lake Bluff, Harper relied on Elissa's directions for a route through the winding streets. He had suggested Baker might have gotten free by now and could be out hunting them.

But as they crossed the line into Lake Forest, Harper refused Elissa's directions for a left turn toward Lake Road. Instead, he accelerated.

"What are you doing? You missed the turn," she said.

"Tighten your seat belt," he advised. "And hunker down."

Perceiving a reason for his abrupt acceleration, Elissa looked back. There was another Thunderbird right behind them, dark green and moving too fast for residential streets. It appeared to contain two rough men — an uncommon mix for a bedroom suburb in the late morning.

Elissa confronted two fears — the other car and Harper's tire-screeching burst of speed.

Now it didn't matter which roads Harper took. He swung left, right, punched straight ahead — whatever gave the agile Mercedes an advantage over the other car.

Elissa shut her eyes and clenched the handgrip.

Then she decided blindness made it worse and opened her eyes.

Immediately she saw a stone archway spanning the drive ahead. "That's not a road!" she shouted. "It's a driveway — a dead end!"

Harper tightened his grip but said nothing. He shot through the arch and jammed the brakes, then rammed the gearshift and spun the tires in reverse. Screeching back through the arch, he twirled the steering wheel and just missed getting broadsided by the Thunderbird. It whizzed past them through the arch and attempted a hard U-turn right through the elaborate landscaping.

Elissa pressed hands to her chest and gasped.

Harper had managed to gain a respectable lead while the Thunderbird chewed flowerbeds and mulch. But he had no idea where to go. Lake Forest roads were an intricate maze, marked with signs too discrete to read at his driving speed.

"I have an idea," Elissa said faintly.

"Good! I need one!"

She pointed ahead. "We're coming to a fork. Hang right!"

He did. "Now what?"

"Go past that blooming magnolia tree on the left. Just beyond, you'll see a high stockade fence with the gate open. Turn in and stop. I'll jump out and close the gate — and maybe they'll miss us."

There was no time for deliberation. Harper checked the mirror and obeyed her directions. He swerved into the drive and braked hard. Elissa popped her door and was out before the car settled. Pushing and stumbling, she managed to close the gate. It was six feet high and, like the stockade fence that bordered the entire property, it was made of tightly joined cedar poles.

Elissa rejoined Harper and stood beside the car.

They waited and listened.

They heard a car racing past.

Soon it was quiet, and Elissa's breathing settled down.

Harper looked about. The property was expansive and wooded, festooned with shrubbery. The driveway led to a pair of large greenhouses and a clapboard garage. Beyond that, a manicured lawn rolled toward a broad stone house.

"It's the Junior Donnelly estate," Elissa said respectfully. "We came through the service entrance."

"So we did," Harper noted. "How did you know the gate was open?"

"We passed it twice," she said, "while racing around. I think the gardener has gone out for his supplies. Otherwise, his station wagon would be parked there by the garage."

Harper looked at her appreciatively. "You, Mrs. Pope, are an unexpected treasure."

Elissa returned his gaze. "Why *unexpected?* Don't you think I have good eyes?"

"You have whopping eyes. I was noting your enterprise."

"Don't you expect that from a woman?"

"Is that what you think I implied?"

"Did you?"

Harper showed a little exasperation. "Mrs. Pope, are we going to conduct this conversation entirely in questions? All I did was give you a compliment — or so I thought."

"Don't bother." She proffered a handshake. "Truce."

After a moment, she said, "As for compliments, I must acknowledge you aren't a bad driver, Mr. Harper. Where did you learn to handle a car so well?"

"Have you heard of Laguna Seca?"

"Who?"

"It's a place in California. They have these auto races —
near Carmel-by-the-Sea. They attract the finest drivers and
instructors... " He shrugged. "It was just a hobby of mine."

From down the road, they heard a vehicle slowing.

"It might be them," Harper said. "Get into the car."

She did, and they sat quietly, listening.

The vehicle stopped just beyond the gate. A car door
slammed and footsteps approached.

Harper shifted the Mercedes into gear and whispered,
"Where's the front drive for this estate?"

"I think... Um... " She gestured decisively toward the
right side of the greenhouses. "That way."

Behind them, the gate swung open.

Harper had almost tromped the accelerator when Elissa
clutched his arm. "Stop!" she urged.

She added, calmly, "It's okay. It's just the gardener."

Chapter 7

DRIVING AGAIN toward Lake Road, Harper said, "Whatever made you come up with that story?"

Elissa had told the gardener they'd sneaked onto the estate to indulge a lunch-hour passion snack. She had offered to pay the gardener if he wouldn't mention this to anyone. The gardener had refused money but warned them to keep their wretched affair off private property.

"It just came naturally," she told Harper. "The servants on these estates have seen it all."

"Oh?" Harper seemed disappointed.

"It was not wishful thinking!" Elissa asserted.

Harper flipped a hand. "Okay. I believe you."

"You're getting on my nerves."

"I'm kidding, Mrs. Pope! Loosen up. Your improvisation was a delight. A virtuoso performance." Harper glanced at her. "I'm only making another attempt at a compliment."

Elissa's response was mild. "Forget compliments. Just don't start having any wild fantasies, Mr. Harper."

He sighed. "I'd say the present reality is wild enough. Um, would you take a good look at the car behind us? Does it look like that Thunderbird?"

Spinning, Elissa took a hard look at a green car following two blocks behind. As she watched, it turned off. Exhaling, she said, "A Mercury. Not them."

Harper's posture relaxed. "Every green car I see looks like that T-bird."

"I know."

"On the other hand," Harper added, "every other car looks like this silver Mercedes. Thank God for Lake Forest."

"I'm beginning to wonder how many of the wrong cars they've chased," Elissa mused.

"Even so," said Harper, "I'll need to scrounge up some other vehicle. I don't think we'd get very far in this one."

"There's our vacant house," Elissa said. "The second gate on the left — the Mark and Misha Drier residence."

"It doesn't look vacant," he said. "Are you certain it's the right one?"

"Yes. The owners haven't moved out. They're just spending a few months in Europe."

Harper pulled up while Elissa dug keys from her handbag. On the ring was a small infrared transmitter. She pressed a button, and the iron gates swung open. Farther on, another button opened the doors to a four-car garage.

"Well, look there!" Harper said, pointing.

In the garage was another Mercedes 500SL — a red one.

"That's new," Elissa said. "I don't recall seeing it before."

Harper inclined his head. "Do you suppose they'd mind a swap? Silver for red?"

"These people seem to acquire new cars the way ordinary people buy loaves of bread," Elissa said. "By the time they return, I doubt they'd even notice the difference."

Chapter 8

THE DRIVEWAY between the garage and house was covered in Missouri River gravel. Stepping along in her high heels, Elissa held onto Harper for balance — and felt his right arm was solid. She peered up at his profile, a copper etching softened by sensitive blue eyes.

Those eyes were studying the house, a two-story cube with vertical panels of stone and glass. Tree reflections on the glass made the structure seem transparent within its wooded setting. "It's a Charles Moore concept," he said. "That's quite a break from Lake Forest tradition."

"The owners wanted to make a statement," Elissa said. "It's the new rich, asserting itself against the old money."

Harper laughed, those clear eyes twinkling at her. She felt a momentary sensation of warmth. And trust.

And then she told herself to grow up.

After bypassing the alarms, Elissa escorted Harper into a spacious room occupying two-thirds of the main level. The furnishings were an eclectic blend of modern and French Provincial, in tones of pale peach and frosty blue. In the center was an atrium containing a forest of exotic plants and a pair of full-grown trees, with leaves touching the skylights.

"Well, Mr. Architect," Elissa said. "Will it do?"

"Umm... What can I say?" He lowered his satisfied gaze from the skylights to her eyes. "Any port in a storm?"

Leaning back against a pillar, Elissa studied him. "What *is* your home port like, Mr. Harper? What sort of house do you occupy in Carmel?"

"Well... " He shrugged. "Compared to this palace, mine is fundamental. I built most of it myself."

"By yourself? Alone? How is that possible these days?"

"Well, for example, I avoided awkward materials like four-by-eight-foot plywood sheets, and I laid subfloors with wood planks. Then, of course, I hired equipment subcontractors for placing the laminated beams and plate glass."

Elissa smiled. "I'm impressed. How long did it take you?"

"Years. The slowest part was the stonework."

"I see. Did you lay it yourself? And was it a lot of stone?"

"Quite a bit, mostly decorative. But the fireplace is a monster, fashioned after those in medieval castles, but lower and wider. Of course, bearing walls are reinforced concrete, and the footings are anchored in bedrock. All the beams and posts are pinned together with rebar and carriage bolts." He smiled. "If the big quake hits, and the California coast splits away from the continent, I expect my house to remain in one piece — even though I may need a boat to reach it."

"You're kidding, Mr. Harper."

"Yes, I'm kidding, Mrs. Pope."

She waved an arm. "Do you want to see the rest?"

"Lead the way," he said.

An upstairs inspection revealed six bedrooms and seven baths (the master bedroom had two), plus a peaceful sitting area commanding a view of Lake Michigan, undulating in steel blue ripples as far as the eye could see.

"Well, Mrs. Pope," Harper said. "Which room would you like tonight?"

"I... " Her eyes widened. "You really expect me to stay?"

"Well, of course," he said, looking incredulous that she'd think otherwise. "I thought that had been settled. You can't return to your apartment, obviously."

"But... " Her mind raced in search of options, of answers. Of objections. She could think of only one. "But, I have nothing to wear!"

Harper dropped his head and spread an arm. "There are six closets full of clothes up here," he said. "I'm sure you could find *something*."

"Oh — but I couldn't... "

"Why not? If the owners won't notice that a silver Mercedes has replaced their red one, they surely won't miss a few articles of clothing."

"Really, Harper. They're not all that dense."

"Well, it doesn't matter," he said. "What matters now is your safety. Your integrity comes second."

Elissa stared at him and felt a shiver course through her body. "Oh, good grief," she said. "Harper, I can't handle this! I wasn't prepared for anything like this. For God's sake, Harper, I was a *debutante!*"

Harper twinkled his eyes at her. "Honest to God?"

She abruptly clutched the arm of a wicker chair and sat down, her back to the sitting room's windows. She clasped both knees and gazed sadly at Harper. "Damn, I wish I hadn't told you that. I just want to go home."

He planted a hip on the arm of a chair and studied her.

She said, "Quit staring at me like that."

He nodded. "I'm sorry. I just never pictured you as a debutante."

"I'll take that as another attempt at a compliment."

"Well, perhaps it is. I know very little about debutantes." Harper paused. "Except that almost all of them are royally rich."

Elissa waved a hand past her face and sighed. "Well, I'm the singular exception."

"You told Officer Baker you live in an apartment. No family estate?"

"Not anymore."

"Well... " Harper dropped his hands and stood. "It doesn't matter to me whether you're a poor little rich girl or a poor little poor girl. I've gotten you into a lousy situation. If you go off alone, you'll be in danger. And then I won't be able to help you."

Elissa looked at him sadly and said, "... *Girl?*"

Harper slapped a palm to his forehead. "That's just an old expression! Mrs. Pope, I am very much aware that you are a full-grown woman." He offered a serious expression which placated her and added: "In any case, I'm only sug- gesting a temporary refuge, until we think of an alternative."

"How long will that take?" she asked. "How long before you conceive some brilliant escape from this madness?"

"I don't know. A day perhaps? Possibly a week? Or maybe never."

She hesitated. "In that case," she sighed, "do you mind if I change into something comfortable?"

He smiled.

"Mr. Harper," she said, reading his smile. "Do please try to control your lecherous impulses."

"I've been trying," he insisted.

"Then try harder."

***

When Elissa strolled downstairs after changing, she found Harper stretched out on an Eames recliner, deep in thought, his gaze fastened on the lake. His profile was intellectually handsome. His jaw, and the hand that propped it, both looked strong.

"May I disturb you?" she asked.

He casually appraised her. Elissa was wearing white slacks with gold-thonged sandals and a loose-fitting blouse of bulky silk threads. She also sported dangling gold earrings and a wristful of bracelets. He commented: "Robbed the family jewels, I see."

She jangled the bracelets and smiled impudently. "It's just costume jewelry," she said. "They don't leave the good items scattered around. Besides, I'm only having a little fun. I'll put it all back before we leave."

"I never doubted that," he said. "Meanwhile, I'm glad you've decided to relax a little."

"If I didn't, I'd collapse like a marionette." Elissa settled into a chair facing him, wondering briefly if she were the first person to occupy it since the bride of Louis XIV. "Well," she said. "Have you come up with any solutions?"

Harper swung his long legs off the footstool and sat up straight. "No, I'm at a loss," he admitted, clasping his hands. "All the proper things to do seem — well, foolhardy. Calling the police, for instance. We might get another Officer Baker — or Baker himself. Or worse."

"Speaking of Baker," Elissa said. "Had you noticed something odd about his face?"

"Now that you mention it... yes."

"I mean, even before he fell on it."

"Yes," Harper said. "It had an artificial quality — as if he'd had plastic surgery that didn't quite succeed."

"Whoa," Elissa said. "For some reason, that gives me goose bumps." She shivered. "But I think you've defined it. Anyway, I was thinking about why he might've staged an elaborate frame-up instead of just shooting you. And I may have found an answer."

Harper raised an eyebrow.

Elissa folded her hands in her lap. "Well, if he or his people were to kill both Munro and you, there'd be a police investigation — which might uncover the secrets they're trying to hide. But if they first killed Munro, then framed you, and then shot you while you were supposedly trying to escape, or something like that — that'd be the end of it. Case closed. Right?"

They looked at each other inquisitively.

"Perhaps," Harper said. "But then for him to shoot me, and get away with it, he'd have to be a real cop."

"But not an ordinary Lake Bluff cop." A quirky smile formed on Elissa's face. "Harper, Lake Bluff is a small town. I don't know all the policemen, but I know many, and I've never seen one in a Thunderbird."

Harper abruptly stood. He paced. He stared at her with renewed awe. "Mrs. Pope, that's amazing! It reminds me... I

was leaving SFO — San Francisco International Airport —
about two years ago, driving along the frontage road after
collecting my car from long-term parking. Suddenly, three
cars converged on a minivan and forced it to the side, stopping traffic in both directions. As I watched, a bunch of
husky young men in jeans and blue windbreakers leaped
from the cars, waving pistols, and they yanked the van's
driver out of his seat and slammed him to the ground and
handcuffed him. Then they holstered their guns and clipped
I.D. badges to their jacket pockets and began talking into
hand-held radios as various police cars arrived on the scene.
It became clear that those husky fellows were federal offi-
cers, and this was a federal bust."

"That's... an alarming story," Elissa said. "But what's the
point?"

"All three of the federal cars were Thunderbirds," Harper
said.

"Good grief! Are you suggesting that Baker is a fed?"

"I don't know. There are so many different breeds. But
he certainly has a lot of resources. He was able to intercept
my call to the Lake Bluff police, probably by tapping elec-
tronically into my phone line outside the house. He found a
way to get keys to the cottage and enter without my aware-
ness. He showed me authentic-looking police credentials.
And I'm sure the gun he planted was the same one that
killed Keith Munro. That's all big-time stuff, Mrs. Pope."

"Oh, damn! Oh, shit! Harper — what've you gotten us
into?"

"I wish I knew," Harper said. "... On the other hand,
maybe I don't want to know."

***

ELISSA'S SECRETARY looked up as Attorney Donald Rogers entered the office. "Hello, Gloria. Is she here?"

"She was. Did you have an appointment?"

"No, but one of my clients did," Rogers said. "And Elissa missed it. Do you know where she went?"

"Well, she had another client with her, one of her rentals I think. She might be showing a property. She took keys from her cabinet, and they left an hour ago."

"I see. Could I borrow your keys to the cabinet?"

"I don't know," Mrs. Weinberg said. "You keep forgetting my name isn't Gloria. It's Glorietta."

"Of course. I'm so sorry. I'll bring you flowers."

"In that case, here's the keys," Glorietta said.

***

ON LAKE ROAD, while they were browsing two upright freezers for meal selections, Harper became solemn. "You know, it's all very cozy here — but what if the police come around to check out this place? Some arrangements must have been made for that."

"That's no problem," Elissa said, gathering utensils from a drawer. "I can prove who I am, and I can show that I have the owners' consent to enter this house."

"Splendid. But can you also prove you have their consent to wear their garments and raid their pantries?"

"I did not raid Misha's panties! I would never do that!"

"Not panties, food *pantry*, plural. They have two."

"Oh hell!" She dropped the utensils on a green marble counter. "A fraternity pantie raid once got into my drawers and... forget that. The police? Why can't we call them now?"

Harper twisted a corkscrew into a bottle of wine. "Have you forgotten what happened the last time you urged me to do that?" He jerked out the cork.

"Don't be paranoid." She snatched the bottle from him and dribbled wine into a leaded crystal glass. "This is *Lake Forest*. If that doesn't impress you, then consider that it's a different jurisdiction. And Baker can't tap the phone if he doesn't know where we are."

Harper tasted the wine and read the label. Although the product was from Alsace rather than Napa Valley, he nodded his acceptance and extended the glass for a full portion. Then he said, "We know nothing certain about Baker. If he has any jurisdiction, federal or otherwise, he could mobilize all the North Shore police agencies to come gunning for me, just because I assaulted him."

"Then what do you want to do?"

For a moment, they gazed at each other...

Then, "It's getting late," Harper said. "Let's have dinner and sleep on it. Maybe our options will seem brighter in the morning."

After a bit of contemplation, Elissa asked, "Shall we dine formally or informally?"

Harper glanced about. "Dinner on the terrace? It may be safer if we don't display any lights in the house."

Elissa considered, then said, "Actually, it's the opposite. The lights are on timers. It's more suspicious if they don't come on. Also, they have these marvelously soft lights in the formal dining room, and the most discrete candles."

"It does sound romantic," Harper suggested.

"I only meant it to be *practical*," she asserted.

"Oh." Harper produced a melancholy smile.

"However, I admit to another purpose," Elissa said. "Can you finish microwaving? I need to return upstairs briefly."

***

Fifteen minutes later, as Harper entered the dining room with Wedgwood dinner plates in both hands, he nearly dropped them. The maroon drapes had been drawn, candles were aglow, and Elissa stood between drapes and candles in a rich burgundy one-shoulder full-length evening gown.

"My God," Harper said. "Is that you?"

With her eyeshadow and lipstick sparkling in the candle-light, Elissa touched three silver and golden brooches on her shoulder swathe. "I'm astonished she left these attached. They're at least a thousand dollars each. And yes, I'm me."

Harper wagged his head, smiling. "I almost thought you were *she*. Would you also know the price of the gown?"

"I assume it cost more than my entire wardrobe. However, the only clue is a Bergdorf Goodman box on the shelf. Anyway, I'm satisfied it serves my purpose."

"And that is...?"

"I have always wanted to be wrapped in Armani or Oscar de la Renta while dining on a Paul Newman frozen pizza."

He laughed. "Does *she* happen to be a friend of yours."

"Misha Drier and I remain friendly, but not friends. We circulate in different social orbits now, after my divorce."

"I see. At first, I assumed you had mixed feelings wearing clothes worn by someone other than a close friend."

"Women do it often in department store dressing rooms, panties excepted. It's a mess, and it all goes back on the racks. But *these* people send all their clothes to dry cleaners after each use. And they don't buy ready-to-wear. So you better not pass food to me that's likely to spill or stain."

"They have no ketchup. Do you buy ready-to-wear?"

"Yes, with care. Ladies do split seams stuffing their butts into smaller sizes; so some makers use cheat labels to save their inventory. A six label is really size eight. I avoid those."

As they passed plates to each other, Harper said, "This has been entertaining. But after we've finished, I suggest we gather up some bedding and sleep in the garage."

Her Wallace butter knife fell onto her plate. "What?"

He forked an asparagus from a side dish. "If we receive visitors tonight, they would attack the house first. From the garage, we'd have a better chance to escape."

She picked up a narrow pizza slice and stared at him. "How could they possibly discover where we are?"

"How did they know which keys in your office belonged to the cottage?"

"Well... " Her posture slackened. "The number code for each set is identified on a chart — in the key cabinet."

He waited expectantly.

"So, if they guessed that we might be hiding in a vacant house," Elissa realized, "and they've already displayed access to that cabinet, they could simply check the drawer to find what keys are missing. The address would be on the chart."

Harper drank the rest of his coffee, set the cup on its gold-rimmed saucer, and folded his arms. He said, "It's a fifty-fifty chance they'd think of that." He took a coin from his pocket. "Heads, the bedrooms. Tails, the garage."

Elissa looked anxiously toward doors and dark windows.

"Tails," she said. "Don't even bother to flip."

Chapter 9

IN THE GARAGE, as they stuffed the trunk of the red Mercedes, Elissa said, "This is dreadful, Harper. Taking their food and clothes was *bad*. Switching cars is *insane*. On top of that, swiping two sets of Hartmann luggage is *criminal!*"

Harper pushed and pulled the luggage into the tight space. "Is it our fault they don't have any old duffle bags? Why do they own so many of *these* sets?"

"The longer their trip, the less luggage they take outbound. Then they come home loaded. It just accumulates."

She rested her hands on her hips. "I just hope to heaven we won't need any of those, that you can enter the house in the morning, work the phones, and stop the madness."

Harper slammed the trunk lid and gazed down at her in sympathy. "Me, too," he said. "I had no desire to corrupt you in this way."

"Or any other way, I hope."

"Well, perhaps just one other way."

She glared at him. "What in hell do you mean by that?"

"How would you like to help me vandalize the house?"

"Do *what?* Oh, God! Not another lunatic enterprise!"

"Well, let's just call it 'redecorating'."

*** *

Elissa followed Harper through the house as he started removing garments from closets and rigging them in various odd locations. He seemed engrossed in this mysterious project — without explaining any of it to her. Why was he now setting up an ironing board?

My God, she thought — *what if he's a fruitcake with a fuse! No, Elissa, don't smile! This isn't funny. He could be murderous!*

She drifted carefully toward the back terrace, her mind wandering. Unlatching a sliding door, she slipped outside and stood on the flagstones. She could hear Lake Michigan lapping at the base of the bluff — a soft, lush sound that made her acutely conscious of the night's serenity.

Would she ever again feel serene?

Could she believe whatever Harper had told her?

She knew nothing about the man except what he himself had provided. He had come from California, and Elissa had no knowledge of his friends or associates or enemies. Renting the cottage to him had required only a cursory check of his identity and credit references. And those merely indicated that he was solvent and lived alone.

Today, she had met him for only the second time. And yet, she would almost immediately spend the night with him, isolated in the garage of a vacant house, on a big estate, from which no amount of screaming or shouting could possibly attract anyone's attention. And the garage was fully equipped with heavy hammers and sharp saws...

Harper had told her that men were chasing him because he had found radon at Fort Sheridan. But it seemed improbable that anyone wanted to kill him because of that.

Officer Baker, obnoxious or not, might have been a genuine officer acting on perfectly reasonable suspicions — Harper's possession of a gun that might have been a murder weapon. As for allegedly going straight to the right door for the bathroom, had Baker actually done that? Or did Harper only claim he did? Elissa hadn't paid enough attention to know what Baker did. And yet, before Baker had made any formal charge, Harper had kicked him down the staircase.

Then Harper had shown Elissa some sort of white substance on Baker's shoes — spackling compound that exonerated Harper and incriminated Baker. But was it? As far as she knew, those spots could have been bird droppings.

And that legendary rat? Elissa had never seen it.

Sensing movement behind her, Elissa turned slowly and observed Harper inside the house. He was fiddling with the stereo system in the living room, selecting and then inserting a cassette, now touching controls. Suddenly a huge *boom* cracked through the house and Elissa jumped.

Quickly, Harper cut the volume on a whole series of booms and glanced around, apparently searching for Elissa.

And then he saw her on the terrace.

"Sorry about that," he called to her. "I needed to test the full effect — the *1812 Overture*. I hope I didn't startle you."

Startle? He had scared the sh-- out of her! She was still trembling like an aftershock, and not merely from a thundering eruption of Tchaikovsky.

She became rigid and watched as Harper disappeared into another room.

She began wondering about those men in the car chase. She had no clue who they were. They might have been police — federal or otherwise — seeking Harper for his assault on Baker; and as a suspect in Munro's murder.

And, as Elissa began to contemplate, perhaps Harper did fire the bullets that killed Munro! Perhaps she was in no danger from anyone... *except Grey Harper!*

Elissa pivoted in the direction of the lake and peered into the trees edging the rim of the bluff. She remembered there was a path that wended through the trees, a wooden stairway that went down to the beach. If she ran now, if she exerted all her energy, she might get to the stairs, down to the beach, then to a neighboring estate where she might find help... all before Harper caught her.

She was hesitating, wondering whether to take the risk, when a strong hand gripped her arm.

She froze.

Harper said, "I've startled you again. Sorry, I keep forgetting how wound up you are."

I must humor him, Elissa thought.

"Oh... that's... quite all right," she said. "I'm perfectly fine. Thank you for your concern."

"Come inside," he said. "I'll show you what I've done."

Harper led Elissa by her hand through an inspection tour of the house, showing his preparations for unwelcome guests. The arrangements were so basic, so simple, so effective... they seemed almost diabolical. He let go her hand.

Elissa, oddly entranced by this display of Harper's imagination, forced down her fears and gazed up into his eyes. In them, she found no madness or malice, only humor and intelligence. She released an inner sigh.

Perhaps sensing her confusion, he said nothing.

*

Her thoughts wander. She realizes she has grown attached to Harper's voice, with its deep and non-threatening resonance. It is a voice loaded with calm assurance. She also is tantalized by his lean and agile frame, which she imagines striding confidently across beams on skyscrapers. And his crystalline eyes seem always filled with creative visions and, at the same time, warmth.

*

Elissa shook her head.

She said carefully, "I don't know why I keep getting spellbound by your activities, Mr. Harper."

He waved at the wild disarray he had created in the house. "Well, all this mischief may seem ridiculous in the morning. I hope so. This is not what I would commonly do for relaxation."

"Well, that is a welcome relief." Elissa managed a smile. "Mr. Harper, I'm not an intuitive person, and you often mystify me. But what you've done here — I have to admit it makes a little bit of sense."

"Does that mean —" he leaned toward her expectantly — "that I can hit the sack now, close my eyes... and not be afraid that you'll wallop me with a monkey wrench?"

Curiously, that remark dispelled Elissa's tensions. With growing confidence, she said, "That all depends on whether you've had your fill of mischief, Mr. Harper. If not, you'd better sleep with one eye open."

***

It was Elissa who couldn't keep both eyes closed.

Despite Harper's preparations, or because of them, Elissa had become increasingly worrisome in the dead of night. Breezes had begun stirring the leaves and wires, toying with her senses.

At one point, alert to any strange sound, she imagined she had heard whispers in the wind.

Now, when a metallic creak at the front gate cut into the night, she was mentally prepared for it.

She was about to nudge Harper when he murmured, "Yes, I heard it, too."

They stood up together, shuffling out of the piles of blankets and pillows they'd used to cushion their bodies on the concrete floor of the garage. Listening, they heard footsteps crunching across the gravel outside. Elissa clutched Harper's arm as they crept through the shadowy stall to a small window facing the house.

Moonlight revealed numerous dark forms darting across lawn and gardens, encircling the black cube of the residence. First here, then there, shadows rushed silently to ground-floor doors and windows. Elissa counted five men and whispered that total to Harper. He nodded agreement.

Inside the house several hours earlier, Harper had switched on lights in various upstairs rooms, had loaded cassettes into stereo music systems, had activated alarms — and then had cut off power to it all at the electrical panel in the garage. Now, with intruders poised at doors and windows around the house, Harper went to the panel and threw the main breaker.

Instantly, the house came alive with brilliant lights and loud noises. In startled reaction, the assailants smashed through doorways and crashed through windows. The clamor was amplified with the crackling of automatic weapons as the men shot at each scarecrow Harper had scattered about the house. The burgundy gown, draped over an upright ironing board, was punctured with bullets. Two beautifully tailored men's suits, on hangars suspended from door headers, were shredded into rags. And the blasts continued up staircases, down hallways, into bathrooms and closets, all accompanied by the Russian composer's earth-shaking orchestration of carillon and cannon volleys.

Meanwhile, moving within a weird mixture of gunfire flashes and deep shadows, the red Mercedes coasted from the garage and out the gate, while Elissa's tap on an infrared transmitter button dropped the garage door behind it.

The car continued silently, without lights, down the wooded stretches of Lake Road, then onto Westminster where Harper finally clicked on the headlights. They proceeded at a casual pace, like a romantic couple enjoying a late drive on a balmy summer night.

But Elissa was not enjoying the ride, at all.

She had half-feared, half-hoped all through the night that looming events would prove Harper was, indeed, a madman. Instead, five men with powerful guns had demonstrated otherwise.

Someone certainly did want Harper shot dead.

And her, too.

And that was the most devastating of all realities.

After ten more minutes of quiet driving, they rolled onto the TriState Tollway — and goosed the speed limit all the way to O'Hare International Airport.

Chapter 10

PARKING CLOSE to Concourse H, Grey Harper pulled the bags from the trunk, stashed Baker's gun there, and escorted Elissa toward the American Airlines terminal.

"Wait," she said. "You've left the keys in the car."

"Doesn't matter," he said. "We won't be back for it."

Elissa waved her arms. "Hey, it's just one more gorgeous eighty-thousand dollar car — the second one you dumped tonight. Why the hell should I care?"

"I'm sure the owners will recover both of them sooner or later, Mrs. Pope."

"Owners? I thought the silver one belonged to you!"

"No," he said. "Mine's at home. The silver one belongs to Hertz."

"I can't believe this," Elissa said. "You could be charged with two counts of grand auto theft!"

"And don't forget the Hartmann bags," he said. "They're surely worth a felony charge, too."

"We're both going to spend years in jail!"

"I'll take a few more years anywhere I can get them," Harper said. "By the way, where are we going?"

Elissa stopped in her tracks. "You're asking me? I thought you had a plan."

"Not yet," he said. "Um — why don't we see what flight's leaving next? Take potluck?" He resumed walking.

"I don't know if I should trust your luck," Elissa said, hurrying to catch up. "Potted or not."

***

FORTY MINUTES later, they were aboard a commuter flight to Detroit. "I hate Detroit," Elissa complained. "Why couldn't we have waited for a flight to San Francisco? That's your destination, isn't it?"

Shrugging, Harper said, "Too obvious. Direct flights to San Francisco are probably the first ones they'd check."

"Well," Elissa said, "nobody would ever think to look for me in Detroit, that's for sure."

It was a short hop, and within an hour they were sitting in the Admirals Club on the second level of Detroit Metro, drinking Bloody Marys. Elissa, munching on her celery stick, thought back to the gunfire and remarked, "Boy, those were really nasty construction workers."

Harper set down his glass. "I doubt that's who they were, Mrs. Pope. Those men specialized in drilling holes with automatic weapons. That's somewhat different from a Black and Decker."

She glanced at him. "Hired hitmen, then?"

He leaned backward. "That raises the question of who hired them."

Elissa tossed her hands. "I've been assuming it was the firm that hired you — Pacific... whatever."

"Pacific Empire Corporation." He swizzled the ice in his drink. "What makes you suspect them?"

Her eyes widened. "Harper, who else has a motive? I mean — it's not as if you were a lawyer. How many enemies can you make as an architect?"

Harper produced a burst of laughter. "You'd be surprised."

Elissa said, "Okay, I know you suspect Baker of being some kind of fed, but it's the corporation that has a big financial stake in this, not the government."

After brief deliberation, he said, "Well, I haven't ruled out the possibility that Pacific Empire could be involved. It's a large and aggressive firm, not noted for widespread kindness and charity."

Harper explained that, aside from luxury housing developments, the corporation oversees a multitude of highly technical international enterprises — oil refineries, military bases, seaports, even nuclear power plants.

"Sounds like the wrong outfit to pick a fight with," Elissa noted.

Harper smiled. "And I admit I still haven't the guts to call them. They could be waiting for that call with one of those instant phone trace gadgets."

Casually setting aside the swizzle stick, he added: "The corporation's world headquarters are in San Francisco, and they have regional offices in nine cities, including Chicago. The Chicago boss was Keith Munro, and this housing project was chiefly his concern. He acquired the land against fierce public opposition and put the whole thing together — except soil tests, which he either neglected, doctored, or concealed. It was nonetheless his crown jewel, and when I told him he'd have to ditch it, he was infuriated."

Elissa stroked an eyebrow with the nail of her little finger and uttered a tiny sigh. "If that's not a corporation issue, what other entity had a motive to kill him?"

"I have no idea. However, it appears unlikely that the company would act so desperately. Granted, they'd take a financial hit. But compared to their full range of activities, that hit would be only a footnote in their annual report."

Gracefully crossing her legs, Elissa smoothed a hand over her thigh. "Well, I'm thoroughly confused."

"Me, too," Harper said.

She placed her fingers on Harper's wrist. "Can you think of anyone else with a reason to murder Munro and come gunning for you?"

Harper hesitated, visibly aware of her touch. He said, "Well, if it's not the players on the field, it must be someone on the sidelines."

"Sidelines?"

"I have a strange feeling there's someone on the fringe of all this — maybe from the lunatic fringe."

Elissa lifted her hand from his wrist, created a nest with all of her fingers and dropped her head into it. "This just keeps getting scarier and scarier," she whispered.

***

THEY DECIDED it was time to use the telephone, and Harper reserved an Admirals Club conference room for privacy. In the club, he had found a Chicago *Tribune* and looked up the number of the newsroom. As he punched the numbers into a credit card phone, he motioned Elissa to pick up the extension on her side of the conference table.

"City desk, Wisniewski," a man answered.

"My name is Grey Harper, and I have a story for you."

"Lovely. About what?"

"I'm the architect on the Fort Sheridan construction job — the project being built by Pacific Empire Corporation from San Francisco. I closed down that project yesterday, and now it appears somebody has made arrangements to kill me, and... "

"Wait, wait... I gotta grab a pad... What'd you say your name was?"

"Harper — F. Graham Harper."

"Hold on."

The line went silent.

They waited.

Elissa said, "What's the 'F' stand for?"

"Franklin. Don't laugh."

He drummed his fingers on the table...

After another long minute and several clicks, a different voice came on the line. "Are you there, Mr. Harper?"

"I'm here. Who's this?"

"I'm Richard Guthrie, city editor. What do you know about the shutdown at Fort Sheridan?"

Harper told him, and Guthrie said, "I see. How many others know about this?"

"I don't know. But you could tell the world."

"Where are you?"

"That, I can't tell you," Harper said.

"Why not?"

"I'm in hiding." Harper described the shooting attack at the Lake Forest house. After a pause, Guthrie said, "Okay... So how did you manage to escape?"

"I had been hiding in the garage when the goons arrived. I slipped out while they were shooting up the main house."

"The 'goons,' you said. They never saw you?"

"No."

"What about the police?"

"What about them?"

"What did the police do when you reported this?"

"I haven't called the police."

"You haven't?" Guthrie's voice deepened: "If someone ever came after me with automatic weapons, I'd sure's hell call the police. Why didn't you?"

Harper hesitated. "Hold on, please." He put the call on hold and motioned for Elissa to do the same. He said, "Elissa, did I mention *automatic* weapons to him?"

"I don't think so, but so what? Anyone might infer that."

He pushed the newspaper toward her. "Find the editorial page and see if a Richard Guthrie is listed as city editor on the masthead. I'd like some assurance at this point."

He restored the connection and said, "Sorry about that. What was your question?"

"I wanted to know why you haven't called the cops."

"Well, at the risk of sounding paranoid... " He hesitated.

Elissa pointed to a name on the masthead: *Richard J. Guthrie.*

She nodded at him.

"Okay," Harper said. "Mr. Guthrie, as far-fetched as it may seem, someone has made it difficult to go to the police. They've framed me for killing the project's chief executive."

He told Guthrie the entire story.

After a lengthy pause, Guthrie said, "Well, okay, here's how we stand, Mr. Harper. We can't proceed without meeting you and verifying your identity. How soon can you come in here?"

Harper considered his options, then said, "Send a reporter to the American Airlines terminal at O'Hare — to the Admirals Club. I can be there in two hours."

Guthrie said, "I don't think I have a reporter who belongs to that club."

"I'll meet him at the desk and sign him in as a guest. It's no problem — just describe him to me."

There was a period of silence, then: "Okay. But it won't be a him, it'll be a her — Rita Chan. She's Chinese, about twenty-six years old. She carries a big canvas shoulder bag. You can't miss her."

"Okay," Harper said.

Hanging up, he looked steadily at Elissa. Then he said, "Well... Back to Chicago."

"Aren't you going to call anyone else?"

"No time." He pointed to the departure schedules on a wall-mounted video monitor. "The flight is boarding now. If we miss it, I'll miss my date with Ms. Chan."

Ten minutes later, as they settled into first-class seats — the rest of the plane was full — Harper turned to Elissa and said, "Now see? Detroit wasn't so bad."

***

ADRENALIN surged through the compact body of Rita Chan as she crossed the sidewalk from the Tribune Tower on Michigan Avenue to an unmarked government van that had just arrived at curbside and popped a door open. The man who helped Rita climb aboard was thick-bodied and short-haired with a broad mouth and a tight smile.

"Ms. Chan — I'm Inspector George Carlisle of the Federal Bureau of Investigation. Sorry we kept you waiting. We had to verify our subjects were actually aboard a flight."

"I'm pleased to meet you," Rita Chan said without much sincerity. Her briefing had been a little too brief, and she was still playing catch-up. Evidently, some crazed killer was on the loose; her newspaper had agreed to assist the FBI in his capture; and part of the deal was that Rita would have an opportunity to advance her career (and the *Tribune's* image) via an exclusive interview with that killer upon his arrest.

"Well," she said, "I'm happy to join you, I guess. But if you don't mind my asking, what's up?"

The Inspector laughed, showing more humor than Rita had expected from a man of his stature. "Weren't you told?"

"Not enough," the reporter said.

As the van swerved off Ontario Street onto the Kennedy Expressway, the Inspector snapped his fingers at the front-seat occupants, a male driver and female passenger. He said, "Play the tape."

The woman pushed a cassette into the instrument panel. The tape began with Inspector Carlisle reciting a case that involved the shooting death of a major corporate executive on a federal portion of Fort Sheridan and the subsequent FBI search for a suspect linked to that killing.

Then Rita heard the voice of Architect Grey Harper, the suspect, telling his story to Inspector Carlisle, who pretended to be *Tribune's* city editor, Richard Guthrie.

When it was over, Rita said, "That is quite amazing."

"Yes," the Inspector stated flatly. "Anyway, what do you think, Ms. Chan — did I sound anything like your boss?"

"Close enough," she said. "But I think the real Richard Guthrie would have asked many more questions."

"Well, I didn't want to scare this guy off. He might not be so easy to locate again."

Rita asked for a replay of the tape while she took notes. When she had finished, she looked past the windshield and saw the exit sign for O'Hare International Airport. "I'm surprised your ploy worked, Inspector. How did you anticipate that this man would call the *Tribune?*"

"I didn't — not specifically. But we enlisted cooperation from all the local media, anticipating he'd contact one of you eventually."

"Oh? You mean... our cooperation in exchange for an exclusive interview — this deal was made all over town?"

"Yes, but you're getting what we promised. We didn't ask much in return — just a forwarding of his phone call, from your office to ours. Your editor picked you to send with us."

"I understand. But what made you think your suspect would call any newspaper? If he's a murderer as you claim, why does he want this attention?"

"You heard what he said. He's trying to sell the notion that he's not a killer, but a victim in some weird conspiracy."

"Obviously, you don't believe him. But then who shot up the home he described in Lake Forest, if it wasn't someone trying to kill him?"

"Ms. Chan, this guy shot Keith Munro in a dispute over a fiasco at Fort Sheridan. We have ample evidence for that.

As for a Lake Forest home under attack, no such complaints have been reported to local police. But Harper assaulted an officer and took weapons from his car; so he could've done damage on his own. Of course, we'll investigate everything."

"And what about his other claim of finding radiation — are you also investigating that?"

"Not yet. But don't worry, we will."

"Well, if you don't, I certainly will. It sheds a different light on things, Inspector."

"Look, I think the guy's a nut, but suit yourself."

"If he's a nut and a killer, how do you plan to arrest him without danger to me or other civilians?"

"He's in the Admiral's Club, inside the security area; so he can't have a gun in there. But the plan is getting his story on tape first — when he doesn't have a lawyer advising him."

The van had entered the terminal's parking garage and had proceeded up several levels until stopping in a section remote from other vehicles.

Rita was puzzled. "Why are you parking way back here?"

"That's the other thing. This is where we're going to take him — well away from any civilians," the Inspector said.

"Wait. Are you expecting *me* to bring him out here?"

"No. We have someone else, well qualified to do that." He tapped the front seat, and both occupants turned and looked at Rita. The woman had Asian features similar to Rita's but was taller and thinner. The man beside her was a hideous sight, his face swollen and bruised.

Being a reporter, Rita did not hesitate to ask him about it. "Oh, sir — what happened to your face?"

"I fell down some stairs," Baker said.

Chapter 11

ACCESS TO the O'Hare Admirals Club was via an elevator, located beyond the reception desk where credentials are checked. From that desk, a receptionist buzzed a small conference room in the club and announced the arrival of Harper's guest. Elissa immediately went to meet the elevator and Rita Chan of the *Tribune*.

Elissa watched weary executives struggling off the elevator with carry-on luggage. Emerging impatiently from behind them was a slender woman with a canvas shoulder bag.

"Ms. Chan?"

"Yes."

"I'm Elissa Pope. I'm with Grey Harper."

"Call me Rita." Her finely shaped hand offered a card emblazoned with the *Tribune* logo. "Where is Mr. Harper?"

"He's in a conference room. We've been waiting for you."

Elissa led the woman down a hallway past racks where she and Harper had stashed their luggage. She motioned the reporter into a room where Harper was waiting. After brief introductions, they took chairs around a conference table.

The woman extracted a mini recorder from her shoulder bag and said, "This will ensure accuracy. I hope you don't mind." She then proceeded into a series of preliminary questions about identities, times, and places. Underneath it all, Elissa noted, her demeanor seemed oddly tense.

"Now, Mr. Harper," she said, "tell me precisely why you believe someone is trying to kill you."

Unzipping a pocket of his bag, Harper removed a bundle of papers. He unfolded a large sheet onto the table. "This is the site plan for Sheridan Estates, a sixty-million-dollar housing project. It's a fantastic piece of property on a high bluff overlooking Lake Michigan. It's part of old Fort Sheridan, adjoining the wealthy North Shore suburbs of Lake Forest, Highland Park..."

"Yes," Rita said. "I'm familiar with the property."

"Good. Then are you also familiar with its developers?"

"The Pacific Empire Corporation? Yes, of course."

Harper sat back and looked at her mildly. "Let me ask you, Ms. Chan. Do you believe it's the sort of corporation that might indulge in murders to protect its bottom line?"

"I couldn't say," she said. "Are you accusing them?"

"Not yet," he said.

"But you are suspicious? Why?"

Harper turned another document. "Because of this. It's an indication of potentially hazardous radiation, probably radon, on the project site. I explained this to your editor."

"Yes, I was briefed. Where did you get this report?"

"I wrote it."

"I see." She appeared dubious. "Mr. Harper, are you an expert on radon?"

Harper crossed his arms. "Anyone can go to a hardware store to buy a simple kit to test for radon. You collect samples and send them for analysis. I got the results by phone."

"We can verify this with a laboratory?"

"Yes. The name, address, and phone are listed at the end of the report. The company is certified by the Environmental Protection Agency."

She lowered her head to study the listing, then looked up. "Isn't it customary to obtain this kind of information well before starting construction?"

"In fact, it comes ahead of everything. Supposedly this was handled by Keith Munro, Pacific Empire's regional operations manager. Did you know of him?"

"I know that he was shot to death."

"Well, he was capable and thorough. But somehow the copies of his reports never reached me. So I got a kit and sent off my own samples."

"And found radon."

"Well, probably."

"I do not understand. Did you find radon, or not?"

Harper tapped his fingers on the table and said, "I'm also concerned about the possibility of other radiation sources. For twenty years during the Cold War, Fort Sheridan serviced and supplied the Nike antimissile systems."

"I understand." The woman became abrupt. "Now, Mr. Harper, none of this seems reason enough for the corporation to want you killed. I am sure they have dealt with many environmental problems. This is only one more."

Harper laid his hands on the table. "Well, *someone* is after us with a vengeance — for no other reason I can think of."

"Do you or Mrs. Pope have any other enemies?"

"None with automatic weapons."

"In that case —" Rita leaned forward and checked the recorder "— please describe those attempts to kill you."

Harper recited the day's events, from a bloody rat in the morning, his tiff with Baker, a car chase in the afternoon, a storm of bullets at night. "And we flew to Detroit and back."

Rita asked, "Detroit? Why?"

"I have no idea," Harper said. "Call it panic."

She said, "Mrs. Pope, were you witness to these events?"

"Yes, I was."

"Do you confirm what Mr. Harper has said?"

"Yes, I do."

Rita's fingers riffled the documents. "May I have these?"

Harper hesitated. "They're the only copies I have."

"I will take good care of them," she promised. "But I must have these for reference in my story."

Harper flipped a hand. "Okay."

"Good. One more thing. Who have you told about this?"

"About the radon? I told Keith Munro, Mrs. Pope, that Baker fellow — whoever he was. And your editor. Now you."

"That's all?"

"Well, I'm hoping you'll inform the general public. One of your editors — Walasek? He said you wrote a piece on last year's public hearing. It's why they picked you for this."

She looked him in the eye for a moment, then said, "Of course." She switched off the recorder. "Enough. I have a company van and driver waiting for us in the parking garage. We will take you and Mrs. Pope downtown right now."

Harper's eyes narrowed. "Why?"

"Why? Because I have more questions, Mr. Harper, and because traffic is heavy and I have a deadline to meet."

Harper glanced at Elissa. She raised her eyebrows.

"The Chicago *Tribune* will protect you, Mr. Harper, and Mrs. Pope as well. I promise that you will have nothing to fear while you are with me."

"Well, if it's absolutely necessary..."

"It is." She gathered her notes and Harper's documents and stuffed them into her canvas bag. The three stood together and walked out, through the clubroom to the elevator, collecting their Hartmann bags along the way.

On the concourse level, among bright lights and bustling travelers, Harper took hold of Elissa's arm and began slowing her pace, gradually increasing their distance behind the reporter. His eyes roamed the faces in the crowd.

"Harper — what are you doing?"

He said quietly, "Get ready to shuffle. It's a yellow alert."

Her stride lagged a half-step. "*Scusi?*"

"I'm not certain of this; but I think we'll be in deep trouble by the time we reach the parking garage."

"But — *why?*"

"Don't ask; don't look startled; don't look like *anything* but a tired traveler."

"God — I'll try..."

Elissa inhaled deeply and flexed her shoulders. She resumed a pace alongside Harper and focused straight ahead.

The reporter looked back and paused, waiting for them.

Harper displayed indifference, glancing at newsstands along the concourse. But Elissa felt his grip tighten, and she noticed that everything seemed to bother him.

When they reached the escalators, Harper stopped. As Chan turned to him, he said, "Would you mind taking my briefcase? With your shoulder bag, you have both hands free. But with two bags and the briefcase, I don't have a free hand for the railing as we go down. So... would you mind?"

She stared at him a moment as other travelers queued up behind them. Elissa looked impatiently at both of them.

Chan relented and accepted Harper's briefcase, then stood aside, motioning him to go forward.

"After you," he said.

"No, go ahead," Chan said.

"Ladies first," Harper said.

Elissa, also with two bags, said, "He's a male chauvinist, Rita. And we're holding up the line. Just go ahead."

Rita shrugged and boarded the escalator. Harper quickly pulled Elissa away from it. "This way, Mrs Pope!"

They bumped several people while rushing back against the flow, and they heard Chan calling after them until the escalator dropped her out of sight. Elissa's running heels clicked like toy cap pistols against the hard floor as they crossed the ticket lobby to the terminal entrance, where cars and taxis and passengers and luggage were jammed at curbside. They scurried across the traffic lanes without looking back, and Elissa felt the roots of her hair tingling, all her nerves vibrating with her fears of violence in the vicinity.

Bursting into the garage, they came to an abrupt halt. Harper glanced in various directions, catching his breath. He said, "Where did we leave the car?"

Elissa gazed about and pointed. "That way... I think. But you locked it! You left the keys *inside*."

"I know. One thing at a time."

They had parked close to the terminal entrance. But that had been before dawn, when the garage had been only sparsely occupied. Now it was full, and the small Mercedes was buried somewhere among hundreds of larger cars.

"You look left," Harper said. "I'll look right."

"Never mind," Elissa said. "It's right there."

She pointed to a small red patch among several sedans. They threaded their way through the cluster of vehicles and stopped alongside the Mercedes.

"I'll need one of your shoes," Harper said.

Elissa raised an ankle and jerked off a spike-heeled pump. Harper examined the strength of the heel, aimed its point with studious concentration, and swiftly struck the side window. He succeeded in breaking the heel.

"Well!" He said, "When you talked about bonking my head with your shoe, I assumed it was a sturdy weapon."

Elissa rolled her eyes. "It is. Let me try." She removed her other shoe. "It's a woman's job."

Harper stepped aside and waved. "Go right ahead."

She swung at the rear window and splintered it. "It's all in the wrist," she said. "Also, the back windows are easiest."

"So it appears. How did you know that?"

She gave him a blank stare. "It just came to me."

Harper picked away at pieces, reached inside and, with considerable stretching, soon managed to open the latch.

As he opened her door for her, he said, "You also did very well at the escalator. You told Chan my insistence on 'ladies first' was just male chauvinism. And she believed you!"

"*I* believed me!" Elissa said. "I thought you were serious."

"Only when opening car doors," he said. "For the view."

Getting in, Elissa flashed a leg out of spite. Later, as they rolled onto the Kennedy Expressway, she faced him and said, "Would you mind telling me what that was all about?"

"Wasn't it obvious? I thought the escalator offered our best chance to get away from her."

"But *why?*

"Well — I assumed that would prevent her from chasing after us. Can you imagine what it must be like, trying to climb back up an escalator that's going down, with a horde of travelers and luggage jamming onto the thing?"

"I meant, why run from *her?* She was trying to help us!"

"No. I don't think so." Harper checked the rear-view mirror and relaxed his grip on the steering wheel. "She was lying to us."

"Lying? Good grief! She was just asking questions!"

"No again. She was anxious to get us out of the terminal, using an excuse about having to meet her deadline. I happen to know the next morning paper doesn't deadline until six p.m. She had all day."

"You know the deadlines of the *Tribune?*"

"Yes. Keith Munro made them clear to me when he was demanding information for his press releases."

"Okay," Elissa said nervously. "Is there any more to this? I desperately hope there is."

"Well, yes — other things..." Harper was busy reading route signs. He said, "I think I'm going the wrong way. How do we find Interstate 80 from here?"

"East or West?"

"West. Actually, either way."

"Do you prefer west?"

"Yes. I prefer west."

"Then we've come too far. Up ahead, take the Harlem Avenue exit. You can loop back, then turn south on the TriState. That will bring you to the Stevenson Expressway, and that should connect with the Interstate."

Harper made the turn. Then he said, "If she left from the *Tribune* office within an after our phone call, she should have been at the airport by the time we arrived from Detroit. Her delay would have allowed a ringer to replace her."

"Maybe she had a long briefing first," Elissa said.

"From who? Those are questions *one* and *two*. Question *three* regards her keen interest in discovering specifically whom I had informed about the radon. That line of questioning was not in context with the balance of the interview. In fact, it's been the major concern of *everyone* who's questioned us about this affair! First Baker, then Guthrie — if it really was Guthrie — and now her. And none of them should have a reason to be so concerned about it — unless they're somehow involved for the wrong reasons."

Elissa cringed. "Jeez, Harper. That's scary on one hand, but it's circumstantial. Don't you have anything solid?"

"Question *four*. I said an editor named Walasek told me she had covered a public hearing on the project. The editor I talked to is named Wisniewski. She didn't correct me."

"What if she was just being polite?"

"But Wisniewski said no such thing to me. There was no public hearing last year. The real Rita Chan would have known that. This woman just said, 'Of course'."

"Yes, I heard your talk with the editor. And I forgot it."

Elissa hugged herself and stared at the swarm of vehicles around them. Then she said, "God, this is so complicated. In order for your suspicions to be justified, the conspirators must have known exactly where to find us; so why didn't they just grab us in the conference room?"

Harper took note of an exit ramp and followed it onto the south-bound tollway. "Maybe it was too public for them. They could use Chan to pry important information from us, then lure us into the hands of others in the parking garage. Luckily for us, we were parked on a different level."

Elissa felt the quivers returning to her spine. "The bigger question is — how on earth did they manage to locate us?"

"That is a tough one. It suggests they have major clout with one of Chicago's mightiest newspapers."

"That is awfully spooky," Elissa said, her voice trembling.

The tires thrummed the pavement. Elissa's teeth ached from tension. Her body felt like a rotten banana. She said, "What real chance do we have, Harper? Be honest with me."

Harper's response seemed to follow his own convoluted search through highway interchanges and mixed anxieties. After nearly a full minute, he said: "I only know we're still in danger. I can feel it closing in on us. But I don't know where it's coming from."

He glanced at her. In the flashing glow of headlights, he saw a gleam of tears on her face. He waited for her reply.

Eventually, she said, "I thought my marriage trip to hell and divorce was the worst thing that could ever happen to me in my lifetime." She wiped a hand over her cheeks.

"But you know... this is becoming even worse."

Chapter 12

THE GRASSHOPPERS were out in force.

As Elissa hiked across a weedy field above Interstate 80, swarms of the insects exploded away from each of her forward strides, until she stopped. Then they stopped, too.

Looking toward a sliver of daylight on the horizon, she realized she had come a considerable distance from Grey Harper — for the first time in thirty-six hours.

A hundred yards back, Harper was settling into a room at a Holiday Inn in Newton, Iowa. They had come halfway across the state before realizing they were exhausted.

Just thirty-six hours ago, Elissa could not have imagined she would spend a night in this distant location — or stand in a field of locusts. She looked back toward the Inn.

Harper had proposed sharing a single room as the least conspicuous arrangement.

"If you insist," she had replied. "But do get separate beds and keep a respectable distance from me."

In a quiet voice of understanding, he had said, "Don't worry. You can have all the respectable distance you want."

Now, having come a hundred yards, she believed him. She turned back.

She found Harper stretched out on one of the beds, reading a Des Moines *Register*. Elissa plopped on the other bed, facing him, her hands folded between her knees. She extended her legs, noticed that her stolen white jeans and stolen white tennis shoes were grass-stained. "I'll have to send them a check," she said. "I'll have to reimburse my clients for all these clothes — for all the things we took from them. I'm sure they won't want them back. You'll help me with this, if necessary — won't you?"

Harper swept his gaze toward her. "Yes, of course."

"Do you think they'll understand? Will they accept money as restitution? Or will they want us thrown in jail?"

Harper shifted his weight. "I don't know — I've never met them. What do you think?"

"I think Misha will understand. After all, we're running for our lives. I hope they'll both understand."

When Harper didn't respond, Elissa felt fragile. She said, "You'll explain it all, won't you? You'll use the phone tomorrow and explain to everybody — even the FBI. Right?"

Harper held out the newspaper to her. "Here's tomorrow morning's edition, already in hotel racks. Check page three."

Puzzled, she turned the pages, eyes scanning, and then her gaze went rigid. "Oh God!"

There was a two-column headline: *Reporter Slain*.

Beneath the headline was a picture of a young Chinese woman with chubby face and stern mouth, identified as Rita Chan of the Chicago *Tribune*.

Elissa stared for a long time, feeling sickened. "My God... they killed her. You were right. This must be the real Rita Chan, and they... they *killed* her. Oh, God! How awful!"

"That's not what the story says," Harper said.

Elissa raised her eyes to him.

He said, "The story says *I* killed her. It says I killed Rita with the same gun I used to kill Keith Munro. I think they mean the gun Baker took from the toilet tank."

He continued, "The story includes background that Munro's body was found at Fort Sheridan several hours after I had shut down the construction project. It says the FBI has taken the case because Munro's body was on a federal portion of Fort property that was not sold. And beyond that, they're also speculating whether you're a hostage — or an accomplice."

Elissa let her torso fall back onto the mattress. Her hands covered her face. Her voice was feeble. "I can't believe this is happening. Elissa Bennett Pope, former debutante, is now a fugitive hunted by the FBI — for murder! Harper, this is one hell of a mess."

"I'm very sorry."

"You're sorry. I'm despondent. What'll we do now?"

"We should try to get a good night's sleep, Mrs. Pope. We'll need to be fresh in the morning. I'm afraid it's going to be a long day."

Elissa sighed. "I don't think I'll be able to sleep. I probably won't sleep until this nightmare is *over*. I want to pinch myself and wake *up*! Oh shit!"

Harper swung his legs off his bed and sat straight. "Let's wash up and have some food. How about a couple of drinks? I'll arrange a delivery. We'll both feel better, then."

He watched her and hoped for a positive response.

"I'm not in the least bit hungry," Elissa said.

"I'm starved," Harper said. "I'll order for both of us. Whatever you don't eat, we'll save for tomorrow."

"Do whatever you like."

He picked up the restaurant guide. After a moment, he said, "How about Iowa corn-fed steaks? This could be our last chance for really good beef, you know."

A shudder coursed through Elissa's body. "What does that mean — our last chance?"

Harper reached across and patted her wrist. "I didn't mean that to sound like a condemned man's last meal. I only meant the quality of beef declines as we head westward. I think it has something to do with the location of the packing houses. The beef in the Midwest is the best."

"Really." Elissa forced a thin smile. "Well, order what you want. I'm actually not hungry."

"How about a good stiff drink?"

"Okay. Order a gallon of scotch."

Forty minutes later, Elissa did feel better. She had showered and changed into a fresh blouse and a pair of jeans. Her hair was still damp, and she mopped at it with a towel as Harper handed her a drink. The dinner had been set out on a small table. She sat.

Harper lifted his glass. "Cheers," he said.

"Sure, why not? Cheers," she responded halfheartedly.

"All better now?" he asked.

"Better," she answered, turning up a corner of her mouth. "The food almost looks edible."

"Then have some."

Elissa looked over the table setting. "Who arranged these plates and utensils?" she asked.

Harper said, "I did. Something wrong?"

"You've got it all bass-ackwards." She began rearranging everything and then suddenly stopped, both fists full of utensils. "What's wrong with me? What in hell does it *matter* how the utensils are placed?"

"It didn't matter much to me," Harper said. "Obviously."

"It's..." She dropped the forks and knives on the table-cloth and clasped her hands. "I'm reverting to a past life," she said, amazed with herself. "That's precisely what I'm do-ing. It must be a sign that I'm having some serious trouble with... coping."

"That's understandable," Harper said. Then, "What do you mean about a past life?"

Elissa made a throw-away gesture and said, "I mean life before the marriage — that whole different life."

"Oh," Harper said. "The rich debutante life, you mean."

"Right." She waved a hand. "And first year of marriage."

"I see." Harper picked up his utensils and started eating.

"Now I suppose you think I'm a flake."

Harper stopped eating and looked at her in surprise. "Not at all, Mrs. Pope. I know exactly what you mean and how you feel about it."

"Do you? How could you?"

He touched his chest with a thumb. "It's been the same with me. I led one sort of life until some years ago. Then I started over — almost a brand-new life."

"Seriously? Tell me about that," Elissa said eagerly.

Smiling, Harper said, "This conversation started with you, as I recall. So tell me — the transition from debutante to fugitive must be a walloping good tale."

"Actually," she said wistfully, "the fugitive part would be the most fun — if it weren't so darned real." She hesitated, then added, "I was raised on the edges of Lake Forest society. Meaning that my family was well-to-do, but hardly — as you put it — *royally* rich. No matter how they tried, you see, they never quite managed to penetrate that very thin upper crust. Until..."

"Until...?" Harper prompted.

An embarrassed smile flitted across her mouth. "Until I passed puberty. That's when it dawned on my mother — based to a notable degree on her own experience — that sexual attractiveness can be as effective as financial strength in achieving social alliances. Of course, that all started before I was old enough to know what it was all about."

"So," Harper guessed, "crash course in debutantism?"

"Looking back, I think I'd call it female robot programming. My school courses were geared to those wifely liberal arts — you know, music, literature, painting, theatre, etiquette — *table arrangements* — that won't earn you a dime in the real world. The only part I enjoyed was theatre. I still do that, in fact. I participate in summer stock. I suppose I like losing myself in a totally different character."

"An actress," Harper said. "I thought I recognized that talent in you." He lifted the bottle of scotch. "Refill?"

Elissa, chewing on her salad, nodded. Then she swallowed hastily and said, "Thank you."

"It's okay," Harper said, "to talk with food in your mouth. This is informal."

She looked at him in surprise. "Of course! By gosh, I'll burp and fart if I wish! I'm a *fugitive* now, not a debutante!"

"Exactly," Harper said, smiling agreeably. "So — was anything achieved by your mother's grooming and polishing?"

Elissa's expression saddened. "My 'coming out' party — as they called debutante balls in those days — it was a smash. It had to be. I, personally, had to convey all the fine qualities of a marriageable ingénue. And it didn't end there.

"For the next four years, my meaningless education continued and various wealthy young men were strewn in my path. I was so dumb, I played along with it. I pretended it was all a part in a play, and I acted it out to the hilt. It wasn't all bad, though. It wasn't a complete tragedy, not at that point."

"Are you implying it became a tragedy?"

"Yes."

"Do you want to talk about it?"

She lifted her glass. "Give me another refill."

He trickled some scotch into her glass. "Ice?"

"Don't bother."

She drank, said, "My father and mother had accumulated enormous debts, partly from their investment in me. You probably think this sort of thing ended in the dark ages, but it didn't. It didn't end in the 'Eighties, either."

"What sort of thing?"

"Arranged marriages."

Harper looked briefly befuddled.

Elissa saw the look. "That's right, Harper. In those days, this country was still split over Vietnam. I had uncles who fought and cousins who ran to Canada. I had older friends who marched for the environment, friends who carried placards in front of the White House. Friends who burned their bras! What did *I* do?" She shook her head. "I consented to marry Patrick Livingston Pope." She gazed at him.

"I even convinced myself I had a romantic affection for Patrick Livingston Pope. After all, he was handsome and heir to the Pope machinery business in Chicago. And he could easily bail out my parents from their debts. In fact, he was quite generous about that. He and his family didn't want to be embarrassed by my family's insolvency; so they were more than happy to buy out my father's struggling little public relations enterprise—" her voice dropped "—for three times its market value."

She swallowed another sip of her drink.

"And so," she continued, "with those two little words, I achieved the grand destiny my parents had planned for me all along."

"Two little words..."

"I do."

"I see."

An ironic smile crossed Elissa's mouth.

"Obviously," Harper said. "It didn't work out."

"No," Elissa said with a shudder. "No, it certainly did not work out. End of subject."

"Okay."

After a hesitation, Harper said, "I've noticed that rather imposing ring on your left hand. Is it black onyx?"

Elissa nodded. "Yes, notably presented on the middle finger, next to my now vacant wedding ring finger. You're probably wondering if it has significance."

"Well, yes."

Elissa said, "I obtained it for the divorce settlement. I'd heard that onyx reduces negativity at times of separation. My bridal rings were worth twenty thousand dollars, and Patrick said I could keep the set, that pompous bastard; so I signed papers that gave me almost nothing. I yanked off those big diamonds, threw them at Patrick and then..." She held up her middle finger, aimed the black onyx toward Harper and grinned. "...I showed him the replacement!"

Harper laughed. "Good for you."

She said, "Now it's my turn to ask you a personal question. How are you paying for everything?"

Harper put down his fork. "Interesting you brought that up. I paid cash tonight, but I don't have much left. I'm afraid to use credit cards — they'd leave a trail."

"I have a charge card you can use."

"Thanks, no."

"Really, it's okay. It's in my maiden name — Elissa Bennett. Well, actually, my family's true name is Benedetti — but that's beside the point. This is a real American Express Gold Card with no preset spending limit. It'll supposedly take you anywhere."

Harper shook his head. "That's generous of you, but I've imposed on you far too much. I can't accept your offer."

"What other option do you have?"

"Well — I can call my bank, have the manager wire some funds..."

"Don't you think the FBI or somebody has frozen your account?"

Harper shrugged. "Probably. I'll contact some friends."

"Mr. Harper," Elissa said. "Listen to me. Right now, I'm the best friend you've got. We're in this together. You have convinced me — whatever they do to you, they'll do to me. We're hunted by men without faces, which scares the *hell* out of me. Until we clear up this horrid situation, it's in my best interests to help deliver the financial means to travel wherever we need to go."

"That's a point."

Elissa stretched a languid arm across the table. "Besides, I need a wardrobe. I didn't take half enough clothes from that house... Not for the distance we're going. I don't even have anything decent to sleep in."

Harper raised both brows. "Well, Mrs. Pope. You've almost convinced me."

"Almost?"

"Even in your maiden name, I'm not sure your charge card is safe. They could know everything about you by now."

"They might," Elissa agreed sullenly. "But I've saved this card for... well, real emergencies. All my other business is under the name of Elissa Pope. I don't think it would occur to anyone that I have this card. And I think this is a totally real emergency."

She paused. "Anyway, whatever we do is a risk. This seems like the least risk."

Harper touched the back of her hand. He said, "Mrs. Pope, I'm going to name you as beneficiary in my will."

"Harper, that's an awful thing to say."

"I meant, of course, I'd gladly marry you first."

"You never stop kidding, do you?"

"I'm not kidding, Mrs. Pope."

Chapter 13

AWAKE IN THE DARK, Elissa Pope was acutely conscious of Grey Harper's presence on the other bed. He was too quiet to be asleep. This made her nervous.

She squirmed on top the bedding in a tanktop and jeans, too timid to remove them. Last night in the garage, fully clothed for travel, laying among blankets and pillows on a concrete floor, she hadn't slept at all. This was no better.

"Harper?"

"Hmm?"

"This isn't working."

She heard his body shift on his bed, and then his voice: "Are you uncomfortable?"

"I think *tortured* is the word. My clothes are biting me."

"Then why don't you take them off?"

Elissa reconsidered this option. Perhaps under different circumstances, she wouldn't have balked about getting undressed in the presence of someone like Grey Harper. Under *really* different circumstances, she might have agreed to share a bed as well as a room.

But this wasn't a night of romance. This was a night of fear and doubts, and her daytime garments were too heavy to wear under the covers.

"Harper," she said.

"Yes?"

"I've never — not once — gone to bed naked in a room with a total stranger."

He said, "Neither have I."

"They say there's a first time for everything," she said, "but this is ridiculous."

"That's true."

She raised a brow. "Are you suggesting *I'm* being ridiculous?"

She heard a grunt. He replied, "I agreed our situation is ridiculous. That's all."

"I can't help it if I feel awkward, Harper. I was raised a Catholic."

"I have my standards of decency, too," he said.

"Then let's stop bickering! Let's both get undressed!"

Lurching out of bed and raising her top, Elissa became aware of similar sounds and movements in the darkness behind her. *God*, she thought, *I can't believe I've got us doing this!*

Harper said, "Does this remind you of a certain old movie?"

Elissa paused. "Which one?"

"*It Happened One Night,* from 1934 — with Clark Gable and Claudette Colbert. It's a classic."

"The one where they hung a blanket between the beds?"

"That's the one. Would you like me to hang a blanket, Mrs. Pope?"

"Oh please! Don't make fun of me, Harper."

"I'm not. Seriously, I'll do *anything* to put you at ease. We need a good night's sleep, or we'll never get through the day."

Standing there in panties, Elissa suddenly felt liberated. She pivoted toward Harper. The drawn window shades admitted a faint glow from outdoor lighting, and she glimpsed Harper's backside — a silhouette with sturdy shoulders and tight buttocks.

"Harper," she said. "Turn around. Look at me."

He turned, then said, "You can relax — I can't see you well enough to know whether you're wearing anything."

"The bare minimum," she said. "My point is — when we're this close, neither my clothes, nor darkness, nor a *blanket* strung between our beds can protect my privacy. Only your respect will do that."

She quickly lifted her sheets and slinked beneath them.

Softly, Harper said, "Good *night*, Mrs. Pope."

Tolerantly, she replied, "Sleep well, Mr. Harper."

Elissa stretched her limbs to the extreme and plunged her head into the pillow. Immediately, she felt luxuriously cozy. Her thick hair became a gentle cloud, and she felt a pleasant tingle along her spine and a warmth in her tummy..

"Harper..."

"Yes..."

"I'm sorry I got touchy. The truth is... I'm beginning to suspect what a rare kind of gentleman you really are. Is that naive, or what?"

"I hope you are not naive, Mrs. Pope."

"If not, what am I?"

"You're probably *exhausted*. I know I am."

"Oops... Good night, Mr. Harper."

"Good night *again*, Mrs. Pope."

After a long silence, she said, "Harper..."

"*Wha*-at!"

"I just wanted to say thank you."

"Yes... Well, thank you, too," Harper mumbled. "I hadn't been getting any sleep in my clothes, either."

Elissa tried to relax and listened to the steady rumble of traffic on the Interstate. She imagined thousands of normal people passing in the night with truckloads of goods, heading for vacations in the Rockies, or driving to sales calls in cities and villages throughout the West.

Drifting towards sleep, she mused over a movie titled *Ordinary People*, which had been filmed in Lake Forest the year she became engaged to Patrick Pope. The film won the Academy Award for its stunning portrayal of private suffering among people who seemed well off... ordinary people in extraordinary difficulty... people... like... her.

Elissa awakened suddenly to the cold of air-conditioning on her exposed knee, the rest of her body barely wrapped in a tangled white sheet. Her motel surroundings were revealed by a sliver of dawn light around the edges of the window drapes. A green-glowing digital clock indicated 5:48 am.

A blanketed form lay breathing quietly on the other bed.

Her predicament came forefront in her thoughts. And her prospects of an ordinary life seemed hopelessly remote.

Chapter 14

THE MISSOURI RIVER was behind them, they had passed cleanly through Omaha, and they were crossing wide Nebraska at a steady clip. The Midwest's hazy skies and summer greenery had given way to the sharp blues and golds of the Great Plains. To Elissa, it felt like a different country. Lolling her head against the back of her seat, she propped her sandals on the instrument cowling and gazed dreamily at far horizons. "It's a wonderful sky," she said suddenly. "It's so wide open — and so totally *blue*." She elbowed Harper's arm. "I feel good about it," she said. "*Away* from it all. Don't you feel good?"

Without waiting for his answer, she turned on the radio, began searching stations. "What kind of music do you like, Harper?"

"Oh — all kinds, more or less. Put on whatever you like."

Most of what she auditioned was country music. After several passes, she paused at a knee-jerker until Harper said:

"— Except country."

She arched a brow at him, then fiddled through more stations until finding *Go Your Own Way* by Fleetwood Mac.

She started to move her body with that, snapping her fingers, rocking her shoulders, nodding her head. Her gold sandals tapped the cowling, her hips wriggled in her tight white jeans and squeaked against the leather seat.

The car swerved a little. Harper quickly recovered.

"Oops," she said, "Did I distract you?"

"Immensely."

She contracted her movements to shoulder sways and foot taps. She said, "Harper... Do you like to dance?"

He shrugged. "Well, it's been years. How about you?"

Her gaze sailed skyward. "I *love* dancing. Two summers ago, I did *My One & Only*."

"... Your one and only what?"

"It's the title of a musical — *My One & Only*, choreographed on Broadway by Tommy Tune. Haven't you seen it? Or heard of it?"

"No, I haven't seen it," Harper said.

"I was with the Highland Park Players at Ravinia, and I had the female lead. There's a lot of fast dancing in that show, one number that's danced in a pool of water, right on stage, and we splashed all over each other, dancing and kicking up a storm. God it was fun!"

Harper laughed.

She said, "I was frightened to death when they gave me the part. I didn't believe I could do it — the hectic dancing, I mean. I'm thirty-six, Harper, thirty-three at the time, and I was terrified I'd collapse on stage — in front of the entire audience!"

"Did you?"

"*No*, thank God. But..." She hesitated.

Harper gave her a glance.

She continued, "I don't want to boast, but I had worked out, whipped myself into shape. I mean, I got *buff*, and I had the *moves!* It was all quite good for me. Especially then."

"Why especially then?"

Fleetwood Mac finished playing, and Elissa's body went limp. Cocking an elbow against the windowsill, resting her temple on her fingertips, she said, "My parents split up that year. It was a year after my divorce from Patrick — a year without connections to the Pope dynasty. That's all it took to scramble my father's finances and send their thirty-year marriage down south. Of course, in his eyes, it was absolutely all my fault. I was the one who blew the fortune, simply because I couldn't stay married to it." She stared ahead.

"After that, we all went our separate ways."

"Where are they now?" Harper asked.

"My mother is living in Florida with a new husband whom I haven't met. My father has a job in Italy — I don't know what kind, and I don't care."

She straightened up and poked radio buttons for fresh music. "Anyway, that hot dancing gig in that musical saved my tush, Harper. I lived for every performance, and then I got my own act together... but darn it! I lost that rock and roll station! Where the hell did it go?"

***

Much later, a change in the car's motion jarred Elissa from a nap. They were among mud-colored hills and eroded bluffs, somewhere far off the Interstate. Seeing no sign of civilization, Elissa was somewhat startled.

"Harper? Where the hell are we?"

"I'm looking for a place to dump the top," Harper said.

Elissa sat straight up. "Excuse me?"

"The hardtop. I'm worried about the broken rear window. Sooner or later, a cop will pull us over — it looks too much like a stolen car. If he asks to see the registration, he'll discover that it *is* stolen."

Elissa had seen enough of these Mercedes two-seaters to know that the hardtops were removable, that convertible canvas tops were stowed in their boots. "I guess it makes sense," she said. "But do we have to trek way out in the boonies?"

"Yes — so no one will find it for a while. These hardtops are expensive. No rightful owner of a Mercedes would throw one away because of a broken window." He stopped alongside a ditch and shifted into neutral. "This top identifies the make, the year, and the color. That's all a cop needs." He glanced into the ditch, about twelve feet deep. "This looks okay," he said. "Can you lend a hand?"

With Elissa helping, it took only moments to remove the top and drop it into the ditch. Then Harper startled her by bringing out Baker's handgun.

"What are you doing with that?" she demanded.

"Have you ever fired one of these?" he asked.

"Never."

He ejected the ammunition magazine and checked it. "I think the time has come."

Startled, Elissa said, "Time... for what?"

"For you to learn to shoot."

"Oh, Lord." Elissa backed a step away. "No way. Those things are dangerous."

"Of course. But it's prudent that you learn — for your own protection."

The air all around them was dead still. The sky above was cold blue. The surrounding hills, in somber tan, were naked of life. Harper carefully inserted the magazine. He cocked back the hammer, aimed into the ditch, slowly squeezed the trigger.

Elissa, expecting to jump like a frog, was surprised she hadn't flinched. The crack wasn't nearly as explosive as she had feared.

"It's that easy," Harper said. "A child can do it — as we've heard too often."

Shuddering at such evil simplicity in so deadly a device, Elissa turned away and hugged herself. "I hate that kind of demonstration, that kind of thought. Can we just forget this and proceed to our destination?"

"I wish we could," he said. "But I'm concerned for you. I may not seem devoted to your well-being after dragging you out here, so far from your home and friends. But think of Rita Chan. She didn't know half what you know. You've come within inches or seconds of that kind of fate several times since you've been with me. We're fortunate no bullets have found us. But good fortune doesn't last indefinitely. You need safeguards, Mrs. Pope, and I can't drive another mile until I've done my best to prepare you for the worst."

Elissa's visions on this day had progressed from dancing in a pool of water to dying in a pool of blood. She sat down on the rim of the ditch, not caring that she was soiling the white jeans, and wrapped her arms around her knees. "What do you want me to do?" Her question was a whisper.

Harper said, quietly, "A few points. Cock the hammer, like I did, on the first shot with a full magazine. You need to draw it all the way — two notches. After that, firing is semi-automatic — just pull the trigger each time. This lever is the safety. When it's flipped up into the notch, the gun won't fire. Thumb it down, like this, exposing the red dot. Now it's ready to shoot. Don't point at anything you don't want to hit. Have you got all that?"

She swallowed her saliva and nodded.

He tripped the safety lever and held the gun out to her.

She stared at it. Her hand trembled as she accepted the weapon. She had anticipated a leaden weight. Instead, she felt a comfortable balance as natural as a kitchen utensil. Her small hand fitted easily around the grip.

Harper watched silently as she adapted herself to the instrument of death.

After awhile, she raised her head. "Will it kick? What if I drop it?"

"You won't. Go find a target in the ditch and take a shot."

Elissa stood. Her instincts were beginning to come forward in her mind, advising her to be brave and stand tall. She looked into the ditch, saw an old hubcap. She gripped the gun in both hands and raised it. "Am I holding it right?"

"If it's comfortable, that's fine. But keep your fingers below the barrel assembly. The slide recoils backwards with each shot."

Elissa lowered the pistol. "Ugh!"

Harper touched her hands and pointed to segments along the top of the gun. "The explosion that sends the bullet out the barrel has a recoil. That recoil snaps back this slide, opening a slot for the next bullet to spring into firing position. It happens in less than a blink of an eye."

"And you expect me to hold onto this... dragon? While all that's happening?"

"Just focus on your target, and you won't even notice."

"You're sure."

"I'm sure."

"How do I aim this thing?"

Harper raised one finger. "Imagine this finger is the front sight, the small blade at the tip of the barrel." With his other hand, he spread two fingers into a 'V', saying, "These fingers are the rear sight, the notched one. Do you see?"

She saw.

"As you aim, imagine a bar stool constructed of that blade and this 'V', with the blade centered in the notch. Your target is perched on top of that stool."

Elissa's shoulders sagged. "We're shooting at *drunks?* Harper, are you kidding me again?"

His crinkles gathered around his eyes. "Just trying to lighten you up."

Her head wagged. "Okay, I'm light. What's next?"

"Aim and shoot."

"Now?"

"Whenever you want."

Elissa sucked in a deep breath. "*Okayyy...* Here goes... "

She raised the weapon and tried to aim it. The barrel wavered in circles, and she couldn't steady it. In desperation, she blinked her eyes and pulled the trigger.

Nothing happened.

"Harper."

"The safety," he said.

"Oh, yes. How stupid of me."

She turned the gun towards her, seeking the little lever.

"Stop!" Harper's hand clamped her wrist. "Please don't point it in your own direction — not even slightly."

Elissa's jaw dropped. "God, this is frightening! Take this thing away from me before I blow one of our heads off."

He squeezed her shoulder. "It's all right, Elissa. Relax. You'll do fine."

She closed her eyes and bit her lower lip. She said, "All right. I'll get the hang of it. It's the *prudent* thing to do. Yes?"

"Yes."

"This is the safety."

"Right. You can flick it with your thumb without changing your grip. You can do it while you're aiming. Up is on, down is off."

She experimented. Down, off; up, on. "Okay, I've memorized that part. Here we go again." She peered along the barrel, centering the front sight in the rear notch, thumbed the safety off, jerked the trigger. The gun cracked and jumped in her hands like a creature suddenly alive. It was an awesome sensation.

But she hadn't hit anything.

"Where'd the bullet go?" she asked.

"Were you aiming at that bush?" Harper asked.

"That bush? No... "

"Well, that's where it went."

Elissa slumped. "Not even close... I'm no good, Harper."

"Be patient. Firing a handgun is tricky. But you'd improve rapidly if you'd keep your eyes open while shooting."

"Did I blink?"

"Intensely. Try again with your eyes fastened to the target. Instead of jerking the trigger, try squeezing it lightly, as unconsciously as you can."

Elissa flexed her shoulders. She lined up with feet spread apart. This time, with eyes open, she saw the bloom of dirt where the bullet struck the embankment — about four feet above the hubcap. Another shot hit far to the left.

She said, "Harper, this *gun* is no good. It's not accurate."

"Handguns seldom are," he said. "But maybe you're aiming too hard."

The remark annoyed her. "How am I supposed to aim? I can't keep this thing steady. It floats all over the universe."

Folding his arms, Harper looked at her seriously. "Well, it takes practice, and we don't have much ammo. There's five rounds left in the magazine."

"Then let's save them for a better cause."

Elissa stepped up to Harper and offered the gun.

He said, "I have a better idea. Elissa, point your finger at the target. Don't aim it — just point naturally."

Shrugging, she shifted the gun to her left hand and pointed her right forefinger at the hubcap.

"Hold it there." Harper stepped behind her and sighted along her arm and finger. She shifted her weight onto one foot, but kept pointing.

"Ah," Harper said. "Your target is that hubcap."

"That's right."

"And without even trying, you're pointing to its exact center."

Elissa dropped her hand. "Oh, great. If I have to defend myself, I'll just point my finger and shout bang-bang!"

Harper smiled. "There's a shooting method that works for some people. It's called *instinctive* shooting. Let's try it."

"You mean, shoot from the hip? Like the trick-shot artists in the old Wild West shows? Like Annie Oakley?"

"From the hip, from the shoulder, from wherever you'd normally point."

Elissa transferred the gun to her right hand, raised it about level with her chest and — not really expecting results and not caring — nonchalantly fired.

Wang!

The hubcap went skipping down the ditch.

Harper nodded pleasantly at her. He said, "You've got the job, Miss Oakley."

"That was luck. I couldn't do it twice."

"I'd bet otherwise, but let's save the last four bullets."

As they went to the car, she said, "Where'd you learn so much about guns?"

He scratched behind an ear. "I don't know so much. I've owned a similar handgun, a Beretta Model 84, for years. I read the manual that came with mine, took it to a range, picked up some tips from other shooters, practiced several times, then locked it away and forgot about it."

"But now, when you need it — it all comes back to you?"

"Like riding a bicycle."

Elissa gave him a considerate look. "Harper, you drive fast sports cars, build houses with your own hands from rocks and redwood, you know how to handle guns. Do I detect a rugged man beneath that mild-mannered exterior?"

He said, "I'd rather you notice only the mild manners."

***

Considering the perfect weather, they agreed to proceed with the car's canvas top stowed away.

By the time they reached the Interstate, Elissa had managed to find another radio station suitable for her sizzling dance exercises on her leather seat.

With wind rushing by, the sun on her shoulders, loud music in her ears, she filed away the experience of shooting a powerful gun with her bare hands. Instead, she focused on moving her hips and snapping her fingers, and she called out to the hills: "Come on, Nebraska — let's rock!"

•••

BEHIND THEM, about three hundred yards farther than they had ventured from the Interstate, there was a settlement of farm structures and a flatbed truck.

The area was not as remote as it had seemed.

****

FROM THE CHICAGO SUN-TIMES (AP Wire)
North Shore Edition, Sunday, June 11, 1995

Lake Forest woman abducted?

Elissa Bennett Pope
(Photo Courtesy Highland Park Players "Taming of the Shrew")

LAKE FOREST (IL) After friends noted her failure to show up for three days of appointments, Lake Forest property manager Elissa Bennett Pope, 36, has been the subject of a widespread FBI search that may implicate her in a June 7 murder.

The victim is 47-year-old Keith Willis Munro of Wilmette, a local executive for the Pacific Empire Corporation of San Francisco. His body was found June 8 on federal property near the former Fort Sheridan army base, where Pacific Empire is building a $60 million luxury housing project.

Highland Park police said Munro's death resulted from gunshot wounds.

According to FBI sources who claimed jurisdiction for the case, the chief suspect in Munro's murder is a California architect, F. Graham Harper, who reportedly stopped work on the housing project Wednesday morning and was last seen in a heated argument with Munro.

Ms. Pope is the ex-wife of a prominent Lake Forester, Patrick Pope, of the Pope Machinery business in Chicago. She had been scheduled to meet with Harper the morning of her disappearance. A car registered in her name was found parked in front of a cottage on the Lake Bluff estate of Mrs. Arthur Barrington. A Barrington attorney, Donald Rogers of Lake Forest, said the cottage had been rented to Harper by Ms. Pope, in her role as property manager. Her car, a dark green Volvo sedan, contained numerous real estate papers and personal items, but no purse or handbag.

FBI sources declined to speculate whether Ms. Pope went with Harper, either as an accomplice or as a hostage. But Atty. Rogers described Ms. Pope as an exceptionally attractive woman, whose divorce from Patrick Pope had startled the Lake Forest social circuit. "They were a storybook couple, in the beginning," Rogers said. "But the divorce had been a bitter feud, and Elissa took refuge in the Highland Park Players theatrical troupe at Ravinia, where she is, or was, a popular performer, most recently in a contemporary comedy version of Shakespeare's 'Taming of the Shrew'."

Asked if Ms. Pope's divorce might have spurred her to run off voluntarily with a fugitive suspect in a murder investigation, Rogers replied, "Elissa was always a spectacular delight in posh Lake Forest, and she is much too smart to pull anything that foolish. It's more likely she has been taken against her will."

(Carol Vanark of The Lake Forester staff contributed to this story.)

****

****

****

Chapter 15

THEY WANTED desperately to keep moving, and so they continued into the night, taking turns at the wheel.

Elissa was driving, Harper napping, when struck by a downpour. The first sweeps of the wipers smeared bug residue across the windshield, obliterating her view of the road. Body rigid, she resisted an urge to hit the brakes.

"Wake up, Harper," she said. "I need to pull over."

He didn't stir.

A monster truck roared past in the adjoining lane, blasting the windshield with more spray. The Mercedes suddenly felt very small; Elissa prayed that another big rig wouldn't rear-end them while she drove onto the shoulder.

Then she saw an exit looming ahead, quickly decided it would be safer than stopping beside the road. She steered onto the ramp and tried to decipher the signs and arrows — all blurs. The ramp kept going, over the Interstate, then joined another Interstate heading south. There was no road where she could get out of traffic to clean the windshield. Distressed, Elissa pulled onto the shoulder and stopped.

Flicking on the emergency blinkers, she looked at Harper. Even though his head was canted against the door frame, the bumping of the car onto the shoulder hadn't awakened him.

The rain was battering the canvas top, it was flooding the windshield, but still the stubborn smears would not wash away. She wondered how long this downpour could last, decided it might continue all night.

No choice; she would have to get out of the car and scrub the damned windshield, before some fast-driving idiot plowed into them.

She was grasping the door handle when a sudden sweep of blue light crossed her vision. In the rearview mirror, she saw the source — a patrol car had pulled up behind her, its light bar flashing. *Oh no!* she thought.

Footsteps crunched on the gravel alongside the car, and a white beam of light struck her face. There was a knock on the glass. Elissa lowered the window.

Outside, behind the glare of a flashlight, she could make out a huge officer in a black slicker. A quiet voice said, "Something wrong, ma'am?"

"No... well, yes," she said. "I had to stop, because I couldn't see." She flicked her hand. "The windshield..."

"If it's not an emergency," the voice said, "it's illegal to stop on the shoulder."

Please don't ask for a driver's license or registration!

"But if you can't see," the officer added, "I guess that qualifies." He aimed the flashlight past her. "Who's the guy?"

She hesitated. If she would say Harper is her husband, and if the officer checked IDs, there could be trouble. "My fiancé," she said. "Please don't disturb him now. He's had a very long day."

The officer lowered the flashlight beam. Rain was spattering his helmet, coursing down his face, but he lingered and inspected the interior of the car. There was nothing to see except Elissa's handbag on the rear boot (everything else was in the trunk). He said, "Classy car — but even a Mercedes needs new wipers now and then."

Elissa smiled. She gave him a *nice* but humble smile. "I realize that. And it's my fault — it's my car. Are you going to give me a ticket?" *(Did I say that?)*

"Wait here," the quiet voice said. "Don't move."

I shouldn't have said that!

Elissa felt her heart thumping as the officer's boots stomped gravel, back to the patrol car. She looked at Harper, debating whether to awaken him now.

The ponderous footsteps returned. The voice said, "Switch off your wipers, ma'am."

She did. And she watched as the officer misted the windshield from a spray can and then scrubbed the surface with a coarse pad. She felt her heartbeat ebbing.

"Okay," the officer said, returning to her side. "Give the wipers another try."

She watched the wipers slash away the rain, and now she could see clearly through the glass. Ahead was a highway marker identifying Interstate 76.

"That's so much better!" she gushed. "Bless you!"

"No trouble at all, ma'am," the officer said. "Be careful pulling out." He touched the front of his helmet. He added, "Welcome to Colorado."

Joyously, Elissa flicked off the emergency lights, checked behind for an opening, then accelerated onto the pavement. Behind her, the patrol car followed, its protective lightbar flashing until she reached cruising speed. Then it passed.

Beside her, Harper's voice said: "Colorado?"

"You're awake!"

"Yes," he said, straightening.

She swiveled her eyes to him, back to the road. She said, "Harper, how long have you been awake?"

He stretched. "I think I was fully awake when you told the officer I was your fiancé."

Elissa considered the implications of that. She said, "And you immediately decided to leave the entire situation in my hands? I'm not sure if I like that."

"I heard you tell the officer not to disturb me," he said. "I took that as my clue to stay out of it. Furthermore, I have learned to trust your talents as an actress."

She thought about it briefly. "Well, I wasn't really acting. I was only following my instincts."

"Then I'd say your instincts are based on intelligence."

She drove in silence for about a quarter mile, then said, "Intelligence? Harper, I don't even know where we are!"

"In *Colorado*," he reminded her.

"I mean, I don't know where we're going. I got onto the wrong highway, and now we're going in the wrong direction."

Reflecting a moment, Harper said, "No, this is okay. It's probably better to get off Interstate 80 for a while. It seems too direct, too predictable."

Elissa nodded. "Then maybe we should cut even farther away — hit the backroads."

Harper said, "But then I wonder if this car would attract too much attention in the small towns we'd drive through. Some local lawman might pull us over just to see if you're a movie star. The patrolman we just encountered — who sees all kinds of cars on the Interstate — he stopped despite the rain. And if just one cop asks for the registration..."

"...We're stir-fried," Elissa agreed. "So what's your plan?"

"Well, in Colorado — we should be able to find a resort where this car won't be so conspicuous. We could hole up for a few days and reconsider our options."

Elissa saw a sign indicating the distance to Rocky Mountain National Park. "Well, there's your resort," she said.

"Splendid. Your side trip into Colorado was a brilliant idea. I congratulate you again, Mrs. Pope."

Chapter 16

AT MID-AFTERNOON, they were settling into an alpine lodge at Estes Park, Colorado. It overlooked the picturesque valley and the dazzling eastern slopes of Rocky Mountain National Park.

"This is *gorgeous*," Elissa declared on the balcony. She spread her arms wide and pivoted, deeply inhaling the crisp mountain air. "I could spend a month here, Darling, I...."

She stopped suddenly, pressed her hands on the railing, and sighed. "I didn't mean to say exactly that." She smiled feebly. "I guess I'm a bit delirious. It must be the altitude."

Harper joined her on the balcony and handed her a cocktail. "I know just how you feel. It's a wonderful break."

She said, "Oh, how I wish we could get hired on a ranch and live out in the country forever, completely anonymous."

Harper smiled gently. "Then we'd have to give the ranch our Social Security numbers for payroll deductions. And what about credit cards, and bank accounts?"

"Or rental contracts. I know. There is no escape, sadly."

They clicked glasses and took seats on redwood chairs with bright yellow cushions. For awhile they sat in silence, enjoying a fresh breeze on their bare arms, watching traffic moving through the quiet town below them.

"For just that moment," Elissa remarked, "I felt as if we were in another life. After all, as fugitives, we're not crawling into dark hideouts. We're actually traveling in decent style."

"I'm glad you're able to enjoy some of this," he said.

Elissa stood up and leaned her hip against the railing. "I wonder, though... if it's for the wrong reasons."

"How do you mean?"

"Well, that old Biblical phrase, '*Let us eat and drink — for tomorrow we die...*' I hope that's not what's influencing us." She sipped her drink. "Because if that's why we're pursuing these pleasures, it's a sadly fatalistic mentality."

Harper shrugged. "To tell the truth, Mrs. Pope, I have a much simpler reason for traveling in decent style."

"And what is that?"

He said, "I simply don't know any *other* way."

Her eyes and mouth sparkled at him. She waltzed away from the railing and placed a feathery touch on his shoulder.

She said, "Are you also a decent architect, Mr. Harper?"

A tentative smile formed. "Well, I wouldn't describe myself as *indecent!*"

She smiled back and pointed to a wooded patch on the lower slope of a nearby mountain. "Tell me what kind of house you would build on that spot."

"You mean on that knob over there, where the rocks resemble sleeping elephants?"

"Why, yes — they do, actually. Yes, Harper, that spot."

Harper focused a sharp gaze on the site. "I don't know if I could describe it. But I could sketch it."

"Would you? Please?"

"Well... all right."

Harper went inside and dug into his travel bag. He returned to the balcony with his sketch pad and felt-tip pens. He put his feet against the railing, propped the pad against his knees, and started circling one of the pens above the paper, as if getting a feel for shapes, dimensions, concepts. Elissa watched his face come aglow with concentration, watched his hand relax its grip on the pen, watched the pen descend directly to the pad and streak across its surface.

The pen made angular slashes, sharp strikes, bold jots. Each mark enriched the substance of the image until it morphed into a bold structure. He glanced sideways at her.

Harper then selected a different assortment of pens. He began filling spaces with various densities of ink. A skeletal outline grew into a solid three-dimensional form. It expanded into a brilliance of horizontal tiers and vertical thrusts. A mixing of textures became granite, wood, glass.

When Harper began sketching a background, including the elephant shapes of the rocky knoll, the house melted into its terrain, as if it had grown there over centuries, from the same natural forces that had created the mountains, streams, and forests.

Elissa watched it all in silent fascination.

She had felt a distinct tingle rising within her.

"I love to watch you draw."

She said it with a huskiness in her voice that embarrassed her. Nonetheless, she added, "I could spend whole hours or days watching you draw."

"Oh?" Harper turned to face her. "How come?"

She sighed. "I don't know... It gives me butterflies."

"Butterflies?" Harper smiled. "Like when you're riding in a smooth swift car that tops a hill and suddenly sinks into a dip in the road? It makes your tummy tingle?"

"Exactly!" Elissa flashed her dazzling smile.

"And watching me draw gives you that feeling?"

"Uh-huh."

Harper capped the pens and handed her the pad.

He said, "Of course, that's more of a sketching exercise than an architectural study. To approach it as a real job, I'd have to obtain site elevations, weather data, soil samples, sun angles, and I'd need to know everything about the owners' lifestyles. But you asked what I would build for that site, as if nothing else mattered. And that's all I did."

Elissa did not say anything immediately. When she felt capable, she said, "To think I had once questioned whether you were truly an architect... There's nothing else in this valley — not as far as I can see — that comes anywhere close to this. It... it looks so perfect, I could *cry*."

She held the pad against her left palm while gliding an index finger slowly over the surface. Then she clutched the pad tightly in both hands and held it against her bosom.

"May I keep this?" Elissa asked. "The drawing? Please?"

He shrugged. "Fine." He retrieved the pad from her, extracted the sketch and handed it over to her.

She said, "Are you upset? Did I say something wrong?"

"Oh no," he said, his eyes crinkling in sudden warmth. "You were immensely kind. You merely reminded me of things I'd rather forget — of years I wasted, you see."

"Wasted? How? Certainly not by doing work like this."

"Precisely by *not* doing work like that." He hesitated, turning his gaze to the mountains. "I'm sure you've heard all about ambitious young men who get so entangled in corporate politics, they forget who they are. Well, that happens in architecture, too. It's very easy to sell out creative ideals, in exchange for lucrative slices of huge projects. To get them, you must become conscious of the bottom line, and then you become addicted to it. You focus on the lowest bids, literally 'cutting corners.' I had started out wanting to build small homes like that sketch. Before long, though, I was fast-tracking like the others. I fell into a gang of predators, and I almost became comfortable there." He paused.

"Successful architects often regard small homes as 'junk houses' — no real money, no importance to careers." He spread his hands. "It took a long time to learn that money never gave me half as much pleasure as that simple sketch."

Swirling her glass of scotch, Elissa watched the afternoon sun sparkling in the amber liquid. "And now...?"

He faced her and grinned. "Now — it doesn't matter much. It seems stupendously insignificant under our present circumstances."

Elissa took a sip of scotch and put down her glass.

A few seconds later, she glanced again at the sketch. She said, "You own your own company now. If you want to build houses like this, what's preventing you?"

"Heather," he said.

She didn't hear that or understand it. "Beg your pardon?"

"My wife," he said.

"Oh." Something sank deep within her. "Oh, I... didn't think you were married."

"I'm not," he said, shifting his posture. "Heather and I went our separate ways a few years ago."

"I'm... sorry." Elissa sensed he didn't want to talk about it. She went to a chair beside him and sat. "But you did manage to escape that gang of predators? And go off on your own?"

Harper placed his glass on the railing and looked at her. "At the time, about four years ago, I was with a San Francisco firm called Adler, Brown, Kiening. It was a pompous partnership that ridiculed houses like that one." He pointed to the sketch. "They concentrated on commercial projects."

Elissa lifted her brows. "Weren't you ever able to do homes like that?"

"Once. And it proved to be a watershed in my career."

"Please tell me about it."

"Are you really all that interested in my career, my life?"

"Good heavens, Harper, for about three hectic days, I've lived with you more intimately than with any man since Patrick Pope! Darn right I'm interested!"

Harper wagged his head and took a sip of his drink. "Well, the youngest partner at ABK was Ed Kiening, the founder's son-in-law. He was a crew-cutted conservative who wore his eyeglasses on a gold chain around his neck. The drawing board in his office was a prop, never used. His specialty was marketing — taking lunches at the Banker's Club or golfing at Pebble Beach, plucking the firm's commissions from the pockets of the rich..." He winced.

"Vera — his wife, Vera Adler — kept a luxurious office in the firm but rarely used it. I never knew what she did, really. One day they surprised me by calling me into Vera's office and asking if I would consider designing a modest home for a man named Michael Parcheski, a new builder in the area and a new friend of Vera's. They felt the man had potential to bring future business to the firm. Of course, I agreed immediately — and Ed Kiening thanked me and called me a good soldier."

Harper laughed.

"Next, he said they were hiring a designer, a young apprentice they'd uncovered at Skidmore, Owings and Merrill in Chicago. They called him Golden George. A probable genius. And they needed to give him something challenging to work on, so as not to quench his spark. And because I was going to be busy on the Parcheski house, they didn't think I'd mind if they gave him my 'Mill Valley thing' — as they called it. Of course, my 'Mill Valley thing' happened to be a new civic center, the largest and most prestigious project in the firm at that time."

"Oh, no," Elissa said.

Harper laughed again, his head angling toward the sky.

"How can you speak so lightly about it? Didn't you feel cheated? Abused?"

"By that time... I had felt mostly amused."

"You're kidding! They swiped your biggest project and gave it to a kid. You should have been insulted and furious!"

"No," he replied. "That would've been like blaming the contour of the land for not suiting the design of a building."

She sat back and looked at him in wonder.

His smile softened. "I couldn't attribute my progress — or blame the lack of it — on other people. It was within my power to decide how to apply my own skills. After I had realized that, the characters around me and their motives became amusing to me. That's all. Just amusing."

"Was Heather with you at the time?"

"Yes, she was."

"Did Heather find it amusing?"

"No, she didn't." He looked at his watch. "I've talked too long. We should start thinking about dinner."

Elissa wanted to whack herself. She had finally got him talking about his life, his career, even his philosophy — and then she had spoiled it with a snotty reference to Heather.

She jumped up, feeling an urgency to run off somewhere.

"I just remembered," she said. "I need to go shopping before dinner. May I have the car keys?"

"They're on the desk," he said, surprised.

Elissa moved swiftly to the sliding glass doors, then hesitated before going inside. "Harper... You don't mind, do you? Can you keep yourself occupied while I'm out?"

"Sure."

"Just don't worry about... you know. Let's pretend we're on a vacation trip. Let's try having a little fun. Okay?"

"Splendid idea," he said.

***

MARCHING toward the Mercedes, Elissa breathed deeply of the pine-fragrant air and smiled happily at the strange little birds flitting among the branches. These were birds of the West, and they seemed more colorful, somehow, than their Illinois cousins.

She turned the ignition key and enjoyed the rich power of the Mercedes engine coming to life. With her spirits soaring higher and higher, she decided to lower the car's canvas top. She shifted into gear and wheeled out of the parking space, fully exposed to a brilliant sun.

Except for the arrant stupidity in her questioning of Gray Harper, she felt she was having the time of her life. The mortal dangers she'd been forced to endure in recent days were far removed. And she was beginning to enjoy a deliciously interesting intellect in that Grey Harper guy.

Entering the Estes Park business district, she encountered a small problem — there was nowhere to park near any of the loveliest boutiques. After several circles of the busiest blocks, she pulled into a parking lot adjoining a Safeway supermarket and stopped in a remote space near the dumpsters.

That's where the loud shot rang in her ears.

In instantaneous reaction, Elissa jumped from the car and scurried behind those dumpsters. She heard another shot and coiled her body into its smallest possible profile, thoroughly terrified.

For a few seconds, there was no other sound or movement. And then...

"Ka-poof!"

Ka-poof?

Slowly raising her head from her fetal crouch, Elissa began to realize that the shots were not producing any damage in her immediate vicinity.

And then she saw why.

Near the rear of the supermarket, an old produce truck was negotiating an approach to the loading dock. It was a tight maneuver, and the vehicle backfired at each shift of its gears.

Bang! It did it again. And then another *ka-poof!*

Elissa slumped against the dumpster hard enough to sting her shoulder blades and waited for the shakes to stop.

Damn it! A minute ago, I was happy as a lark. *Oh crap!*

***

FOUR HUNDRED MILES back, in the middle of Nebraska, a farmer drove a flatbed truck along a gravel road toward Interstate 80. Sitting high in the cab, he inspected erosion along the sides of the ditch, thinking there was a spot along here that needed a culvert.

Something bright caught his attention, and he put his foot on the brake. The truck squeaked noisily and slowed to a stop. The farmer worked the gear shift into reverse, backed up, stopped again.

What'n hell is that? He cut off the engine, heaved the door open, climbed down from the cab.

He stood for several minutes, thumbs hooked into his pockets, contemplating the bright red object that looked like the roof of a small car. Then he scrambled down the embankment, pulled aside some weeds, and rested his hand on the object.

"I'll be damned," he muttered. "This looks like it belongs on a sports car."

He lifted an edge; it was lightweight. It also looked brand-new, except for the missing glass. He decided to drag it up the bank and lift it onto his truck. He had some wire he could use to lash it down. He'd take it to the repair shop in town, maybe get some money for it. He wondered what it was worth.

Chapter 17

THE MIRROR in the ladies' room finally cooperated, by presenting a decently adjusted view of Elissa's form-hugging, cream-colored silk cocktail dress with a knockout neckline.

Clutching her handbag, she strolled self-confidently into the restaurant lobby and then paused at the entrance to the dining room. Seeking Harper in the crowd, she caught sight of him at a far window table, gazing at a sunset view.

A happy host approached Elissa and proffered his help. "I'm okay," she said, smiling. "I found him, but thank you."

She walked ahead briskly, trying to ignore the attention she aroused at every table she passed. When Harper looked her way, they locked eyes and instantly forgot all the others.

From his viewpoint, Elissa's dress seemed almost alive, the way it was clinging so tenaciously to all her body parts in motion. He tried to conjure a sublime remark as he stood to greet her, then said, "Mrs. Pope, you have just overwhelmed a very hard working sunset. That hardly seems fair of you."

She suppressed a smile at his awkward pun and leaned close to him. "I'm sorry I've kept you waiting. But it does require a ton of effort to compete against a sunset." Elissa reached out for a handshake and raised her cheek for a kiss.

But Harper missed her signals. She had barely caught his right forefinger before his hand skipped away to pull out a chair for her. And her kiss invitation had simply evaporated.

Elissa rolled her eyes and bent forward to sit down.

That was the moment when he noticed a chain of pearls fastened from one side of her plunging neckline across to the other. The chain grew taut as Elissa bent forward, then slackened as she straightened up. *Fascinating*, he thought.

Elissa said, "I see that you've been studying the menu. Anything interesting on it — besides me?"

He looked at her curiously.

She said, "I'm sorry. I'm reacting to the people who are drooling over me with hungry eyes — as if I'm one of the appetizers. Do you think this dress is worth the attention?"

"Not so much the dress, per se, as what it contains."

"*Per se?*" Her cheeks bubbled out as Elissa suppressed a giggle. "Harper, I have to hand it to you. With that phrase, you managed to turn a potentially *crude* observation into an almost intellectual deduction!"

"My intellect also is curious about those pearls," Harper said, gazing at them. "They appear to have a job."

"Oh?" She glanced down. "Those. Obviously. Well, the boutique madame called it a *modesty chain*. It's adjustable to secure the neckline, to prevent any... fallout. But it bombed."

"Oh? Is that what kept you in the ladies' room?"

"It did. It started with the rain jacket I wore as we drove up here with the top down. I wore it because the dress is so delicate... and also because I wanted to surprise you with this new dress in this kind of romantic setting."

"And you did," he said. "But...?"

"But, when I shrugged off the jacket, the snap-together pearls popped apart! Fortunately, I was in the ladies' room. Because the *fallout* was nuclear. If you get my drift."

Harper had been about to drink from his water glass. He quickly put it down. "Obviously, you somehow fixed it."

A waiter appeared beside Elissa and offered a wine list. She shrugged. "Harper, you choose. I'm too distracted."

"So am I." He told the waiter, "Give us ten minutes."

"*Oui,*" the waiter said and withdrew.

Elissa grinned. "*Oui?* I think he's pretending. Anyway, the pearls were fine in the boutique. It's a shop that caters to wealthy Texans who spend summers up here, and it's like a Neiman Marcus dress — a dazzler."

She looked around briefly before continuing.

"But I don't think it's a Colorado dress," she said quietly. "Or it wouldn't attract a whole posse of lookers like this. Anyway, the madame offered a four hundred dollar discount because I'm the first woman the dress fit after two years on display. Can you believe that?"

Harper said, "Actually, just the way you walk in it can stop a battleship in its wake. Did you train for that?"

She laughed. "Quite the opposite. Debutantes are taught to walk with books on their heads."

"Well, then..."

"My gait simply reflects how I feel. If there's a touch of *samba*... it means I'm jolly tonight."

Harper folded his hands and hunched forward. "Don't look now, but you didn't see the waiter's eyes when you *shrugged* a moment ago. He's at the side of the room, keeping both eyes on you. Better be careful with those shrugs."

Elissa laughed again. "Don't mind him. That's what good waiters do. They wait. The moment you lift a finger, he'll pop right over here. He's been well trained."

Harper tugged an earlobe. "I hadn't been aware of that. Are you sure his attentive behavior is due to his training?"

With a tiny smile, Elissa said, "Well, maybe it's more."

"So tell me how you fixed the dress," Harper said.

"In the shop, the pearls were joined perfectly. I refused to believe I could've gained weight while running for our lives; so I decided one pearl had somehow escaped."

"I see. Were you able to recapture it?"

"No. I sat there for awhile and fretted. I finally managed to compensate by lowering the back zipper half an inch."

Harper's brows lifted. "That's an ingenious solution."

"I wondered how it looked in back, but everyone's eyes seem drawn to the front. Anyway, you're the expert about designs. Take into account the exquisite silk embroidery across the front and tell me what you think, overall."

"Honestly?"

"Of course."

"The moment you entered the room, every heart stopped beating for a moment. I think that's what they mean by the term drop-dead gorgeous."

"I was afraid you'd say something like that."

"You asked for an expert and honest opinion. And, Mrs. Pope, being gorgeous is not a crime."

"Perhaps not." She hesitated. "But beauty can be a *curse*. Decent guys tend to be shy and afraid to approach, while the aggressive types often are beasts. It's scary. In movies, it's always the beautiful women who attract serial killers."

She added, "Thankfully, you appear the decent type. I noticed in the way you sized up the dress, you don't leer — you appreciate. That's a major difference to women."

"I'm so relieved," Harper said, smiling. "It's bad enough being perceived as a singular killer."

Elissa winced. "Seriously, men aren't the only problem. Female friends can be difficult to find and harder to keep."

"Would you rather be unattractive?"

"Ouch. All right, I'm like the actors who strive for fame and fortune and despise the paparazzi who come with it. Or lottery winners who fall into total despair. Yin and yang."

"Your beauty makes you more bitter than better?"

"It has. But, thankfully, my life improved after I joined the theatre set. They taught me to accept pulchritude as a plus. And I did, at times — but seldom in real estate transactions and never when a wife is involved..." She stopped.

Then she said, "Am I talking too much? This is my first real date in so many years... and I'm overboard, aren't I?"

"No. This is good therapy. For both of us," Harper said.

"Thank you, Harper. That helps."

She raised her handbag from an adjacent chair and said, "I used my four hundred dollar discount for this. It's from a new designer in New York named Kate Spade. Like it?"

"It's fresh," Harper said. "Like modern architecture."

"Exactly. It's small but holds my entire survival kit, also known as my very personal effects." She held up a wrist. "I also loaded up on bangles. If the FBI insists on casting me as a moll, why not enjoy the role? And bangles offer something to stare at besides my bust. *God!* I do talk too much."

Amusement filled Harper's eyes.

Gazing around, she said, "I am starting to get annoyed, though. Some of these people won't ever stop looking."

"Of course not. You have arresting looks."

"Or maybe they think I should be arrested! Could you imagine if they think I'm a... prostitute?"

"If so, they'd think I'm a John. We're in this together."

Elissa leaned back, wide-eyed. She tried to hide a huge grin with a hand over her mouth, but the crinkling of her eyes gave her away. Harper smiled, and Elissa dropped her hand, revealing a surprising panorama of sparkling teeth.

"What?" Harper said, brows raised.

Encouraged, she chirped, "Jumping *cats!* When I raised my face to you for a kiss, in public... isn't that what call girls do? And you, the noble architect, a John?" She deepened her voice to a baritone: "*Why — excuse me, miss. I must compliment your horizontals and verticals!*' How funny is that?"

"Well! With that vocal range, you're a delight tonight."

"Actually... except onstage, I can't recall having so much fun. But if you wonder about that kiss invitation? It's what everyone does at Lake Forest functions. It implies nothing."

"Zip? *Nada?* I am deeply disheartened!"

"Don't be. You're adorable in that business suit. If I were a call girl, I'd offer you treats for free. Or is it tricks? And if I'm not mistaken, the suit is made-to-measure Savile Row sharkskin? So perhaps, you'd leave me a handsome *tip?*"

"You're right about the suit," he said, surprised.

"I had been assigned to Patrick's wardrobe. But forget that. I'm having a fantastic time and do not wish to spoil it."

"Then let's test your theory about the waiter." Harper raised a finger, and darned if the waiter didn't pop right over.

In Lake Forest...

IN THE GARAGE on Lake Road, Inspector Carlisle rapped the hood of the silver Mercedes. An agent had found Hertz rental papers with Harper's name in the glove box.

"So he obviously switched cars," the Inspector said. "We should have found what other car he took days ago. Go back into the house and search for records on all the cars. Insurance papers, service records, tax claims, anything."

"We did all that," the agent said. "Three of their cars are accounted for, including one at a dealer for service. We don't know if any other vehicle was ever kept in the empty stall."

"Well, hell, they couldn't have just walked away. Did the Pope woman have another car?"

"No sir. Just the Volvo."

"Damn." The Inspector rapped the hood again. "What about tire marks on the floor of the empty stall?"

"We shot photographs, but the marks are all intermixed. It's going to take awhile, and I don't think they'll help much. Is there any progress on reaching the owners of the house?"

"Not yet," the Inspector said. "They're at sea. But we've contacted a lot of agencies, and we expect to have better luck in the morning."

"It's already morning in Greece."

"So it is. I'm heading downtown right now."

Carlisle left in a hurry.

Chapter 18

THEIR LAMP was dim. From their table, they could view lights all along the valley. They preferred to look into each other's eyes.

During small talk, Elissa often touched Harper's hand or forearm. She tapped his wrist now and said, "You never finish telling me about your watershed."

"Hmm?"

"You said the house you did for the Parcheski fellow was a watershed in your career. That implies a major change."

"Well, yes. But... it's a long story."

"Book length?"

Harper smiled. "Not that long."

"Unless you're weary of my company, I'd like to hear it."

Harper sipped his coffee and said, "Well... The Parcheski house gave me an opportunity to create a minor wonder — thirty thousand under budget, cover story in *Architectural Record*, and Parcheski was thrilled. When I told him I was considering leaving ABK, he insisted on giving me the commission for a redevelopment project on the wharf in Monterey. I grabbed Barney Hochhalter, the firm's HVAC expert, and we went down there for a look."

"That's a great start," Elissa said. "I'm enjoying this."

Harper spread his hands. "So, Barney saw all the rich beauties strolling among the boutiques in nearby Carmel-by-the-Sea, and he was sold. We moved there, and the Parcheski development won national awards for all of us. It also gave me the means to start my own house, on a piece of Parcheski's coastal property, and I've been there ever since."

"That's wonderful!"

"Yes it was."

"And what about the young genius — Golden George? How well did he do with your civic center?"

Harper's eyes saddened. "Unfortunately, construction bids for the Mill Valley Civic Center were much higher than the bond issue, and the entire design had to be economized. Some of George's best ideas were scrapped. Within a year, he quit architecture entirely. He went to Europe to take up sculpture and painting. That was the last I heard of him."

"How ironic. You must have felt vindicated, knowing the firm had blundered badly by taking you off the project."

"No," Harper said, his expression wistful. "I had grown to like George very much. I'm sorry he quit the profession. There are few architects with his vision, and his departure was a loss to all of us. I've often wished I could find him, to entice him to work with me."

"Don't underestimate your own talents, Harper. I'm sure you're every bit as good as Golden George."

"Well, George and I have entirely different architectural styles; so there's really no basis for comparison. But when you asked if I were a decent architect this afternoon, I said I wasn't 'indecent', and that's being realistic. I'm not a genius. George is a genius, but he had picked the wrong firm to join — just as I had."

Elissa smiled. "You've obviously been doing well, though. A sixty-million dollar housing project at Fort Sheridan — that's a long way from Carmel."

Harper nodded. "Well, the contract was initiated in San Francisco. I'm not so well connected that I attract clients as far away as Chicago."

"Still, sixty million..."

"Yes. I sometimes accept large projects, provided they're a few basic structures multiplied and rearranged. That's all there is to Fort Sheridan."

Elissa folded her hands and leaned forward. "Are you sure you aren't minimizing your talent?"

"Yes, I'm sure. Within my range of specialties, I'm good at what I do. In that sense, at least, I've been happy with my work for the past several years."

"Happy without Heather?"

Harper looked at her without answering.

Elissa raised a hand to her face as her heart sank. "There I go again! I'm so sorry — that was utterly stupid of me."

Harper cocked his head and smiled. "That's all right — it's a natural question. My answer is that I have adjusted my definition of happiness a bit, and under that definition I am happy without Heather."

Elissa bit her lip. "That sounds like you still love her. Have you thought about trying to get her back?"

"That's impossible," Harper said.

"Why?"

"Because — Heather is dead."

***

***

STUNNED, Elissa dropped her spoon. She gazed into her soup. She couldn't touch her soup. Her mouth curled, and she struggled to say the word: "...Dead?"

"I'm sorry," Harper said.

"No — *I'm* sorry. I thought you were... just divorced. I had no idea that... that Heather was... dead."

Harper left his hands on the table, keeping them steady. "Yes, we had been divorced. Her death came afterwards."

"Dear God," Elissa said. "I'm really so sorry. I shouldn't have pestered you about it. God, I am so sorry."

"No need," he said. "I'm more sorry for you."

She reached across the table and took his hand. She held firmly for a moment. "No need to be sorry for me, either."

He said carefully, "I'll tell you about Heather — if you care to tell me about Mr. Pope."

For a moment she gazed steadily into his eyes, then nodded. "All right. To know me, though, you get the good, the bad, and the ugly."

He said, "That's all very important. But if you'd rather not... I just thought it could help."

"Yes," Elissa said. "I think it would help, actually... Yes, I am finally ready to talk about Patrick Pope."

The waiter arrived at that moment with their entrees. He made a production of it, placing each plate before them with a flourish. He described the dishes, arranged items on the table, dusted crumbs, offered refills of wine and water, and waited endlessly for dismissal. It would have been grand if his patrons had been in the proper mood.

When he finally departed, they breathed in relief.

"Patrick Livingston Pope," Elissa said with a slice of bitterness in her voice — then stopped.

"Yes?"

Behind them, a piano player had taken his seat and began stroking the chords of Errol Garner's *Misty*.

"Patrick was a Yale graduate in business administration and economics, the eldest son in a prominent Lake Forest family. He had been groomed to take control of the Pope machinery business in Chicago. He also was good-looking and twenty-seven years old when he plucked me from the various offerings — and married me."

There was a tremble in her hands as she waved a fork over her dish.

She said, "I thought we were a good couple in the beginning. Maybe it was the thrill of being widely admired and accepted within the top echelons. Or maybe it was Patrick's good looks and personal power. And it felt good, matching the expectations of his father, and especially his mother, who was more meticulous. Whatever, I enjoyed a brief bliss, then a long period of contentment. Just not long enough."

"What spoiled it?" Harper asked.

"I was *so* nice to Patrick. But the idiot didn't want nice."

The piano notes struck a melancholy chord, causing Elissa to raise her eyes upward before settling them onto Harper's concerned expression.

"Patrick apparently wasn't doing well in the business. Unlike me, he wasn't fulfilling his father's expectations. They began having furious brawls. That led Patrick to tamper with various mixes of alcohol and drugs, until one day his alter ego emerged like... a *monster*. He began staring at

me, thinking his troubles were my fault, and then he started taking it out on me."

"By doing what?"

"First, he started jealously blaming me for compliments I received from other men. He accused me of flirting if I used lip gloss..." She dropped her head, raising it slowly. "...And he started beating the hell out of me."

"Good Lord."

"That's what I actually meant by beauty being a curse. It's all Patrick ever saw — my exterior. Never what's inside, up high, like my heart. I realized he didn't love me, he loved sex, and strictly — I mean strictly — his definition of it."

Realizing her hand was bending her fork, she suddenly dropped it. "He equated sex with pain. He had gone so far as lessons in how to apply it from a prostitution ring that specialized in it..." She stopped as if frozen for a minute.

The piano covered her sudden silence with music, and Elissa lowered her face into her hands for that quivering interval, then abruptly straightened. "Harper, if I continue with this story, it's going to get miserably bitter. I think I'd prefer to quit while I'm ahead."

He gazed at her affectionately. "By all means, stop then."

"Thank you," she said. "I'll put an end to it by stating simply that I managed eventually to save myself from him. It wasn't easy, though. For a long time, I was a nervous wreck. I had started drinking scotch, then smoking, then driving too fast. I did everything, work or socializing, at a terrible frenzy until... One day I realized I was destined for some treatment facility unless I got Patrick into one first. Somehow, I managed to do that. Then I sued for divorce, and I won a restraining order to keep him away from me. Naturally, his family was furious that *I* did all that to *him*..."

A lock of hair fell across her left eye. With two fingers, she whipped it back in place. She stared at the dark window.

"In response, the family rigged the settlement so that I received no substantial part of their fortune. In church, they opposed my divorce on religious grounds. They claimed I was *frigid* and used contraception to avoid bearing his children. How does a *girl* — that's what Patrick insisted on calling me — disprove lies like those?" She shook herself.

"I went on the offensive. I had to make semi-public my scars and bruises. But Lake Forest hates scandals, and to even hint at one — I became an outcast for months. It seemed the whole male gender was afraid of my looks, my notoriety, or Patrick's wealth, or all three. Well, it didn't matter anymore. I didn't want any of that family's money."

"But you kept the name," Harper noted. "Why?"

"Strictly for business," she responded, raising her chin. "Going into North Shore real estate, the Pope name was an asset, at least publicly, whereas the financially foggy Bennett name had become a liability."

Elissa stared down at her black onyx ring. "And I guess it was another defiant gesture that gave me a bit of satisfaction at the time. Like this ring did. It's because onyx dispels grief, they say. Because black is the absence of light. They say it's used at the end of unhappy relationships. They say it boosts self-confidence..." She hesitated, then added...

"And who are *'they'*? I really don't give much of a damn."

Her eyelids fell closed. Her mouth fell open, quivering.

"I just think of it as my courage ring."

The pianist began playing *It's Easy to Say,* a richly romantic Mancini melody. Feeling how the music throbbed within her heart, Elissa elevated her gaze into Harper's clear blue irises and saw a glint of moisture there. Leaking tears from her own sparkling eyes, she whispered, "Darn my runaway mouth. Sometimes I get so *emotional* — I'm so *sorry.*"

"Never apologize for having a soul," Harper said. "It's a good thing. I wish everyone had one."

"I did try to stop but I couldn't. It's just... those days and nights of Patrick have been... my obsession. Can we go?"

"Yes," he said, straightening. He signaled the waiter.

Her hair fell across her eye again. This time she ignored it. "I ruined our first night of vacation, going from a delight to a *dud!* All because that bloody obsession won't go away!"

"It might prolong an obsession," Harper suggested, "by keeping it bottled inside. Pour it out. I'm a good listener."

"You're also very sweet, Harper. But I know full well that everyone detests hearing other people's issues."

"Inconsiderate people *are* the issues," he said. "Refusal to consider the misfortunes of others is an ice-cold barrier to social harmony." He gathered her hands in his. "I'm glad you shared your story. Every word of it." He released her hands. "And I'm glad to get out of here. Let's take a drive with the top down and see the mountains in the moonlight."

Eyes still misty, Elissa managed an oblique smile. "I'm so grateful you understand me. Perhaps now we can move on."

The waiter arrived and Harper accepted the check. It was snatched instantly by Elissa. "I'm paying, remember?"

"But —"

"Don't you dare quarrel. I have gone into tough mode."

Harper withdrew his fingers. Elissa conducted the transaction, shunting aside her loose hair and personal grievances
and calculating a generous gratuity. She paused to smile at
the kindly, mature pianist who had tried hard to impress her.
She added a solid tip for him as well... then blew him a kiss.

Harper noted and silently approved the tip amounts,
which he intended to fully reimburse. And he studied
Elissa's profile against the lights on the piano platform...

*

*Harper has found himself mesmerized by the musicality in
Elissa's voice, the precision of her speech, the deep breath in her em-
bellishments, and the occasional low-key resonance of her tone. He
marvels at her graceful hand gestures, the ways her lips form her
words, the way her large eyes convey her deepest emotions.*

*Now, with her surprising toss of a kiss, Elissa has thoroughly
delighted the pianist — a gesture that demonstrates her uncanny
sensitivity to the needs of others — even while enduring her own
grievances of fates and circumstances.*

All that — plus her extraordinary courage.

*

He said as they rose from the table, "It may not be my
place to say it, but Patrick Pope is the world's worst fool
since Nero."

In Virginia...

THE PHONE chirped softly in the study of an Alexandria
residence, where General Lyman P. Norgan worked late

hours on a pet project. He slapped down a pencil, shifted his manuscript aside, and lifted the receiver. "Who's calling?"

The receiver emitted a series of tone codes.

The General activated his personal scrambler. He said, "Yes, Inspector. What've you got?"

FBI Inspector George Carlisle said, "We've finally got a description of the car Harper took from the garage of that Lake Forest mansion."

"It's about time. What in god-damned hell took you so long?"

"The car wasn't registered with the owners of the mansion. It belongs to a friend who joined them on their European tour. All of them were on a chartered yacht in the Greek Isles. Just to locate them, we worked through the owners' law firm, the State Department, the Greek embassy, the CIA, and American Express. Believe it or not, it was American Express that came through."

"And?"

"The car is a Mercedes 500SL. That's a two-seater sports coupe, just like one Harper had rented and left behind. But the rental car is silver, and this one is red."

"Did you manage to get the license?"

"Oh yeah, we got it. The plates are personalized. They spell H-I-S-O-W-N — *His Own.*" The Inspector snorted. "It's one of those dumb-ass Yuppie plates."

The General rapped his pencil on the desktop. "This should produce results. I suggest that you link up with Baker and get ready for travel. Like *now.*"

"Done," the Inspector said.

Hanging up, the General returned to his manuscript.

Chapter 19

HIGH ON Trail Ridge Road, Grey Harper drove onto a scenic overlook and switched off the headlights. The moon was behind them and bright. Snow-crested mountains stood in sharp relief against a star-filled sky.

Elissa, leaning back against the headrest, said softly, "This is incredible. I've never seen so many stars. Have you?"

Harper did not answer, and she saw that he was staring straight ahead and frowning.

"Harper?"

"Mmm?"

"Hello. Have you ever seen so many stars?"

He glanced upward briefly. "Only a few nights like this in places like this — ten thousand feet above smog and haze."

He shifted in his seat and faced her. "You know, I've been thinking all day about the killing of Keith Munro. And I just can't imagine who might have done it — or why."

Elissa was puzzled. "I assumed they wanted to frame you and conceal your discovery of the radon."

"But who's 'they'?" Harper rapped the steering wheel. "I'm nearly convinced that it's not the Pacific Empire Corporation. They relied on Munro to look out for their interests, and he was good at that. If they had wanted a cover-up, Munro would not have stood in their way. Quite the contrary, he would have taken charge of it."

"But who else could it be?"

"I have no idea. All I know is that whoever's doing these things... they're not afraid of involving the FBI."

Elissa cringed. "That's creepy."

Harper sat for a moment, staring, then opened the car door. "I need to take a walk. Want to come along?"

"If you'll hold onto me," Elissa said. "I'm wearing heels borrowed from Lake Road. They fit with adjustable straps, but not well enough for stumbling around in the dark."

Harper went to her side of the car, opened the door, and held out his hand. Her legs swung into view, and he smiled.

As they strolled, the car park was approached by a lone vehicle, a camper. It stopped nearby, illuminating Elissa and Harper with its headlights. Its engine remained running, and no one stepped out.

Harper made a chopping motion with his hands, signaling the driver to cut off his lights. There was no response.

"How rude!" Elissa said.

Harper said, "Wait here."

Elissa felt a sudden fear. "Where are you going? We don't know who they are. Wait!" She stumbled after him.

He ignored her, marching toward the vehicle.

It began backing up, onto the road, and turned. It moved off, and its engine drone disappeared around a bend.

Elissa arrived in her heels. The silence became intense.

With a tremor in her voice, she said, "I wish you hadn't done that. What if they were the men chasing us? You would've walked right into their guns!"

"I doubted that our enemies would have a vehicle with Arkansas plates, Mrs. Pope. I'm sure the driver was just a country boy who wanted a good look at the woman in the silk dress — the best scenery he could see tonight."

The tightness in Elissa's chest faded a bit. "I hope that's all it was. But please, don't be so impetuous. Country boys can be big and mean."

"I'll be careful, Mrs. Pope."

They came to a waist-high parapet. Beyond it, the mountainside fell away in a steep tumble of rock and timber.

Harper, drawing Elissa closer to the edge, said, "Look — the moon has filled the canyon with the mountain's shadow. You can't see anything down there. It's pitch black."

With her heels nudging the pebbles, Elissa clutched tightly to his arm and gazed downward — into an abyss. Instinctively, she recoiled. "That is *scary*," she whispered.

Elissa quickly turned away, toward the moonlight.

"It's the army," he said.

She looked at him. "I beg your pardon?"

He slipped out from Elissa's grip and rested both hands on the parapet, his shoulders bending over the cliff. "It has something to do with the army. Those men who attacked the mansion, they were moving like soldiers. The way they dashed about, held their weapons, used hand signals. It's exactly the way we were instructed at Fort Ord — another fort that's closing, by the way."

Elissa hadn't thought of Harper as a former soldier. She tried to visualize him in battle fatigues... and couldn't. Of course, that would have been twenty years ago, long before he became this distinguished looking architect. She said, "Harper? What sort of work did you do in the army?"

He inclined his head — his driving glasses reflecting a spark of light from somewhere — and smiled. "Camouflage."

"Camouflage? You mean, like painting tanks?"

"Well, I worked on patterns and paint formulas for them, but mostly I designed fake structures to fool enemy bombers. Leave it to army intelligence to employ my architectural skills on buildings designed to be blown up."

They both laughed, and Harper said, "Seriously, this affair must have some direct connection to Fort Sheridan. Not just the old woods, but the military base. In a way, it reminds me of something Barney often talked about."

"Barney?"

"Did I mention him — the HVAC specialist in my firm?"

"Oh — the guy who ogled the strolling girls in Carmel."

"That's him. Anyway, he's a conspiracy buff, and he believes a secret government exists in the United States — a government run not by elected politicians, but by powerful generals and industrialists. I sometimes got tired of this and told Barney he was going off the deep end. Then he'd remind me of Eisenhower's warning against the military-industrial alliance and argue that Eisenhower was in a position to know."

Elissa took a moment to process what he had said. Then:

"Are you suggesting we're being hunted by such secret and powerful men?" Her voice sounded brittle.

"Well, I hope not," Harper said. "But the attack by men who moved like soldiers — and a possible link to Fort Sheridan — has me wondering." He stared down into the abyss.

"But the old military base is *closed*," Elissa said. "It was shut down after the Cold War ended. There's absolutely nothing there any more."

Harper lowered his voice. "There are similarities to Fort Ord, environmental and otherwise. My experience at Ord is one reason I got this job. There might very well be *something* there — something beyond the mere presence of radon. I just wonder if it's terrible enough to set off a chain of cold-blooded murders."

Elissa shivered. She was becoming dizzy from the altitude, the darkness, from Harper's menacing implications.

One of her heels caught a stone, and she tottered off-balance. Instantly, Harper's arms clamped around her tightly, and her body felt — *frail*. She sensed the parapet at her hips, a cold wind from the chasm slicing across her naked back.

Suddenly the horrendous abyss seemed to rise up to swallow her.

"*God*, let *go of me!*" she screamed. "What are you *doing!*"

The sound of another vehicle came up behind them and he released her. In the moment when the vehicle's headlights swept Harper's face, his eyes were strange, as if he did not recognize her; his hands fanned outward, awkwardly.

Glaring, Elissa pressed her hands to the neckline of her dress, felt her heart pounding in her palms, her lungs seeking oxygen in the thin air. Then she shuddered. And the terrifying abyss — both behind her and between them — began to recede. "Oh, God — for a moment..." She stopped.

"Elissa, what *is* it?" His eyes now showed nothing but genuine concern. "What's wrong?"

"It's... oh hell," she sputtered. "I just got... bewildered."

In the darkness, his voice seemed soft and distant as he said, "What in the world were you thinking — that I was trying to *push* you — over the cliff?"

"No, not that."

But her reply was too swift.

He said, "I grabbed you hard because you had stumbled to the edge. It was all reflex! I certainly didn't mean to hurt or frighten you."

"Please — I'm all right. Can we go?"

"Yes, of course." He offered a hand.

Elissa hesitated, a heartbeat, before accepting support.

Seated in the car, she crossed her forearms and hugged her shoulders. "I'm thoroughly ashamed, Harper. Why am I continuing to ruin what started out as a beautiful evening?"

Inserting the ignition key, he hesitated and turned to her. "Elissa, it was all my fault. You were having a wonderful time, and then I had you talking about what your ex-husband did to you, and then I pulled you to the brink of a cliff, and I frightened you with conspiracy ideas. I didn't mean to, but I'm afraid I really overloaded you with stress."

She said. "Stress alone has never done that to me. Normally, I just pass out. And forget I said that. It's nothing."

"Then add the effects of a little too much wine and too little oxygen, and being watched from a strange vehicle. In any case, I'm a chump for letting the whole thing happen."

She raised her eyes to him. "Please don't blame yourself."

"Then who should I blame? The Republicans?"

She managed a smile. "Sure, why not?. But hey, all this speculation about soldiers — aren't you content with being pursued by ruthless villains and the FBI? Must we also be hunted down by the United States Army?"

Harper, starting the car, said, "You're right. That seems grossly pretentious."

"It's absurd! It's not as though we're foreign terrorists or invaders from another planet. We're just *ordinary people!*"

As the Mercedes engine rumbled in the dark, Harper gave her an appraising glance, then said, "Forgive me, Mrs. Pope, but there's not a soldier in the world who would look upon you as an *ordinary* person."

She sighed. "I see we're back to your compliments. I'll forgive that one if you'll raise the top before driving back. In my haste to leave, I left the jacket at the restaurant, and this dress just wasn't built for chilly nights in the mountains."

"You can say that again," Harper said like Groucho Marx. "But you were certainly built for that dress. And don't be angry I said that, because those assets brought you a hundred dollar discount."

"Four hundred," Elissa emphasized. "Sometimes, Harper, I could shoot you myself."

"Well then, you'll have to take a number, Mrs. Pope."

She sat straight. "A number! That's right! I need a number to retrieve that jacket." She searched her handbag and found a stub. "Swell," she said, "the restaurant hours are on this, and it's closed. Oh, well, I'm sure Misha Drier won't want it returned anyway. I'll add it's value to the whole list I send them as soon as we get out of this mess — if ever."

Neither of them spoke for a while after that.

Chapter 20

ELISSA SHOOK her damp hair to loosen it, then walked out of the suite's bedroom. She was still troubled by her odd dream of looking outside in darkness, seeing Harper in the car, under its interior lights, doing something... secretive.

No sign of him now; so she went to the sliding doors and looked out. The sun was just now sweeping the ridges.

From behind her, his voice said, "Good morning."

"Yipes!" She spun around. "Where've you been hiding?"

"I've startled you again. Sorry. I brought you a continental breakfast from the lobby." He carried a tray to a round table by the window and pulled out a chair for her.

"Well! Thank you." She sat. "Aren't you joining me?"

"I'm not a breakfast person until I've done exercise. No time for it this morning."

"Hmm. So you gathered all this just for me? Why?"

He sat down across from her. "You had an unpleasant experience last night. I thought you deserved a little boost this morning. Mostly fruits and rolls. Did I miss anything?"

"It's perfect." She spread jelly, bit a croissant and gazed around. "But where's all your stuff?"

"Oh yes. I packed my things in the car."

"What — we're traveling again? So soon?" She stared at him. "Why the sudden rush?"

Harper crossed his arms and looked at her. "There's a story with your picture in yesterday's *Denver Post.*" He took a torn-out page from his pocket and showed it.

Elissa grabbed the page. "No wonder those people were staring at me! Good grief... It's that poster photo from *The Taming of the Shrew!* It was a *costume!* But look at that huge wig, that ridiculous necklace! My snooty expression! People seeing this will take me for a supercilious Lake Forest diva who flaunts her filthy riches! The only people hoping for *my* return will be gigolos and kidnappers! Oh God."

"Don't take it so hard. Those people last night were looking at a remarkably beautiful woman. Maybe one or two saw the news photo, and you're right. It's not the real you."

He stood. "Anyway, thinking about what I said last night, I'm anxious to get to Carmel. All my preliminary work is there — the Fort Sheridan site plans, historical records..."

"Harper."

"Yes?"

"They know where you live!"

He nodded. "Nonetheless, I need to go there."

"Why?"

"Why?" His eyes widened. "Mrs. Pope, I've been telling you — we need answers, explanations. We can't live forever on your American Express card."

Her hands fell onto her lap. "We might live longer," she moaned. "If we go to your house, that could be the end."

Harper gazed sadly at her face. "Well, I hadn't planned to take you there. We'll split up somewhere along the way."

"The hell you say!" She jumped up, knocked her chair back, paced away, and spun to face him.

"Is that why you brought me breakfast? To soften the blow? To play me for a silly fool?"

"No, Mrs. Pope. That was not the reason."

His voice was soft but firm. She looked into his eyes and saw how steady they were... and also how disappointed.

Elissa relented. "All right. I guess I'm sorry."

He nodded, shrugged.

She waved her hands loosely. "But damn it all, Harper — you have this maddening way of..." she caught her breath, "...of taking action that appears spontaneous, but isn't, because you've been secretly *pondering* these choices all the while. Then you spring these... these intensely calculated surprises on me. I don't know how your mind manages to be in two or more places at the same time, but I won't let you get away with it. I won't have it! I refuse to be dumped somewhere *along the way* like a piece of garbage!"

"But it's for your own safety, Mrs. Pope."

"That happens to be my responsibility, not yours."

Shrugging, he said, "It's a thousand miles to Carmel. We'll have plenty of time to discuss it later. For now, if you want to come along, you'll need to pack in a hurry."

"Fine." She moved toward the bedroom. Passing the desk, she glanced down and said, "What's all this?"

"Hmm?"

"These license plates. What are you doing with them?"

"Oh, those." Harper glanced down at the set of personalized plates from the Mercedes. "It's rather embarrassing driving a red sports car with plates that spell 'HIS OWN' — don't you think?"

"Ordinarily," Elissa said, "I wouldn't be caught dead."

"That's precisely what we hope to avoid." He smiled. "I had thought about smearing mud on these — which would get us stopped in twenty minutes — or switching them with another car. But 'HIS OWN' is so outrageously conspicuous... I can just imagine the other owner's double-take and swift call to the police. So this is the best I could do."

Harper lifted one of the plates and briefly described how he had taken a small hammer from the car's tool kit and had pummeled the words "Illinois" and "Land of Lincoln" into flat metal.

Next, he had inverted the plate and re-lettered it with the marking pens from his drawing kit, topped with a sealant of spray fixative. Finally, he had peeled off the stickers with a razor and transferred them to the opposite corners.

Now he turned the plate upside down for her inspection.

Scratching his jaw, he said, "It won't withstand close scrutiny, but from twenty feet away... what do you think?"

Upside down, the lettering spelled 'NMO SIH'.

Elissa wagged her head. "There are a lot of ways people could interpret that, especially a junkie. It will either get us arrested or save our lives. I think you're almost a genius!"

He spread his arms. "*Almost* a genius? That, Mrs. Pope, sounds like the story of my life."

She was about to say something when he added, "But I'll have you know, I've also repaired the heel of your shoe — the one I broke at the Chicago airport."

"You *did?*" Elissa's whole appearance brightened. "Two favors this morning? And you managed to repair an Italian-made spike-heeled woman's shoe without spending a hundred bucks? Wow. That is what I call *genuine* genius!"

Chapter 21

THEY SLICED through Colorado along U.S. 40, intending to rejoin Interstate 80 at Salt Lake City. This route, although slower, was more direct and more scenic. It brought them to Steamboat Springs for lunch.

The ski village was less enchanting during the summer, but its restaurants were charming. They selected a Swiss-styled cafe on the mainstreet. From a window table, they observed townspeople in western clothes strolling lazily about their business. And they kept watch on the car.

Elissa had volunteered to drive the next leg of their journey, giving Harper freedom to enjoy a stein of ale with his House Special sandwich. His serving was huge, the sandwich two inches thick, embedded among salad greens and deep-fried potato wedges. Even so, Harper had consumed most of it before Elissa had pegged five bites from her fruit plate. "Where on earth do you stash it all?" she queried. "If I ate like that, I'd be a female walrus."

"It runs in the family," he said casually. "Generations of Harpers have eaten like hogs without gaining much weight."

"Lucky stiff."

Settling back in his chair, Harper said, "Please, Mrs. Pope. Don't call me a stiff — yet."

Her eyes flared, and she dropped her fork. "God, what a thought! At times, your sense of humor is mind-boggling."

"Yes, well — I've also been *pondering.* Rejoining Interstate 80 for the rest of the trip doesn't seem like a good idea now, and I'm wondering if we should take a more devious route..." He waited for a comment. When none came, he said, "I'm trying to include you in my pondering so that you won't feel left out."

"Are you being sarcastic?"

"If that's what it sounded like, forgive me."

Elissa shook her head — and then suddenly reached for his arm. "Harper," she whispered. "Look outside. It's a state trooper. He's stopping by our car!"

Harper switched his attention to the patrol vehicle, which was gradually slowing as it approached. The officer clearly was inspecting the red Mercedes. He stopped his vehicle, consulted a clipboard, glanced again at the Mercedes — then drove on.

Elissa sighed with relief. "It appears your doctored license plates passed the test," she said. "And that cop was closer than twenty feet."

"I hope you're right," he said. "But he might be playing it cool."

"You mean — driving on, but radioing for assistance? Setting up roadblocks? That sort of thing?"

"Yes, that sort of thing," Harper said.

Elissa pushed her hands together and frowned. "Shouldn't we get out of here?"

Harper sat quietly for a moment, then said, "No. Relax. Finish your meal."

"But, Harper..."

"If we rush out," he said, "we might encounter that officer again. I would rather not give him a second look at us."

"But if he's setting up roadblocks..."

"Then they'll catch us, whether we leave now or later. We might as well enjoy our lunch, Mrs. Pope. I'm sure the food here is better than the food in jail."

"Good God! Now my appetite is ruined." Elissa's large eyes became sorrowful.

"Well, give it a few minutes," Harper said. "If we're not surrounded by police with megaphones in the next ten minutes, we'll probably be okay. Then you can relax and eat."

He smiled at her.

She smiled back. "You're about the steadiest person I've ever met. I've never even heard you *cuss*. Don't you ever get excited, or angry, or scared to death — or *anything?*"

"Yes, of course I get excited," he said.

"When?"

"Every time I look at you."

Elissa rolled her eyes.

"Anyway," Harper said, "I suppose this little brush with law enforcement has answered the question I brought up a moment ago."

"Hmm?"

"We can assume that *they* know what kind of car we have. If they know about it in Steamboat Springs, they know about it everywhere — and we'd gain nothing by deviating farther from Interstate 80. We'd only lose time."

"Maybe it's time to abandon that car and catch a plane," Elissa suggested.

Harper considered this. "Maybe. But there might be surveillance at the large airports and bulletins at the small ones." He leaned across the table. "Actually, I wish there were a way we could switch cars again."

"You mean steal another one?"

Noting her disapproval, he said, "I guess not. It would be reported, and we'd gain nothing."

Elissa nodded in relief. "How about getting the Mercedes repainted or something?"

"Wouldn't that arouse suspicion — asking a shop to repaint a brand-new car? A car that has a perfectly spectacular finish? A car with hand-lettered license plates?"

"You're an artist, Harper. Why don't *you* paint it?"

"Mrs. Pope — painting a car is not like painting a picture. To achieve a proper finish, I'd need spray equipment, buffers, heat lamps..."

"It doesn't have to be a *good* job, Harper. It just needs to be different."

Slapping the table, Harper said, "Why, of course! That's absolutely brilliant! You're almost a genius, too, Mrs. Pope!"

She smiled brightly and picked up her fork. "I believe I've also regained my appetite." She savored a bite of fruit and said, "It doesn't appear that anyone is attempting to surround us."

"No," Harper said, glancing out the window. "No police, no FBI, no battalion of the U.S. Army." He turned back to her and sighed. "In a certain romantic Sundance Kid sort of way, it's almost a letdown."

Chapter 22

THE HARDWARE CLERK, a heavyset old wrangler with white mustache and gruff demeanor, fussed over the collection of spray cans in Harper's shopping basket. He seemed annoyed by the quantity and variety, because none of it made sense to him. "Whatever it is you're paintin'," he declared, "I'd surely like to see the results when you're done."

"It's for a mural," Harper said. "I paint large murals."

"Is that so? You doin' the side of a building, then? Maybe like that old brick wall next to the Exxon? I hope you ain't another one of them hippie peace-freak painters."

Harper said, "Actually, my technique is more like Cubism — like Boccioni, sort of."

"*Hrmmph*," the old clerk grumbled. "Can't say I ever took much personal likin' to Boccioni, or any of that other so-called modern art." He gazed at Harper's face. "Where're you planning to do all this mural paintin' — if I might ask?"

"Not in town," Harper promised, leaning on the counter. He waved a hand in a westerly direction. "It's for a barn — way out that way, somewhere... I can't tell you exactly, my friend. I've only just arrived here from my last commission, in Paris... Paris, France."

"You don't say." The clerk wriggled his mustache and gave Harper another stern look. "Didn't know they had any barns in Paris, France. You sure it wasn't Paris, Texas?"

Elissa thrust forth her card. "Please, we're in a hurry."

The clerk looked more kindly at Elissa, then frowned. "Um, I'm frightful sorry, ma'am — we don't take American Express in here. Only Visa or MasterCard, if you got 'em."

Harper produced his Visa. "This one okay?"

Elissa bumped his arm in a silent warning.

"Yeah," the clerk nodded. "That'll do, Picasso, provided you got some photo identification. Like a driver's license? Or maybe in your case — a passport?"

Harper laughed and handed over his license.

The clerk inspected it, then bent over and filled out the charge slip. "Now, if you'd be so kind to sign your autograph, it will make a nice addition to my celebrity museum."

Harper jotted on the slip and pushed it back. "This has been fun," he said.

"You made my whole day," the clerk said.

After they had left the store, lugging bags of paint, Elissa said, "You're absolutely *insane*, Harper!"

"You think so?" He seemed surprised. "But the store didn't have any credit card electronics. Visa won't know of the transaction until the proprietor mails it in — probably not before the end of the week, when he has a batch."

"But good grief — a *mural?* On a *barn?*"

"Do you have a better story?"

"I'm surprised you didn't say you were going to spray graffiti on a highway overpass!"

Harper smiled. "You're right. That is a better story."

***

THEY HAD PARKED on barren soil adjoining the main lodge of the ski mountain. In summer, it was the loneliest part of Steamboat Springs. The buildings were locked, the chairlifts were dismantled for maintenance, and the roads were strewn with fallen rocks.

Harper selected a couple of rocks and went to the car.

Elissa watched him curiously.

He picked one section of the left front fender and bashed a rock into it. Elissa stiffened.

Next, he backed along the side, eyed the driver's door, and hauled back for another bash.

"Harper!" Elissa shouted.

He banged the door twice and examined the results.

"Hmm," he said. "This isn't working."

Elissa said, "Harper, for God's sake..."

"It looks fake," he said, then brightened. "Of course! There's an easier way." He climbed into the car and started the engine. "You wonder what excites me? Watch this."

Elissa lifted her palms and dropped her jaw as Harper wheeled the car across the parking lot and climbed a low embankment. He drove into the trees and sideswiped a boulder, spun around and grazed the boulder again. He shifted into reverse and crashed the rear of the vehicle into a tree, threw the stick forward and charged another boulder. *CRUUMP!* He threw his arms up outrageously.

"Harper!" Elissa shouted, running at him. "Harper! Stop!"

He stopped. He rested an arm on the door and cocked his head toward her. "I'm sorry — I should have asked you to join the fun. Hop in, Mrs. Pope."

She drew herself to a halt four feet away and stared at him. "What in the hell are you doing!"

He looked a bit surprised. "Why — what does it look like I'm doing? I'm disguising the car."

"Harper — you're going to kill yourself!"

"No way," he said, his expression confident. "I know this car. I know what it can take."

For a minute, she watched his face. He watched back.

"I thought..." she said. "I thought you had only intended to paint the car."

"I'll get around to that," he said. "Climb aboard. It's like riding the bumper cars at an amusement park."

"I don't know why I'm doing this." She strutted around the car and opened the passenger door.

"Buckle up," Harper said.

Elissa clipped the seat belt. Harper hit the accelerator.

***

Twenty minutes later, Elissa watched him picking at the car, breaking off ornaments and trim, spraying it with oxide red and gray primer. He was particular with dented areas, shading them with tones of rust and raw metal, striving for a certain effect. He also was attentive to the canvas top, using chromium yellow to suggest years of neglect. He struck a side window with a jack handle, enough to create a web of cracks. And he plied the hood off-center with a tire iron.

"Well? How's it look?"

"Horrible," she said.

"You're not just saying that, I hope."

Deciding to do more, he selected two spray cans of flat red Rustoleum and began circling the car, shooting a mist over the entire shell. He picked two more cans of flat gray primer and circled it again.

Finally, he stopped. He dropped the last of the spray cans and ambled over to the boulders where Elissa sat and watched. He sat beside her and waited for a reaction.

After a moment, Elissa cocked her head and widened her eyes. "I am..." she announced "...awestruck."

"Oh, well..."

"That car," she said, "...looks like a fifteen-year-old heap."

Harper was pleased. The basic body shell of Mercedes roadsters had changed little in recent years, and he had knocked off the parts that had defined the latest model.

"You've done a remarkable job of aging and weathering," Elissa marveled. "It looks convincingly natural — not faked. It's... actually rather exquisite."

Harper nodded. "Most owners treat a Mercedes as an investment, and they strive to protect it against rust and busted trim. Nonetheless, I wanted to make it blend with all the ordinary cars in America. I had to really trash the thing."

"You've certainly done that," Elissa said. "But I'm a little astonished that you could bring yourself to actually do it!"

"Unavoidable," Harper said. "Well... I'll send the owners my Mercedes to make up for their loss. It has just as few miles as theirs did. It's a fair trade."

"I know. But this one — it *had* been such a gorgeous and valuable automobile in and of itself."

"Well, yes," Harper said. "But not nearly as valuable as our own lives."

Chapter 23

THEY CROSSED PATHS with two patrol cars on U.S. 40 en-route to Salt Lake City. Neither officer noticed the decrepit "old" Mercedes cruising at a moderate pace with Elissa at the wheel.

Harper, studying maps, inquired, "Have you seen Arches National Park?"

Elissa diverted her attention from the road. "Never. Why?"

"It's about three hours south, near Moab. But I don't suppose we could justify the time."

After a moment, she said, "Is there a particular reason why this occurred to you?"

"Well, there's a huge arch that has started to crumble. I thought it could be interesting to see it — before it falls."

Her brow cocked and her hands tightened on the steering wheel. "For some reason, I rather like that idea, Harper. Let's do it."

***

IN A HOTEL farther west, Baker was on the carpet doing push-ups, his injured face twisted with exertion. "Hundred and *four*... hundred and *five*... hundred and *six*..." he counted, his voice getting louder with each number.

Inspector Carlisle was talking into a phone and rustling through road maps on a desk. "That's Baker," he said into the receiver. "He's driving me nuts, General, exercising all afternoon... As I was saying, we've mapped Harper's rate of progress to and from the point where that Nebraska farmer found the cartop. It should bring him to Salt Lake City tonight. Salt Lake is like a hub. We've got eyes on all the spokes, and there's no way Harper can come through here without being spotted. If he tries backroads or anything like that, he'll get lost, run out of gas, and fry his ass in the heat out here. It's all wasteland."

"Hundred and *nine*... Hundred and *TEN!*"

"Baker, for cryin' out loud..."

Baker flopped flat on his chest and lay still.

The Inspector just sighed and spoke tiredly into the phone. "What? Of course, General... I'll call you the minute we get a fix on him." He hung up.

Baker sprang to his feet, looking disappointed. "Damn, I'm losin' it. I used to hit a hundred and twenty five, at least."

"Who cares?" the Inspector said with immense fatigue.

"*You* should care!" Baker snapped. "You're miserably out of shape. Can't get your dick up, much less push your fat body off the floor."

The Inspector looked at Baker in surprise. "The hell's the *matter* with you?"

Baker balled his fists and whirled his arms in wide loops. He looked like a gorilla wanting to break out of a cage.

"This thing's taking too long. You don't even know what you're doing. You're letting that Harper guy outfox you."

"You got some better ideas?" the Inspector shot back.

"Yeah, I do. I say we shouldn't be so lazy, hanging out in a hotel room waitin' for some stupid cops to do the job for us. I should be on the road with Harper's mugshots, checking gas stations and roadside cafes — coming up behind him. That's what I think. That's what I do!"

The Inspector wagged his head. "By God, you want him *personally*. Does saving Norgan's ass mean so much to you?"

Baker looked surprised. "Norgan? Screw it. The General sends me nice jobs and referrals now and then — that's all. Otherwise, I couldn't care less what happens to the asshole."

"Then why do you want Harper so damned bad?"

"He needs to be taught nobody does what he did to me and gets away with it. Nobody ever has. Nobody ever will."

The Inspector flapped his arms at his sides. "Jesus Christ, Baker. I thought you were a pro. Now you sound like a punk from a street gang."

For a moment, Baker coiled up and looked like a cobra ready to strike. Then he settled down. He said, "You're right, Inspector. Forget it. I enjoy my work so much, sometimes I get a little carried away."

The Inspector studied Baker briefly, then said: "You'll get your kicks, Baker. We're going to find Harper."

"The lady, too," Baker said. "Don't forget her."

"Like I said, Baker, you'll get your kicks."

***

ELISSA'S EYES traced the long curve of Landscape Arch, soaring across a violet sky. She felt a pull from it, as though the arch were drawing her spirit toward some eternal realm.

Elissa had spent her years in the densely populated and mostly wooded flatlands of metropolitan Chicago, where long-distance inland views were sparse. This road trip had introduced her to many grand vistas. In the region of the Arches, the panorama was astounding.

Farther west, the sun was squatting on a vast and bizarre horizon of rocky pinnacles and monstrous slabs. The light grew vivid with pinks and reds, the air so quiet that Elissa's ears were filled with the sound of her own breathing.

Standing beside her on the sandy pathway in front of the Wall Arch, Harper looked across to Landscape Arch and said, "Isn't it strange to think how that magnificent formation has been taking shape longer than the human race — and might be gone in our own lifetime?"

Elissa, who hadn't said a word since her eyes found that arch, turned to him and asked quietly: "Is that why we came to see it — for that kind of reassurance?"

He looked down at her. "What do you mean?"

"Well, we didn't plan to set aside our other urgencies to see a tourist attraction, no matter how gorgeous. What if we're really seeking a hope, a conviction, that huge structure will fall before we do?"

Harper gently embraced her shoulders. Seeing the arch outlined in crimson as the sun went down, he said, "I've always been fascinated with arches, as pure structural forms. In Greek, the prefix arch- means 'master' or 'principle', and so the word architect means 'master builder.' In the same way, I think of the arch as the most dominant form in architecture — graceful and amazingly strong, and mathematically... " He stopped. "I'm boring you."

"Not yet," she said. "What are you trying to say?"

"Well, look..." His other arm swept the horizon. "There are many arches here. Behind us is the Wall Arch, a shape so massive it's hard to believe it was created by haphazard winds. I'm amazed it's still there with all the weight on its span." He turned and looked at her.

"In any case, some of these natural arches are more artful and durable than all the arches conceived by deliberate human intelligence. Now, don't ask why I'm intrigued by that — I don't know. But I think it's why I came."

As they gazed into the great bowl of shimmering light, their eyes took on a look of enchantment. Fiery rays gave a sheen to Elissa's face and lips, a dazzle to her hair.

She took hold of Harper's hand.

"I've been suffering a fatalistic streak for years," she said, resting her cheek against his shoulder. "But this experience sends shivers into my heart like a whole orchestra of violins."

As the sun dipped lower, its rays became briefly more intense against the high cloud formations, soon followed by the inevitable drift toward darkness.

Harper gave Elissa a nudge. It was time to leave, and she clutched Harper's hand the whole distance to the car.

Settling behind the steering wheel, gazing ahead, she said, "Thank you, Gray Harper. You have restored some of my childhood joy in just being alive. I won't forget this day with you." Her lips quavered. "Not as long as I live."

She quickly brought the engine to a muted roar.

Chapter 24

THE NEXT day, Elissa emerged from an indoor mall, wearing a dark olive dress and heels, crossing the street to where Harper was reading a newspaper on a bench in front of Temple Square. It seemed a peaceful place, despite traffic and tourists circling the square. She dropped a large canvas bag at her feet, sat beside him, and embraced his arm.

He said, "Another new dress?"

"Sale rack. It's my disguise. I needed to shop the mall for refills of feminine necessities, but my picture is *everywhere*. I didn't want to be obvious that I just came off the road. This working girl attire blends me with the city." She lifted the bag. "Also, I did laundry while I was out. Yours and mine."

"Oh?" He flipped a page in the *Deseret News*.

"You brought me breakfast and fixed my shoe," she said. "I wanted to return the gesture, and I hope you don't mind. The laundromat was convenient, and I was discrete."

"I'm grateful then. But you shouldn't feel subservient."

"Doing tasks for someone who expects them is subservient. Freely doing unexpected favors is not subservient; it's fun. I enjoy doing domestic things. Like playing house when I was a kid. I think you enjoyed bringing my breakfast."

"Yes I did," he said. "Thank you for knowing that."

"I'm very sorry I had doubted your sincerity. I know how that can hurt. So what's in the paper? Anything interesting?"

"Oh, yes," Harper said. "The new governor's under attack already, and there's a movement to revamp the liquor laws, and a woman has been indicted for stabbing her former husband's third wife..."

"I meant," Elissa said, "something of concern to us."

Harper dropped the newspaper onto his lap. "I think the liquor laws concern us, Mrs. Pope. I dislike going to a state store to bring a bottle in a paper bag into a restaurant."

Elissa laid an elbow on the backrest of the bench and rested her cheek on her hand. A breeze riffled her thick hair, and she smiled. "I love it," she said. "I love sitting here, among these relaxed and delightful people... And I love the thought that we're on the doorstep of a great religious sanctuary. I love the serenity of this place, the normalcy — and I just don't give a damn about cocktails in a restaurant!"

Harper laughed. He leaned back — then suddenly lifted the newspaper and pulled Elissa behind the sports pages.

"Harper, what...?"

"There's a man carrying a paper bag toward the hotel," he muttered. "— It's our old friend, Officer Baker."

Elissa peeked over the newspaper and caught her breath. "Oh my God," she breathed. "They've *found* us..."

Watching Baker walk through the entrance, Harper's eyes became steely. "Maybe not. He was moving casually, not deliberately. If we stay clear..."

"Harper, all our things are in that hotel — all my clothes, all your stuff, your drawing instruments — that beautiful sketch you did for me in Estes Park..."

"And Baker's gun," Harper said.

"Harper," she said, "we can't just leave it all..."

He hesitated. "You're right, Mrs. Pope. We could replace the clothes and most of the rest — but with the FBI on our trail, we'd have a devil of a time getting another gun."

Elissa clutched his arm. "And you couldn't replace the sketch. Even if you drew exactly the same thing, it would never truly be the same. I want that sketch, Harper."

"Well," he said, "that's flattering. But the gun is my only reason for going in. I'll try to take whatever else I can manage — including the sketch if it's that important to you."

"No," she said.

"No?"

"You take the gun and stuff, and I'll take the sketch."

Harper shook his head emphatically. "No, Mrs. Pope. I'm going alone. There's no sense in both of us taking the risk. You take a hike across town, and I'll try to catch up with you later."

Elissa shifted on the bench, stared directly into his eyes. "Do you remember when we were searching for the car at O'Hare airport?"

"What about it?"

"Who saw it first?"

"Why — you did."

"Remember before that, when the green car was chasing us in Lake Forest and we ducked into the Donnelly estate?"

"Yes..."

"Who saw the open gate?"

Harper sighed. "You did, Mrs. Pope." He shuffled the pages of the newspaper. "But who spotted Officer Baker just now? Who saw the Spackle on his shoes in the cottage? Who caught on to Rita Chan's impostor?"

"That's exactly my point, Harper."

"What point?"

Elissa crinkled a corner of her mouth. She said, "Four eyes are better than two."

"Well, of course they are, but..."

"It took both of us to get this far, Harper. At any of the times we listed, one of us missed something important — something that could have gotten both of us killed. We need all four eyes, Harper. We're a team. We've survived because we're a team. If you go in there alone, and miss something, you'll end up dead, and then I'll be alone, and then I'll end up dead. Let's stick together, pal. It's our best chance. And then I can also manage a quick change into jeans for travel."

After a moment, Harper said, "You know? You should have been a lawyer!"

Elissa looked at him curiously, and despite her anxiety, she managed a feeble smile. "And do *you* know — I actually had thought about that at one time." She said, "It was during my battles with Patrick Pope. I had seriously considered studying law — actually becoming a lawyer — just so that I could send Patrick to the cleaners in his dirty shorts. But I decided against it, of course."

"Why? Did you have any doubt you could do it?"

Her smile collapsed into a frown. "No. I was just... I was deep-down terrified of working inside any environment full of criminals!"

Chapter 25

HER BIGGEST FEAR, crossing to the hotel, was that Baker might have accomplices unknown to them. Her second biggest fear was encountering Baker or his associates aboard an elevator, where they'd be trapped.

"Look," Elissa said, "there's no hurry. Why not find a hidden spot where we could observe the lobby for a while. We might see if Baker is with anyone. We might catch him leaving, or going into the restaurant, and that would give us a chance to get in and out of our room more safely."

"I agree," Harper said. "That's a good plan. But it might require a lot of patience. It might get hard on our nerves."

"I can handle it if you can."

As they entered the lobby, they tried not to appear furtive. Harper scanned left while Elissa looked right for suspicious persons. Harper motioned to a seating area partially concealed by plants. "There?" he suggested. "We won't see the elevators, but we can see the approach."

They strolled to the couches and tried to make themselves comfortable. Harper gave Elissa a few sections from the *Deseret News*. "It's something to hide behind — but don't let the stories distract you."

"Don't be flippant, Harper. It's not helping."

"Sorry," he said.

They lifted their newspapers, and Harper whispered, "Don't forget to turn a page now and then."

"Will you *stop?*" She raised the paper to hide her smirk.

For the next twenty minutes, they didn't speak. Nor did they see anyone suspicious. The lobby provided an interesting parade of people, though. While Harper watched an attractive woman checking in, Elissa elbowed him. "Forget the blonde," she said. "Keep your eyes peeled for Baker."

Later, Elissa nudged him again. "Take a glance at the man who just came from the elevator hall, the heavy guy in the blue suit."

"What about him?"

"Doesn't he sort of resemble a cop?"

"I don't know," Harper said. "What does a cop look like?"

"Check his suit — the color, the cut, the shine. It's a Chicago suit. I can spot Chicago people anywhere by their clothes. And the shoes. And especially the way he looks at people, with that suspicious sneer."

"You could be right, Mrs. Pope. Maybe we had better stop looking at him, before he sees us."

They shifted postures, raised the newspapers, and kept out of view until they caught sight of the heavyset man pushing through the doors to the street.

An hour passed.

"This is getting awfully brutal," Elissa said.

"Yes.. My bones ache. I wish something would happen."

"Uh-oh," Elissa said.

"What's the matter?"

"You might be getting your wish. There's another man in a blue suit, and — God, he's seen us, and he's coming right for us. Harper..."

"Sit tight," Harper said. "Pay no attention."

The man stood in front of them.

"Hello," he said. "This must be the only place they allow smoking in the lobby." He indicated the ash trays on the tables. "Do you mind?"

"Go ahead," Harper said. Elissa sensed Harper's relief and tried to adopt it.

The stranger sat and lit a cigarette. "The name's Steve Downey," he said.

"Clyde Franklin," Harper said. "And my wife, Bonnie."

The man reached across the table to shake hands. He said, "Vacationing?"

"No, just passing through," Harper said.

"Do you travel often?"

"... Lately, yes."

"I'm in sales," Downey said. "Travel Club of America. We get you discounted rates at hotels all over the country. Plus a lot of other benefits. It only costs a small annual membership fee. Would you be interested in something like that, Mr. Franklin?"

"No, and if you don't mind..."

"No problem. Let me give you my card. If you change your mind and want more information, just call the toll-free number. No obligation."

Harper accepted the card.

"Well," Downey said, stubbing out his smoke, "thanks for the break. It was good meeting both of you. Have a safe trip."

Harper nodded. Downey got up and left.

"Jeez," Elissa said. "We could have done without that. I almost missed him."

"Who?"

"Baker."

"You saw him?"

"Just a glimpse. He came from the elevator hall, stopped, and then went into the gift shop. He's still in there. Now what, Harper?"

"Did he look this way?"

"I couldn't tell — wait, there he is."

Baker emerged from the shop and started stripping open a pack of cigarettes.

"Uh-oh," Harper muttered, peeking over the newspaper. "It looks like he might be hunting for ash trays, too."

"God, if we stand up to move, he'll *see* us," Elissa said.

Baker looked in their direction. He pulled a cigarette from the pack and started walking toward them.

"I think we're in big trouble, Mrs. Pope."

Elissa became frantic, searching for a way to escape.

"Wait," Harper said. "Don't move. He's stopped. He's turning — he's walking toward the entrance."

Elissa shifted her news pages. Through the doors came the heavy man she had suspected of being a cop. Baker walked straight to him, and they began talking. Then they turned to the doors and left the hotel.

"*Whoa!*" Elissa breathed. "That was close! I'm *shivering*."

"You've amazed me yet again," Harper said. "You were dead right in spotting that big man as a cop. You could make a living as a criminal."

She pulled herself together and stood. "That is *not* a compliment. Let's collect our things and get out of here."

***

OUTSIDE the hotel, Inspector Carlisle briefed Baker as they walked toward a waiting car. "We got a break. Actually two. Night before last, a woman resembling the newspaper photo was seen at a restaurant in Estes Park, Colorado. Then yesterday, one of Harper's credit cards turned up — a charge at a hardware store in Steamboat Springs. Just *yesterday*. It was odd the way it happened. Usually, the store doesn't send off the charge slips until the end of the week. But the clerk was suspicious, because Harper bought so many cans of spray paint."

"Spray paint?"

"That's right. Said he was an artist. Said he was gonna paint a mural on a barn."

"A barn?"

"That's what he said. Of course, the clerk didn't buy that. He does business with all the ranchers and farmers in the area, and there isn't one of 'em who'd want any kind of mural. And the lady with Harper, she didn't want him to use the card — got nervous about it. So the clerk thought he'd better check the credit, and he called Visa."

"Why would Harper spray-paint a barn?" Baker asked.

"I think he intended to paint the *car*," the Inspector said patiently. "He bought a lot of Rustoleum and gray primer."

The Inspector opened the car door and introduced the driver. "This is Special Agent Jim Kelly — works from the field office here."

Baker nodded at Kelly and climbed into the back seat. He said, "Okay. Are we going back there — to Colorado?"

"No need. Kelly has lined up a couple of conference calls at the field office. There's a state trooper with a possible lead, and we'll talk directly to that clerk. I got a strong hunch we're real close to Harper. Damn, I feel like we could just reach out and touch him. Until then..." He reached over and touched Kelly. "You bring that report with you? The background on Mrs. Pope?"

"Right here," Kelly said, taking it from his jacket pocket. "Not much in it, though."

After a few minutes, Carlisle folded the document and said, "I don't get it. Her mother moved out of Lake Forest and lives with Pope's step-father in Florida. Her birth father moved out of Lake Forest and lives in Italy. Adjacent to Lake Forest, the Fort Sheridan project gets this California architect who's running like hell out of Lake Forest with Mrs. Pope. Three nights ago, that couple stayed in a house whose owners left Lake Forest to hang out in Greece. What's *with* all these people? Lake Forest is one of America's richest communities — and it's not good enough for 'em?"

"Hey," Baker said. "Don't you like chasing 'em all over?"

"I had enough of that game. We'll nail 'em tonight, and I'm on tomorrow's flight back home. I guarantee it."

Chapter 26

IN THE ELEVATOR, Elissa suddenly pressed a hand to her chest and propped her body against the wall. "It just came to me, what you told that salesman."

"Hmm?"

"You introduced us as... as Clyde Franklin and wife Bonnie. *Bonnie and Clyde!* Jesus Christ, Harper!"

He smiled. "Sometimes I can't help myself."

The elevator hummed to a stop and the doors slid aside. They stepped off and went quickly toward their mini-suite, nodding at a bellman along the way.

Harper hesitated, then called after the bellman. "Young man..."

"Yessir." The bellman came back.

"We've had an emergency," Harper said. "We need to cancel. Do you have express checkout at this hotel?"

"Did you check-in with a credit card?"

"Yes," Harper said.

"Fine, then; no problem, sir. I'll tell the cashier you're leaving, and she'll mail your statement. What's the name?"

"Bennett," Elissa said. "Elissa Bennett. The room is charged in my name."

"Oh." The bellman raised a brow slightly. "The room number?" He was writing on a small notepad.

"Nine-oh-seven," Elissa said.

"Got it. You're all set." He looked at them. "You need help with the luggage?"

Harper opened his wallet. "No, thanks. But... is there a direct way into the parking garage? Without going all the way down to the lobby and back up the garage elevator?"

The bellman pointed. "You can use the fire stairs at the end of the hall. The bottom four levels open to the garage."

"Thanks." Harper handed the bellman a tip.

***

Driving out of the parking garage, Harper said, "I need to find another hardware store before it closes. I'll stop at the curb, and you can ask some pedestrians. Okay?"

"Don't stop here," she said. "Go into the next block. There's an American Express office there — see the sign? I can get some cash or travelers checks."

"Good idea," he said. "But hurry."

It took about ten minutes, and Elissa returned with a booklet of travelers checks and climbed into the car. She said, "I asked, and they said there's a hardware store on East 400 South near South 700 East. Now, can you find *that?*"

"Sounds perfectly logical," Harper said with a wink.

They entered the store just before closing time.

"We're about to close," a pretty clerk said.

"I need just a couple of minutes," Harper said. "I need spray paint and a large tarp."

"How large?"

"Oh — about thirty feet square."

"I think the biggest we have is maybe eighteen feet."

"That's okay. I'll take two."

After they had gathered the supplies and dumped them on a counter, Elissa started signing travelers checks. The clerk based an assumption on the checks, and she said, "It seems like an odd way to spend a vacation."

"What?" Elissa looked at her.

"Painting," the clerk said, gesturing at the cans.

"Well," Elissa said, sadly. "We didn't plan it. We arrived at our vacation cabin and discovered it had been vandalized. Somebody had sprayed obscenities all over our walls."

"Aw, golly," the clerk said. "I'm real sorry to hear that."

"We can't get painters in there before Tuesday," Elissa continued. "I can't stand to look at those walls for all that time. My husband thought we could spray over the graffiti — make the place livable until the painters arrive."

The clerk nodded and accepted her checks. "I don't know what this world's coming to — these kids and their spray cans. There's talk about making it illegal to sell spray paint to minors, but that won't stop 'em. If they can get liquor and drugs and guns, they'll get spray paint, too." She handed Elissa her change.

In the car, Harper said, "From now on, I'm letting you do all the talking. Your story was better than my tale of painting a mural on a barn."

"By a long shot," she said. "But now I can't wait to see the results of your next paint job — whatever the hell it is."

Chapter 27

INSPECTOR CARLISLE had camped in a small office with a square table, four chairs, six telephones. Waiting for a callback from the Colorado State Patrol near Steamboat Springs, he rapped a pencil impatiently against the Formica tabletop.

The door opened and Baker sauntered in. "Any minute," Baker said, hoisting back a chair and straddling it. "Kelly said the cop's name is Cheever."

"What's the delay?" the Inspector demanded.

"He was thirty miles out when they called him back."

The Inspector pointed his pencil. "There's something curious in what the Colorado hardware clerk said. He said the Pope woman wanted to use her own credit card, an American Express. She didn't seem nervous about that. She didn't get tense until Harper pulled out a Visa."

"It's like they've been using the Pope woman's card to travel, you mean."

"Yeah, I think that's it, exactly. But we've had her cards under surveillance, too. We've had that all along. Something just doesn't jive."

"Maybe you missed a card," Baker said. "She has a card you don't know about — maybe in her maiden name."

"You could be right. It's possible. That's gotta be the answer. What's her maiden name, do you know?"

"I think I do," Baker said, fishing for his notebook.

The phone buzzed, and the Inspector snatched it. "FBI," he said. "Inspector Carlisle."

"Officer Jake Cheever," the voice said, "Colorado State Patrol."

"All right," the Inspector said. "I want to ask if you got a bulletin on a red Mercedes Five Hundred SL, Illinois plates spelling H-I-S-O-W-N — 'His Own'. Did you get that?"

"Sure did," Patrolman Cheever said. "I thought I had your guy, too, yesterday. There was a red Mercedes parked in front of a Steamboat cafe. The plates were wrong, though."

"Did you run a check? Maybe those plates were stolen."

"I did, in fact. Came up blank."

"Blank?"

"There's no record of those particular plates in Illinois. I thought I could've made a mistake, or ran into a computer glitch. I intended to repeat the check, try different letter combinations, but I've been on patrol, haven't had a chance yet. So I filed an incomplete report."

"Those plates were letters? Not numbers?"

"That's right, sir. I wrote them on my clipboard. It's in the vehicle. Want me to get it?"

"Right now," the Inspector said.

While the Inspector held the phone and waited, Baker lifted his notepad and pointed. "Her maiden name. It's Bennett. Elissa Bennett Pope, she told me."

"Good work. Go find Agent Kelly. I'll put him to work on that right now."

The Inspector was still holding the phone when Baker returned with Kelly. The Inspector motioned Kelly to sit. He said, "Listen, Jim. It seems our guy could've come through Salt Lake today. He might be here now, in fact. If this Bennett name comes up on any hotel list, let me know immediately, then get over there with pictures and stake it out. Got that? Okay, get on it."

Inspector Carlisle lifted the phone to his ear while Kelly hurried from the office. "Cheever?"

He listened and started writing on a notepad. "Hmm," the Inspector said. "N-M-O-S-I-H. That is an odd one. You sure about this?"

Baker was sitting opposite the Inspector. As he glanced at the notepad, seeing it upside down, he said, "That's it!"

"Ha, what?" the Inspector said.

Baker reached across the table and flipped the pad. "Look again," he said.

The Inspector looked. "Jesus Christ! That smartass son-of-a-bitch!" He hoisted the phone. "Cheever, you got him. Good work. We'll get back to you." He slammed the receiver. "Damn it, I think we're close. Real close."

They waited.

After awhile, the phone buzzed, and Baker grabbed it and punched connecting buttons. He listened, then shifted the receiver to the Inspector. "It's Kelly."

"Yeah, Jim," the Inspector barked into the phone. He listened a moment, then — "What? I don't believe it! We must've walked right past each other! Christ!"

He picked up a pencil and jotted notes. "Yeah... yeah... Okay, how about the chopper?... Yeah... Right. No, no pilot. Baker can fly the thing. Now listen. By the time we get to the airport, Harper will have a good head start. But he doesn't know we've got an up-to-date description of the car, so he'll stay on course. Yeah — straight out I-80, and that'll bring him into the Bonneville Salt Flats. That's perfect. There's nothing out there but salt beds for hundreds of square miles. There's not even a bush to hide behind. So do this, Kelly — get that chopper fueled up and bring out some firepower. We'll meet you at the Skypark private airport."

He banged down the phone.

"Kelly found Harper?" Baker said.

"He started calling hotels with the Bennett name and found her on the third try. You'll never guess which one."

"You mean — our hotel?"

"Can you believe it? They must've seen us, because they checked out almost an hour ago — just after we left there."

"Hell, he could be across the state by now," Baker said.

"Nah. It's big country and he sticks to the speed limits. Like I told Kelly, we'll catch him in the middle of the Salt Flats. He hasn't got a chance." The Inspector clapped his hands. "Let's haul ass, Baker. This is the part I like best."

Chapter 28

A THREE-QUARTER MOON drifted over the Great Salt Lake as the Mercedes dashed into the night.

With the top down, Elissa leaned back against the headrest and gazed into a starry universe. She felt euphoric at the distance they were gaining over their enemies.

Harper had switched on the radar detector and punched the speed above one hundred. There was wide space between the east- and westbound lanes, and traffic was sparse. Under these conditions, Elissa felt their speed was a risk worth taking.

She closed her eyes and drifted into sleep.

***

AT THE AIRPORT, a Thunderbird sedan jerked to a stop alongside a Bell Jet Ranger with U.S. Government markings. Special Agent Jim Kelly stood near the helicopter and waited while the Inspector and Baker climbed from their vehicle.

"That bird ready to fly?" the Inspector asked.

"A-OK," Kelly said. "The flight plan has been filed and the tower is standing by. You've got immediate clearance."

"What about the weapons?" Baker asked.

Kelly motioned to his own car a few yards away. In the trunk were several canvas bags. Baker zipped them open and inspected an array of automatic weapons. He selected two M16s and handed them to Kelly. Then he lifted out a metal ammunition box. "This'll do it," he said, slamming the trunk closed.

The Inspector told Baker, "I'll help Jim hoist this stuff aboard while you wind up the chopper."

Baker climbed inside and flipped switches. He located the flight helmets and plugged in communication cords. He checked instruments while the turboshaft engine delivered increasing noise and power to the whipping rotor blades.

"Jim," the Inspector yelled over the noise, "I want you at the communications center. First thing — you remind the highway patrol to report sightings of the subject car but take no action. No arrest, no pursuit, none of that. Got that? We'll handle this ourselves. Make sure they understand."

Agent Kelly appeared skeptical. "You don't want any backup?"

"No. Hell no!"

"But..."

"I'm taking full responsibility, Jim. You just take orders — got it?"

Kelly nodded. "Got it."

The rotors were pushing more wind at them. Kelly and the Inspector ducked their heads and slid the weapons and ammo aboard. Kelly assisted the Inspector as he climbed in. The marker lights came on, and Baker double-checked the collective pitch, foot pedals, and cyclic stick. After the Inspector was belted in and helmeted, Baker adjusted the crew com and reported his readiness for liftoff.

The Inspector raised a thumb.

Kelly hastened to his car and ducked inside, avoiding the rotor blast.

The craft lurched upward and canted sharply into the night.

***

AWAKENING, Elissa realized the Mercedes wasn't moving. The driver's seat was empty. Looking urgently around her, she saw nothing but an expanse of gray earth beneath a gigantic mosaic of stars.

"Harper?" Despite her timidity, her voice rang clearly in the desert silence. "Grey — where are you?"

His head popped up in front of the hood, startling her.

"Jeez!" Elissa said, jerking, "Don't scare me like that! What are you doing?"

"Just a second," he said. "I'm almost done."

Elissa opened the car door — noticed the interior lights failed to come on — and got out. She took several steps and realized she was on a hard-packed gritty surface; not as hard as concrete but much firmer than beach sand. This crust spread to moonlit mountains in the distance. Stars seemed to float right down to the earth.

"Wow," she said. "This is like floating in space on a gigantic platform. Where, actually, are we, Mr. Harper?"

He stood up and dusted his hands. "We're on the Bonneville Salt Flats," he said. "As you see, there's nowhere to hide out here."

"I see that. So why are we here?"

"Because everyone else is over there." He pointed to a disjointed string of lights on the highway. "I came out about four miles from the road. We don't really need pavement to travel across this stuff, unless it rains, and I don't think that's going to happen. We don't need headlights, either."

"Or instruments? The interior lights aren't working."

"I pulled the fuse. This is a total blackout operation."

"More like a dark grayout." She looked at the car. The rear half was covered with a tarp that stretched several feet behind. The other tarp was partially unrolled across the hood, hanging over the fenders. "If you're trying to make a tent," she observed, "it's a pretty clumsy job."

***

ABOARD THE helicopter, the Inspector transmitted to Agent Kelly, who had taken his post in Salt Lake City.

"We're at least twenty miles past where the UHP claimed they spotted our target vehicle, and there's been no sign of it, Kelly. Are they sure about that identification? Over."

"Roger," Kelly answered. "However, the next patrol car is stationed thirty miles this side of Wendover, and no vehicle of similar description has reached him. Over."

"So we keep looking. Over and out." The Inspector nodded toward Baker but kept watching the ribbons of highway beneath them. He used binoculars to examine each car they overtook. He said, "They gotta be right along here, then — within the next ten or fifteen miles. Are you ready to do your stuff, Baker?"

"Always."

"I can handle the shooting, you know. You don't have to shoot and fly at the same time."

"Hey, that's the most fun, Inspector. You just watch me."

***

HARPER and Elissa heard the chop of a helicopter. The noise traveled far, but its direction was indistinct. "I can't tell where it's coming from," Harper said. "Can you?"

"No." Elissa felt her fear rising quickly.

"Check back along the highway, toward the east."

"Which way is east?" Elissa said. "I'm lost out here."

"Past the rear of the car."

Elissa peered at the sky above the scattered vehicle lights and saw nothing. "I don't... Wait... It's only a shadow — just above the highway. But.. Now it's gone."

"No flashing beacons? No red or green?"

"Nothing. There was like a reflection on glass for a second, following a car. But the noise seems so much closer than that. I just can't be sure if my eyes are playing tricks, or..."

"Well, they're out there," Harper said, "because we can hear them. They're flying without navigation lights; so it must be them. Get into the car, now, Mrs. Pope — quickly."

She scrambled onto the seat, expecting Harper to join her. The noise seemed to be coming closer. "Harper, what are you waiting for? They're coming this way!"

"Keep still!" Harper unrolled the tarp on the hood. "Duck your head."

Elissa saw the tarp whipping across the windshield. She ducked, and the interior of the car went dark.

Heart pounding, Elissa waited anxiously as Harper moved around outside the car. Then one edge of the canvas bulged, and she felt him squeeze down beside her. He made a puffing sound, then said, "Cross your fingers, Mrs. Pope."

The noise came straight at them — a painfully loud whine combined with a heavy thumping. The canvas rippled against the windshield. A flap lifted away and Elissa gazed straight up.

She was astonished by the stars' sudden disappearance. Instead she saw an oblong blackness hanging directly overhead. "Oh my God," she whispered. "It's the helicopter... It's them!"

Her shout was drowned in the noise. Elissa clutched at Harper, gasped for breath, felt her face stinging as if struck by a fusillade of needle-shaped bullets... until all light and sound and motion whirled away into space.

Chapter 29

"LAND this thing," the Inspector ordered. "I want a word with that trooper."

Baker obeyed. He brought the Jet Ranger on a curving glide around the Utah Highway Patrol vehicle and settled it down smoothly on the salt beds nearby. He shunted the power down to idle, and the Inspector unbuckled his harness and popped open the door.

The patrolman waited for the dust to settle down before leaving his car. Then he went to meet the Inspector partway.

They introduced themselves, the Inspector showing his badge. He said, "How long have you been posted here?"

The patrolman shrugged. "Maybe an hour. Maybe a little more. No Mercedes roadster came past this spot. Not from either direction."

The Inspector winced, shoving his hands into his pockets. "From here back to the first sighting — is there anyplace a car might've turned off?"

"Well..." The patrolman looked around the horizon and waved both hands. "Anywhere."

"Anywhere?"

"Yeah. There aren't any crossroads or paved turnoffs, but the surface of the flats is pretty solid. You can see all the tracks out there, where people go joyriding. Your guy might be tooling around out there somewhere."

"How fast can he travel on that?"

"In a Mercedes Five Hundred SL? I'd guess a hundred and fifty, easy."

The Inspector looked stricken. "A hundred and fifty, on sand? You gotta be kidding. He'd plow down and flip end-over-end."

"Not likely," the patrolman said. "Right out there, a jet-powered automobile set the World Land Speed Record over thirty years ago. It went over six hundred miles an hour. A guy named Craig Breedlove. He still hopes to crack the sound barrier on land."

"Jesus!" the Inspector yelped.

"You want help?" the patrolman asked.

"No. Thanks anyway. That's a fast chopper, and we can sweep a large area in a short time. If our guy's out there, we'll find him. He's got nowhere to hide. That right?"

"I dunno," the officer said. "Big trucks and motor homes have bogged down in heavy rains, leaving some ditches."

"Ditches won't hide him from the air," the Inspector said. "Don't worry. We'll get him, all right."

"Okay. Good luck."

***

HARPER held Elissa until she tapped his shoulders and said, "You can let go now. I'm okay."

"Are you sure? I think you fainted."

"I know I did. It's not the first time." She sat straight, felt her head touch the tarp. It again covered most of the car. "I'm getting sick and tired of being terrified, and fainting, and all this awful rubbish. When will it stop?"

"I'm sorry," Harper said. "I wish I knew."

"And where did that thing go — the helicopter?"

"We were lucky," he said. "When the tarp lifted, the craft was straight overhead. In that position, they couldn't see down to us. I was able to grab the tarp and hold it in place until they moved off. They're now roughly four miles away. I think they landed beside the highway."

He touched her arm. "This gives me a chance to slip out for a minute. I threw the tarps down fast, and I need to check them before the helicopter takes flight again. Are you sure you're okay?"

"Yes — but I want to get out with you. I badly need fresh air. My face stings and I've got sand up my nostrils."

Harper offered Elissa a handkerchief, and she wiped her face while they walked around the car and inspected it.

Elissa observed that Harper had sprayed the tarps in colors that matched the salt beds, blending various shades of whites and grays, adding some shadowing techniques. His army camouflage training and natural artistic skills had really paid off.

The Mercedes was low-slung with its top down, and Harper had laid out the tarps far enough to produce a gradual slope. From overheard at night — even under a bright moon — the car's shallow height would probably blend into its surroundings. And at ground level, from a few miles away, it would be lost against the mountain background.

"Harper, you're an absolute wizard with spray paint," she said to him.

They heard the helicopter engine rising in pitch and saw the craft rising above the flats. They rushed back to the car.

"When we get a chance," Harper said, "we'll drive ahead. I'll roll the front of the tarp onto the hood — to keep from running over it and to let air into the engine. The rear tarp can drag behind. It might suppress sand rising behind us and help obliterate our tire tracks, although that's not so important. There are all kinds of tracks out here."

He watched through a peephole as the helicopter approached. "If we can practice rolling the tarp on and off quickly, we might cover a lot of ground while staying hidden."

He stopped talking as the roar intensified and passed overhead. The wind from the rotors again rippled the canvas, and Elissa wondered why they kept coming this way!

***

THE INSPECTOR nudged Baker. "There it is again — on the right! It *is* a car! I told you so!"

Baker swung the chopper to starboard, toward a distant shape on the flats. It was traveling at high speed without headlights. He caught up quickly and made a pass alongside.

"But it's not a Mercedes," Baker yelled. "I told you *that.*"

"Okay, but it's suspicious. No lights. Get closer."

Baker shifted the controls.

"Spotlight," the Inspector said.

Baker thumbed the switch, and a brilliant disk of light struck the ground near the speeding car. He maneuvered the helicopter skillfully, bringing the light alongside the vehicle, then directly onto it.

The Inspector switched on the loud-hailer. "This is the FBI!" His amplified voice produced an immediate effect on the vehicle, causing it to swerve. "You are ordered to stop! Now!"

The car, a Pontiac Firebird with wide tires, slowed rapidly. Baker swooped directly in front and blasted the car with rotor-driven grit. The car stopped, and doors on both sides popped open. Two figures jumped out, followed by a third from the back seat. They shielded their eyes from the spotlight and dust.

In the Inspector's binoculars, the figures became clearly defined. "Crap — they're just punks," he said to Baker. The words traveled via the loud-hailer to the trio below. They responded with shaking fists and raised fingers.

"They won't be any help. Get back on course, Baker."

Baker wheeled the chopper around and resumed a preplanned search pattern.

Eventually, they had searched ninety square miles.

"Screw it! Nothing!" Baker snapped. "And now we're running outa fuel."

"Damn it, I do not understand this," the Inspector whined. "There's nowhere to hide! We saw that other car for miles!" He scowled and knuckled his helmet. "I think the state troopers blew it, Baker. Harper went some other way, and they missed him. They damned stupid missed him!"

"Whatever, we gotta call it off," Baker said. "Unless you want to hike back to Salt Lake."

The Inspector gruffly summoned Agent Kelly on the radio. "Anything else from the UHP? Over."

"Not a word. Over."

"Are they sweeping other routes? What about I-Fifteen,
One-twelve, One-ninety-nine, Six, Fifty..."

"Most are covered," Kelly said. "Over."

"Most?"

"They can't cover them all," Kelly said. "Not enough per-
sonnel. We could have declared a federal priority and called
in the sheriffs and park rangers. But you said you didn't
want any backup. Over."

"I said... Aw crap-shit," the Inspector groaned. "Over
and out!"

Chapter 30

THEIR ESCAPE from the helicopter should have provided immense relief. Instead, Elissa felt increasingly agitated.

As they surged toward Nevada, the salt flats had become softer and a bit treacherous; the moon had set; a dimness was spreading across the region; and something lurking deep within that darkening landscape was clutching at her nerves.

Elissa gazed at the tape deck built into the instrument panel. Her sudden need for musical relaxation sent her digging into compartments until she found a cassette. "It's Whitney Houston," she told Harper. "Her songs from *The Bodyguard*. Okay with you?"

Steadfastly steering by starlight, Harper said, "I assume that's another movie I didn't see. Sure, go ahead."

Gradually, Whitney's voice, soaring above the noisy flapping of the trailing tarpaulin, had its impact on Elissa. The singer's heart-throbbing rendering of *I Have Nothing,* — especially the lyrics "can't run from myself" and "nowhere to hide" — expressed many of Elissa's own subconscious feelings. With growing emotion, she thought of nothing else...

But then *something else* began distracting her.

An unfamiliar sound had crept into the music.

Something deep and dissonant.

Elissa leaned forward and twisted the volume control up and down. It affected only the song, not the heavy rumble.

"Harper, there's something wrong with this radio. I can adjust the tape volume, but it sounds like there's some other song in the background, and that one keeps getting louder. Do you hear that?"

"If you mean that thumping, it *is* getting somewhat annoying. Isn't it part of the song you're playing?"

"Hardly. It sounds more like heavy metal stuff. I can't tune it out. Could it be interference from a radio station?"

Harper checked the rearview mirror, staring into dust and darkness. "I don't think it's our radio," he said.

Elissa turned around. "Oh God! Not again!"

"What is it?" Harper said. "What do you see?"

"Jeez, Harper — they're coming right up behind us!"

"*Who?*"

"I don't know! It's a car without lights! Go! Run for it!"

Reflexively, Harper jammed the pedal — a *mistake*. The robust acceleration whizzed the tires through the sandy surface like grinding wheels, digging deep. Quickly shifting gears, he tried recovering momentum, to no avail. The low-slung Mercedes had sunk onto its chassis.

Elissa moaned as the strange vehicle chugged up and stopped — a Pontiac Firebird with chrome pipes smoking and glittering in the starlight. Its music quit. Its engine shut down. It sat motionless in the dark, its occupants invisible.

"They're just sitting there," Elissa whispered urgently, "looking at us, and I can't see who they are."

"Don't look at them — look at me," Harper said. "Judging by that car, Mrs. Pope, they're probably youngsters out cruising for fun."

Elissa glanced at them and back to Harper. She said, "You mean like that camper on Trail Ridge Road? I don't think so. This time, I'm not wearing a low-cut dress to attract anybody. This time, Harper, their motives could be deadly serious."

"We'll have to deal with it," he said. "The trick is showing absolutely no fear. Can you do that?"

Elissa took a deep breath. "I need a role model. Name a fearless heroine in a recent movie — quickly!"

"Um — Like I said, I haven't seen any recent movies."

"Jeez. Never mind — I've got one. What are you planning to do?"

"Play it by ear, to start. Here —" He pressed Baker's gun into her hands. "Don't show it unless you have to. Don't point it unless you're prepared to fire it. It's got four rounds. And don't forget the safety."

"Harper, be careful..."

"I will. You stay put."

He got out of the car. To Elissa's surprise, Harper turned his back to the Pontiac and strolled around the Mercedes, bending to inspect the depth of the tires in the sand.

The Pontiac shined two spotlights at the Mercedes, its doors cracked open, and its interior lights came on, revealing three young men. Two got out and slowly approached.

Harper glanced up from the tires and nodded. "Hello," he said into the glare of light. "Glad you stopped. If you've got some spare time, I could use your help here."

The pair exchanged glances. One said, "Uh, yeah, Ace —
it looks like you're real stuck."

Harper casually straightened up. Elissa saw that one
youth was short and hefty, with long curls hanging from a
black cowboy hat and a raggedy mustache hanging from his
nose. The other was lanky, with narrow eyes and bony face.
He had a deerskin vest studded with beads, a belt of silver
disks that clinked as he approached.

Gesturing at the Mercedes, Harper said, "It's down on
the frame, but I have a tow-chain in the trunk. Not too
busy, are you?"

The young man tried to get a look at Elissa, but Harper
had deftly stepped into his line of vision. The fellow's attention shifted to the Mercedes. "What's those things you got
hanging off the car, Ace?"

"Canvas tarps," Harper said.

"Uh, why'd you hang 'em there?"

"Couldn't find room in the car," Harper said.

The young men again traded glances and snickered.

The lanky one said, "Well, you're real lucky we come
along, you know. We're the Desert Rats. I'm Commander
Lucas, and this here's Jonas. Guy in the car there, he's Arnold. He sorta rides shotgun. Know what I mean?"

"It probably means he's too young to drive." Harper
went to the rear of the Mercedes and shoved aside the tarpaulin.

Lucas seemed caught off-guard by this. He briefly studied Harper's motions at the trunk, then looked at Elissa and
liked what he saw. "That woman — she belong to you?"

Harper lifted the trunk lid. He said, coldly, "She belongs to no one, by her choice. Why do you want to know?"

"Well — because she's a real *fox*."

Jonas spoke out irritably: "Shut up, Lucas!"

"Well she is!" To Harper, Lucas said, "And I'm just curious why a fox like her is bein' hunted by the FBI."

"Christ A-mighty!" Jonas swore. "Dumb *ass*, Lucas!"

Harper's hands came out of the trunk with the end of a tow chain and his briefcase. He dropped the chain and said quietly, "Where did you get that idea, Lucas?"

Lucas leaned forward. "Hell's bells, Ace. An FBI chopper was searchin' all over the Flats for you. Forced us to stop — called us punks and got us pissed off. Anyways, a bit later on, we see this *strange* badass object — it kinda resembles a sand dune, ya know, only it's movin' sixty miles an hour. Well, we hadda check it out, you know. And this is it — a damn ol' Mercedes-Benz dune buggy! It's gotta be the first."

Jonas cautioned, "Don't push it, Lucas."

"Hey," Lucas said, grinning toward Elissa, "I ain't pushin'." He abruptly moved to the car and bent over her. "Hey, Foxy, do I look to you like the kinda hardass that'd be pushin' on a pretty woman?"

Elissa adopted her role model and put the gun to Lucas's nose. "Do I look like the sort of woman who'd let you try?"

"*Yee*-haw!" Lucas jumped backwards. "Balls afire, lady!"

From the Pontiac came two sharp metallic snicks.

And there was Arnold, leveling a double-barreled shotgun at the Mercedes, waiting anxiously for Lucas to get out of the way.

Harper didn't wait. He stepped in front of Elissa and held out his briefcase. "Take it, Lucas," he said.

Lucas grinned. "Well, now — what have we got here? A new attitude? You kinda scared now, Ace — just because of an ol' double-barreled shotgun?" Lucas snatched the briefcase from Harper and laughed. "As you can plainly see, Arnold ain't too young to drive." Arnold was very big and thickly bearded. "He's too dumb, maybe, but he ain't too young. Right, Arnold?"

Arnold said, "Move back here, Lucas."

Harper watched while Lucas backed off a few feet.

"Throw down your gun," Arnold said to Elissa. "Now!"

Elissa gave Harper a helpless look.

"You can do as he says," Harper suggested.

Feeling miserable but not showing it, she let the gun fall to the ground.

Lucas examined the briefcase with amused curiosity. "This what the FBI wants you for? Some cash bundle that don't belong to you? How much you got here?"

Harper held up a hand, revealing a small black device. He pressed a button, and the briefcase began emitting a series of high-pitched beeps.

Lucas jerked, and he stared at the briefcase in his hands.

"It's what the FBI wanted, all right," Harper said quietly. "But it isn't cash."

'Beep-beep-beep-beep-beep...'

"What the hell is it?" Lucas demanded.

"Plastic explosive," Harper said. "The beeping means it's armed. If I release this button before setting the right combination on the briefcase lock, that explosive will make a crater here the size of a football field."

'*BEEP-BEEP... BEEP-BEEP...*'

Elissa couldn't believe this!

But Lucas did. He started shaking. "You'd kill us all? Even your own self?"

"Without a doubt," Harper said convincingly, "— unless Arnold drops the shotgun — now!"

Arnold was bug-eyed. The shotgun landed at his feet, and he scurried backwards.

"Everyone stand perfectly still," Harper said.

Lucas, his voice trembling, said, "What about the damned briefcase?"

"I suggest you hold it very tightly."

"Oh, Lord Almighty!" Lucas said.

Jonas said, "I told you not to mess with them, I *told* you!"

Elissa lunged from the car and recovered Baker's handgun. She hurried to Harper's side. "What are you doing?" she whispered to him. "Are you *crazy?*"

Harper smiled faintly. He collected Arnold's shotgun, instructed Lucas to put the briefcase on the ground — carefully — and move away. After twirling numbers on the lock, he released the transmitter button.

The beeping stopped.

"Okay," Harper said, not showing his relief. "Let's talk."

"Who'n hell *are* you?" Lucas asked breathlessly.

"Are you sure you want to know?"

"Uh — maybe not," Lucas said.

"You've been calling me 'Ace'," Harper said. "That'll do."

Lucas struggled with his posture, shifting his feet, wagging his elbows. Finally, he said, "Uh, we only stopped to check it out, you know. We didn't intend no harm to you or anything — not 'til *she* pulled a gun. I swear to God."

"You provoked her," Harper said.

Elissa, still dazed by the incredible activity, felt sympathy for Lucas. "He's right," she told Harper. "I over-reacted."

Lucas peered at her hopefully. "We just want to help, is all. We're... like desert Boy Scouts. Good deeds and all that."

Harper said, "Then here's a chance to earn some merit badges. First, we need a tow. I'm willing to pay for it."

"You got the chains? No problem."

"Then we need a route across Nevada away from police patrols. You scouts seem to know your way. Any ideas?"

Lucas looked at Jonas. "Maybe. What d'ya think, Jonas?"

Jonas tugged at an ear behind his curls. "Well, we was aimin' to head on over to Frenchman — that's most of the way. We could get 'em that far, Lucas. That'd be easy."

Elissa was curious. "How?"

"Well," Jonas said, "don't get us wrong. Sometimes we provide service like that for folks in trouble. We got it arranged where we do either tourist class or business class."

"Explain that?"

"Tourist class — well, you know, that's just for assholes, and it costs all their money. Business class is cheaper. It means we do business, don't rob nobody. Would that be agreeable to you folks?"

Harper said, "There's room to deal. Let's hear details."

"Tell him, Lucas."

Lucas grinned, almost comfortable now. "Well, Ace, here's where we could do you a real favor. We'd give you our bandit escort. That's like a police escort — except we're bandits." He snickered loudly. "What we do, we drive out ahead — five, six miles in front of you. We see a trooper, we let you know. Then you just hang back until we signal all-clear. Real simple."

"Interesting. But how do we stay in touch?"

"Ain't you got a CB radio?"

"No," Harper said.

Lucas smiled openly. He said, "Then let's start doin' some business, good buddy!" He motioned at the Firebird. "Come on and look at our selection."

As Harper and Elissa quickly discovered, the trunk of the Firebird contained enough CB radios to stock a chain store.

***

While the young men were busy installing the CB, Elissa pulled Harper across the crusty ground, then stopped and faced him. "Okay, 'Ace' — what's in the briefcase?"

"The beeper, you mean?"

She rolled her eyes.

He said, "It's a good thing they thought we were criminals, or it might not have worked."

"*What* the hell *is* it?"

"It's just a little electronic gadget I found at the Sharper Image store in San Francisco. It's to help find things that you're always misplacing, like car keys. You trigger it with the remote control, and it makes those beeps. I was always misplacing my briefcase, you see."

She stared at him in wonder. "That's *incredible*."

He shrugged. "Not really. They have all kinds of things like that. The only problem is that I often misplace the remote, and then..."

"I mean it's incredible the way you used it. That was amazingly fast thinking, Harper."

He smiled. "Actually, the thought was planted by the clerk who sold me the gadget. She was joking, but she said I should be careful about where I misplace my briefcase. She said other people hearing those beeps, from a strange briefcase — in an airline terminal, for example... they could mistake it for a bomb."

Chapter 31

SOUTHWEST of Wendover, they followed the Firebird into Nevada on Alternate 93, which joins U.S. 50 at Ely. Elissa drove and Harper tried to take a nap. He had faded halfway when the CB started making noises.

"Foxy, this is Star Wars. Talk to me, babe."

"Good morning Star Wars," Elissa responded. "How's the view up there?"

"Three-mile visibility," Lucas said. *"Darth Vader hung a left at McGill and pit-stopped. Use the thrusters, Foxy. Shoot the gap."*

"Ten-four," Elissa said, accelerating.

Harper loosened the shoulder harness and sat up. "Did I just hear you talking CB lingo?"

"Sort of," she said.

"Do you understand it?"

"I knew what Lucas said. He said a cop turned off three miles ahead at McGill to use a toilet. If I speed up, we'll get past before he comes out."

Harper smiled. "I assume Lucas is 'Star Wars'."

"It's his handle," Elissa said. "Mine is 'Foxy'."

"That I guessed. Where was I when you all got together on this?"

Elissa reached over and touched his arm. "Don't worry, you didn't miss anything. I was just faking it."

"Yes, well, you are good at that."

"Not always," she said. "I blew it with the gun moll act."

"By the way, who was your role model?"

"Not the best choice. I used Sigourney Weaver from the *Alien* films."

"Oh. Well, I haven't seen those," he said.

"She's like a female Rambo," she explained.

"— Rambo?"

"God!" Elissa stared at him. "I'm amazed you ever saw *It Happened One Night!*"

"It was a while back. On Turner Classic Movies."

"Well, hooray for the old Hollywood! Where the hell have you been in modern times!"

He flipped a hand. "Immersed in my work, I suppose."

"There's more to life than work," she insisted.

"Yes. I'm beginning to appreciate that."

They rolled along in silence for several minutes.

Elissa said, "You weren't such a bad actor yourself. Maybe we should audition together. Did you also have a role model?"

"I did."

"You did? Who?"

He gave her a glance. He said, "Cyrano de Bergerac."

She was astonished. "Harper — you are a case!"

***

After crossing Robinson Summit at nearly 7,600 feet, they came to an empty stretch of highway where a carpet of sagebrush bled into a purple horizon. On an apparent impulse, Harper urged her to stop the car — in the middle of the road — and turn off the engine.

He said, "Listen for a moment. Tell me what you hear."

Elissa was puzzled. Eventually she whispered, "I don't hear anything — it's dead quiet."

"Yes. Isn't that amazing? This stretch of Route 50 has been called the loneliest highway in America. I'd forgotten about it until Lucas led us this way. With the top down, we should be able to hear a helicopter for miles."

"I see," Elissa said. "For a moment, I had thought you just wanted to experience the peacefulness."

"That, too," he said.

They drove on.

***

After awhile, Elissa said, "Wasn't it lucky — finding those guys?"

Harper looked at her. "Lucky? Mrs. Pope, they charged us five hundred dollars for a stolen radio! They're thieves!"

"They installed it for free," she noted.

Harper laughed. "Well, I suppose they deserve some extra payment for assisting us. It's the first time I've been ripped off and glad about it."

Elissa said, "We still have some traveler's checks and about fifteen dollars in cash."

"That'll get us to Frenchman, anyway," he said.

Elissa mused over their destination. "Frenchman. It's such a quaint name. How far is it?"

Harper checked the map. "Just sixty miles ahead and then it's about a hundred miles to Carson City and the California state line." He leaned back and crossed his arms. "Ask the bandits if they know a truckstop cafe in the vicinity."

"Hungry?"

"Yes, but it's more important to find new transportation. It's time to abandon the car."

"Abandon... the car? And do what? Hitchhike?"

"Well, more or less... yes."

"Good grief," Elissa said.

***

Within an hour, they had reached Frenchman. The Firebird kept going in search of casinos, where Lucas hoped to win a fortune at poker with their five hundred dollars.

Frenchman was just a truckstop. Elissa drove onto the gravel lot surrounding the cafe. It was lunchtime, and there were five interstate trucks and an assortment of local pickups parked there.

Harper instructed her to pull around to the back, where he climbed out and opened the trunk. In a few minutes, he had found what he needed, a sharply pointed drafting compass and a hammer. He wrapped a jacket around his arm and told Elissa to pop the hood release. After raising the hood, he reached down and pounded the compass into the radiator grill until steam started escaping. He backed off and slammed the hood. Elissa tossed up her hands. "You're always doing the weirdest damn things," she said.

"Next," he said, climbing into the car, "before we drive up to the front, can you invent a character that will be noticed — I mean *really* noticed — by a pack of truckers?"

Elissa thought a moment. Then she pulled the tail of her blouse from her jeans and knotted it beneath her bust, exposing her tummy. She grabbed her high heels from be-hind the seat and slipped them on. She added a layer of gloss to her lips and fluffed her hair. Her transformation took less than a minute, and then she flashed her eyelashes at Harper.

"Hello, you fabulous Hunk," she purred. "Could your huge Big Rig accommodate a little ol' pair of buns like mine?"

Harper laughed. "Perfect. Now, here's what we need..."

Inside the cafe, they went directly to a lunch counter and sat on stools, arguing loudly enough to be heard from one end of the counter to the other.

"I told you at least a hundred times, Frankie," Elissa complained. "Have the damn car checked. *But no*. You said it's a Mercedes-*Benz*, and there wasn't nothing wrong with it — you said. And now look! Here we sit, God-knows-where, that old heap of trash gushin' like a teakettle. You should've listened to me, you pin-headed jerk!"

Harper seemed to enjoy behaving like a harried husband. He said, "You're not listening. I said the radiator was hit by a stone — probably thrown by a *truck*."

A hefty female server appeared across the counter with two water glasses and set them down. "Trouble, folks?"

"I'll say!" Elissa said. "This meathead didn't get our car inspected before we set out, and now it's like totally wiped out. We're going to miss my sister's wedding at Lake Tahoe, and it's all his damned fault."

"It was a stone!" Harper insisted.

The server woman could see the car through the win-dow, engulfed in steam. "Damn, that's too bad," she said. "I could give you folks some jugs of well water, but the way that baby's spouting, she'll be dry again inside of four miles."

"Where's the nearest repair shop?" Harper asked.

"For a Mercedes automobile? Hell, you'd have to go to Carson City. Maybe Reno."

"Damn," Elissa said. "For what you paid for that second-hand piece of junk, you coulda bought a brand-new Cadillac." She turned to the server. "What's the chance of hitching a lift with somebody? I gotta get to my sister's wedding."

"Well, I don't know," the woman hedged. "Most truckers ain't allowed to carry passengers... "

Harper said, "I'll pay fifty bucks for a ride to Tahoe — anything to get my little sweetheart off my back."

"I'll ask around. Can I get you folks some lunch?"

"Why the hell not?" Elissa grumbled. "We ain't going anywhere for a while." She snatched a menu off the counter and opened it.

***

Later, while they were munching sandwiches, a trucker in boots and cowboy hat sat heavily on a stool next to Elissa.

"You the folks who need a lift?"

Harper and Elissa both swiveled and faced him. "Yeah, mister," Elissa said. "Can you help us?"

The trucker looked them over carefully. "Your automobile broke down?"

"Yeah, and we're trying to get to my sister's wedding in Lake Tahoe, Nevada. It's tonight."

"Uh-huh," the trucker said. "I understand you're willing to pay fifty bucks."

"That's right," Harper said.

"Cash?"

"Travelers check," Harper said.

"Well, I dunno."

"Maybe the restaurant will cash it for us?" Elissa asked.

"Maybe." The trucker called to the server. "Hey, Brigitte — you take travelers checks?"

The woman held up a hand, finished serving another customer, then ambled over. "What kinda travelers check?"

"American Express," Elissa said.

"Oh, sure," Brigitte said. "How much?"

"They're all twenties; so sixty for the trucker? Forty for the lunch and gratuity?"

The woman nodded. "That's fine, honey."

"Thanks," Elissa said. "We sure do appreciate it."

"You got much luggage?" the trucker asked.

Harper said, "Just a few bags. We planned a short trip."

The trucker could see the car's license plates through the window. "From Illinois? That ain't what *I* call short."

"I meant time-wise," Harper said. "We planned to head right back after the wedding."

"Uh-huh. Then why didn't you fly?"

"He's got a terrible fear of flying," Elissa said.

"Well... yeah, me too," the trucker acknowledged. He held out a hand. "The name's Jim."

"Hi-ya, Jim," Elissa said, throwing her friendliest smile at him. "I'm Elissa, and that —" she hooked a thumb over her shoulder "— that's my good ol' hubby, Franklin."

Jim shook hands with both of them.

"Will you take us, then?" Harper asked.

Jim shrugged. "Sure, why not? With today's fuel prices, your sixty bucks could be my profit on this trip." He nodded toward the Mercedes. "What about your car?"

Harper said, "Well... Maybe we could push it around back — get it out of the way. Then I'll get one of Elissa's relatives to drive us back after the wedding, then hire a tow to Carson City, or wherever they can fix it around here."

"Yeah," the trucker said, "that sounds like a plan. I'm driving that big silver rig out there with the crew cab. Plenty of room. I'm ready when you are."

The server cashed the travelers checks and generously gave Elissa three silver dollars in change. Thanking her, Elissa asked, "Could you direct me to the ladies lounge?"

Brigitte indicated an adjoining room. "Go past the slots."

"Thanks a big bunch," Elissa said. "Be with you boys in a minute. Don't you leave without me."

"No *way*, ma'am," Jim said.

To the restroom and back, Elissa strolled past ranks of shiny slot machines that clattered and rang as people stood and played them. There was one big machine beside the cafe entrance that sported a revolving red light and a glittering sign that advertised BIG BUCKS.

She hesitated, fascinated. *Why not?* She fed her three silver dollars into the machine, stared at it for a moment, and pulled the handle.

In the cafe, Jim told Harper, "You're lucky you found me. This place is scheduled for demolition in a few months. With the Interstate, there aren't enough truckers down here anymore to keep this place going. I'm one of the last, you know?"

Harper was about to comment when he was startled by the howl of a siren. He turned toward the windows, searched the lot — saw no police.

"It's a jackpot," Jim said, pointing to the casino room. "Somebody hit the BIG BUCKS. Let's go see."

They found Elissa in the midst of a small crowd of on-lookers, surrounding a slot machine that had gone berserk with flashing lights and a wailing siren. Harper wedged in beside Elissa as silver dollars continued clinking rapidly into the tray. He said, "Did *you* do that?"

She nodded eagerly. "How much is it? Are we *rich?*"

The display was counting into the hundreds. It indicated that Elissa was one triple-bar short of the maximum payoff.

"Not rich," Harper answered. "But we won't have to sleep under a park bench tonight."

Chapter 32

DUMPING their luggage onto the floor, they collapsed into chairs and looked at each other. They hadn't investigated any of the rooms yet, hadn't gazed out any windows for the Lake Tahoe views. They'd do those things eventually. For the moment, they simply looked at each other.

"Thank you," Harper said.

Her dark eyelashes flicked upward. "For what?"

"For everything, especially today. Without you, I could not have gotten this far."

Her mouth rippled into a tender smile. "That's very sweet, Harper. But it was only luck. Everyone needs luck to survive. Today, we got our share."

"Well, the slot machine was luck," he said. "Everything else you did — managing the bandits and charming the trucker, even finding these accommodations — that was pure skill."

"Well, hey — the slot machine was skill, too. I applied a certain shimmy in my hips when I hauled the handle, and my rhythm was perfectly in tune with the spin of the reels."

"No argument from me," Harper said, smiling.

Elissa had grown fond of that smile.

Earlier, the trucker had dropped them on the hotel strip in South Lake Tahoe, and they had gone to a central reservations office to check on room availabilities.

The better casino hotels had been nearly full, but Elissa thought of a real estate agency she'd employed on behalf of her Lake Forest clients. There, she displayed her credentials and smoothly arranged for a timesharing "cabin" on the west shore, at a spot coincidentally named Lake Forest.

With no gambling on the California side, the west shore remains relatively quiet and secluded, and they found it uplifting to arrive at last in California. Using hundred-dollar bills from Elissa's Nevada jackpot, they paid a deposit and left her American Express Gold Card imprint for the balance. They thought the item wouldn't show on her account until after check-out — when it wouldn't matter.

Tomorrow, they would be in Carmel.

One way or another, the journey would end there.

Hiring a taxi, they had arrived at this traditional redwood two-story residence, set between the road and shore amid a clutter of boulders and tall pines. And now they sat gazing at each other with those smiles.

"What about food?" Harper asked, breaking the spell.

"Well, the basics — whatever isn't perishable — should be stocked in the kitchen," Elissa said. "The timeshare rules require guests to replace what they use, or they may be charged double for missing supplies. Most guests leave a little more than they found, and the stock eventually outgrows the checklist."

"Hmm," Harper said. "Might there be any scotch?"

"I'm sure. That's one of the basics."

Harper stood and glanced about the room, hands on hips. They were in a spacious living area with large windows at the far wall, facing the lake. Furnishings were expensively casual, a rustic modern theme with beige and grey stripes on the sofas and chairs, white pine on the tables and cupboards. He went to one of the tall cupboards that had a key in its lock and twisted it open.

"Another jackpot," he said.

Inside the cupboard were dozens of bottles and glasses and a bartop refrigerator containing ice. "Well, let's see here... there's Ballantines, Johnny Walker Black Label, Chivas Regal, Dewars..." He shifted bottles and looked deeper into the cabinet. "The rest are whiskeys, vodkas..."

"I'll have a Ballantines," Elissa said. "Is there ice?"

"Yes. Plenty."

"Fill my glass with ice, then pour scotch up to the rim."

"Whoa," Harper said.

"Well, okay," she said. "Not so much ice, then."

He seemed about to laugh, then frowned while cracking ice from a tray and clinking the cubes into a glass. One glass.

Elissa said, "Now what's wrong?"

He looked at her, somewhat apologetically. "Would you mind if I don't join you? Considering tomorrow, I'd rather not dull any of my senses."

"No, I... wouldn't mind," Elissa said. "Of course not. As a matter of fact, Patrick always drank a lot more when he had a problem. And that became his problem."

Harper nodded. "I had thought sharing drinks with you would help relieve your anxieties on this trip. Was I wrong?"

"I am relieved now," she said, smiling gratefully. "It's one more thing I don't need to worry about, with you. As for me, is there any ginger ale?"

"There is," he said. He filled a glass and brought it to her. "There are peanuts and pretzels, if you like."

"No, thanks." Elissa took a sip from her glass and stood. "Let's look around."

"Okay. You lead."

Elissa wandered first to the windows at the rear of the room. Outside was a stone-walled redwood deck with planters and benches, wrought iron chairs with cushions, and a wrought iron table with an umbrella. On the right side of the deck was a lower level and a hot tub with a wooden lid. Beyond that were rocks, trees, and Lake Tahoe.

The lake was deep blue under the late afternoon sky, rippled only by gentle breezes and wakes of colorful touring boats. Toward the far side, a flotilla of sailboats was scudding along in some kind of race, white triangles bent at sharp angles against the deep green of the opposite shore.

The forest marched steeply to a jagged ridge and distant peaks. Snow remained in hollows and above the treeline.

"This is so serene," Elissa said, "even better than Estes Park." Her eyes roamed left to right. She said, "What are those mountains? Those to the right, with snow on them?"

"I don't know the names of the peaks," Harper said, "but that's the Heavenly Valley ski area."

"Heavenly Valley," Elissa repeated. She looked longingly at the hot tub. "Do you suppose the tub is full, and works?"

"Let's go investigate," Harper said.

They went to a half-flight of steps leading to a lower level and entered a spacious bedroom with curved panoramic windows. As Elissa's eyes acknowledged the lake view and roamed around the room, she had one basic reaction:

"Wow!"

Across the room was a huge round bed with satin coverings and pillows. A semi-circular console curved behind one third of the bed. The console was equipped with light controls, a TV projector, stereo equipment and speakers, fold-down snack trays, and a mysterious array of push-buttons.

"It looks to me like we're going to have a vicious fight over that bed, Mrs. Pope," Harper said from behind her. "Or we're going to have to share it."

"Well," Elissa said innocently. "We haven't finished exploring. Maybe there's another one like it."

"I think you'd have to go to Xanadu," he said.

Elissa unlatched the sliding door. "I believe the hot tub is right out here, though." It was.

Harper removed the cover and saw the tub was filled with clean water. He found the control panel and adjusted the dials. A pump motor hummed beneath the deck, and the water began to swirl. Another notch increased the bubble action until the water seemed to boil. He said, "The temperature is still cool. It'll take awhile to heat up. Let's look at the rest of the place."

On the other side of the bedroom, they found a luxurious bath with two shower stalls, two wash basins set into a long marble counter, a separate nook with toilet and bidet, and mirrors everywhere. Behind a mirrored door was a linen storage closet stacked with fresh towels and terry robes.

Beyond the living room was a kitchen and breakfast area facing the lake. A door led to a breezeway and another wing of the house containing three mid-sized bedrooms with two mid-sized baths.

"I'm eager for the tub," Elissa said. "Do you want to join me? I'll show you the swimsuit I bought in Estes Park."

"I don't have any trunks," Harper said.

"Good Lord, it's the first time I've found you unprepared," she teased.

"I'll improvise. I'll look through these rooms while you're changing."

He searched through two bedrooms without finding any swimwear. The third room had a locked cedar chest. Looking at the lock, he recognized a similarity to the lock on the liquor cabinet. Figuring it was worth a try, he returned to the liquor cabinet and pulled out the key, went back to the bedroom and inserted the key into the chest. It worked.

The chest contained an assortment of linens and beach clothes. But the only male trunks he found were extra-large and emblazoned with figures of naked females. And the background color was a vibrant chartreuse.

Harper cringed and took the trunks.

Returning to the master bathroom, he knocked.

"Yes?" Elissa said.

"Can you hand me a robe from the linen closet?"

Harper waited until the door came open a crack and Elissa handed out a robe. Her arm was bare except for a thin bronze bracelet. She asked faintly, "Would you have a spare razor? Don't ask what it's for."

"I have a package of disposables. I'll get it."

He returned with the package and placed it in her out-stretched hand, then proceeded to the other wing and changed clothes. A stone path from the breezeway led him to the deck. Everything was still. Elissa hadn't come out yet.

Harper approached the hot tub and tested the water with his fingers. It felt mildly warm.

He stood with his back to the house and looked at the lake. The sun was setting behind him, and the water was taking on a lavender color at the far shore. As he watched, a palette of pink and gold shimmered along the snowy peaks of the mountains and across high ribbons of clouds.

Hearing the door slide open, Harper turned and watched Elissa step out in her Estes Park swimsuit.

She had brushed and fluffed her hair and added gloss to her lips. She had adjusted her mascara for evening light and added touches of eye shadow. And seeing wonderment in Harper's eyes, she walked past him swiftly, her face bright, and halted in front of a large redwood planter. *"Oh, Harper! Did you see these beautiful hydrangeas? Just look at them!"*

"Ah — so that's what they are. I did see them. There's also another brilliant sunset in progress, right behind you."

She spun around, her eyes dazzling. "Oh! That's *breath-taking!* Isn't that just the most *beautiful* sight in the *world?*"

He said, "Among the best, sure. But not at the top."

"No? Okay... tell me, what is more beautiful on *your* list?"

He hesitated. The separate cups of her bikini bra were joined by a jeweled oval ring that encircled her cleavage. A pair of matching rings at each hip joined the front and back portions of her bikini bottom. The stretchy fabric was a translucent blend of orange and pink dots sprinkled over sprays of lavender and gold — almost exactly the colors of the snow in the sunset on the ridges of Heavenly Valley.

Harper's gaze shifted up to her eyes. "Do I dare speak?"

She said, "Try to be serious. You can't mean this bikini? There's barely anything to it!"

"That's *exactly* what I mean. Why does it always bother you to be appreciated for your natural beauty?"

"I'll answer that with a question for you. Has anyone ever compared your body to a Lamborghini?"

"Uh... not even close," Harper said, raising a brow.

"Well, I have a tale for you. It goes back... around the end of our second year of marriage. As he was leaving for a round of golf, Patrick said he wanted cocktails that afternoon by our pool. And snacks. He told me to wear a bikini.

"The previous year, he had the pool installed — there aren't that many pools on Lake Forest estates — for our first anniversary. So I thought he was planning another surprise, with our second anniversary coming up. I got into a bikini, almost as skimpy as this one, and I set up the poolside bar and snacks, and I waited for him. I waited eagerly.

"And then he arrived with his rowdy foursome! These guys were young, rich, and spoiled. They'd had a few drinks at the club, and Patrick started bossing me around like a French maid, 'go get this, do that' — and my stupid brain was still thinking like a dumb debutant!

"So... I was obediently fixing their drinks with my back turned, when I heard a guy say, 'She's got a helluva lot better curves than your Lamborghini, Chuck.' Another said, 'And I bet her rear engine packs more power.' The third guy said, 'How about her headlights! Chuck, does your two hundred and fifty thousand dollar Lambo even *have* headlights?' Chuck says, 'Sure, but they're concealed until you turn 'em on.' So the first guy says, 'Well, her headlights aren't exactly concealed. Does that mean she's turned on?' He yells, 'Hey, Patrick, did you know your wife is turned on? Is she always like that?'" Elissa stopped and looked at Harper.

"You're not laughing," she said.

"Did you expect me to?"

"Those guys expected *me* to laugh. But I felt *humiliated*. I managed a grin for everyone's sake and then... I just *acciden-tally* spilled Chuck's crushed-ice Mint Julep all over his lap."

"Good. I don't blame you," Harper said.

"But Patrick did. His friends had no clue what was going on. They were too drunk. He punished me after they left."

"Good Lord! For what?"

"He blamed me for not behaving like his dainty French maid for his buddies. That's when I finally realized our hon-eymoon was over — how Patrick took pleasure in watching me suffer humiliation in front of other men. It made him feel stronger and superior. And it made me grow up."

She added, "I often think women's bodies are designed to be used and even abused for the purpose of procreation. But we are sentient creatures, having our own desires and hopes and dreams. We shouldn't be forced to lay down for others, for procreation or to satisfy their passions. It blisters me when anyone looks at me as... an object. As a sex toy."

Harper's eyes drifted from her, toward the darkening sky.

She said, "I'm sorry. I suppose I should not have told you all that. You must be very tired of hearing me recite all my issues with Patrick. But you did ask why it bothers me to be 'appreciated,' as you called it. In my case, it all stems from that incident."

Harper reached out for her hand. He said, "I understand and I fully honor your intentions. You are perfectly justified in staking your boundaries regarding me and anyone else. And I ask your forgiveness because my work, my *life* is all about form and function — the beauty that blossoms from bringing it all together. I just can't see beauty as something to be ashamed of. Certainly not in your case."

"Oh, Harper, you're a dear. If it seems I'm training you, it's because it's all happening so fast. I barely know you, yet I find you dangerously attractive! Please don't get me wrong. Women love to give pleasure, too. We only ask for pleasure in return. Is it too much to expect? Is it too much to ask?"

And then Elissa abruptly turned away. Harper waited. When her gaze returned to him, he saw her tears.

He said, "Was it something I said?"

"No. It... *I'm* so *self-conscious* around you! When you try to comfort me, it scares me. Because I'm not used to that."

"You've had a lonely life," he said. "And no one knew."

"*I* didn't even know. Until now." She wiped her eyes with two fingertips and faced him squarely. "Enough sentiment. It's past our *fun* time, and I'm awkward standing here nearly naked, while you're all covered with that robe. *Off with it!*"

Harper adopted a modest expression, shed the robe, and stood before her well-poised in the mammoth chartreuse shorts with pink cartoon nudes in outlandish poses.

Elissa's eyes exploded. Her jaw dropped and she slapped both hands against her cheeks. "Holy *Toledo!*" She burst into musical laughter and began inching closer to him, staring, wrapping her arms around her ribs to contain her body's convulsions. "I... *God*, that's ridiculous!" She was breathless, rocking on bent legs. "My *goodness*, I've just *got* to sit *down!*"

Harper lifted his palms. "Well... it was this or nothing."

Elissa convulsed a second time. "Oh, please! As someone famous once said, I heartily recommend the *alternative!*"

With that, Harper joined into her laughter. It took some time before they settled back on adjacent chairs.

Wiping her cheeks with both hands, she said, "I'll have to repaint my face. It must be a holy mess."

He said, "You look sublime. The sunset is your makeup."

She sat up. "Speaking of that — we've seen an awesome display of sunsets on this journey. How did that happen?"

He said, "We're driving westward, into late afternoon sun, in clear weather and open country, the whole way."

"Harper? I realize that, but it's phenomenal nonetheless."

Leaning back in her lounge chair, Elissa stretched out her glamorous gams and crossed her ankles. "Despite all our troubles, I'm very glad to be here with you. And those awesome swim trunks! I'm not the only one who overwhelmed the spectacle of a sunset! *Thank* you. I needed that laugh. Good Lord, it felt so wonderful!"

"It was good for me, too," Harper said.

"... You're not supposed to say that — until *afterwards*," she squealed.

And that started yet another spasm of mirth until finally they went hand-in-hand to the hot tub and gingerly lowered themselves into the frothy water, while the peaks across the lake faded to silver-gray and the stars came out to glitter.

Chapter 33

THE WOMAN behind the lunch counter put down a glass of water and said, "What'll it be, young fella?"

The "young fella" was in his thirties, in a blue suit and red-striped tie. He had dark blond hair and a thin blond mustache. He flipped open a leather folder and showed a badge and I.D. card. "Billy Clanton," he said. "FBI in Sacramento." He saw her name tag and said, "Please look at the pictures, Brigitte, and tell me if you've seen these people."

Brigitte pressed her hands on her hips in surprise, then looked at the photos. She took a pair of spectacles from her apron pocket and put them on carefully.

In the first picture was a slender man with glasses, standing next to a model of a village, pointing a stick at the miniature structures. "Dunno," Brigitte said. "That picture's kinda fuzzy."

"It's a copy from a newspaper photo," the young man said. "Look at the other one."

The other was a clear portrait of an attractive woman with dark eyes, brunette hair, and a faint smile on full lips.

"Well, now!" Brigitte said. "That one does look familiar, although she's changed somewhat. There, she looks kinda dignified. Today, she was more like a hussy. She had lunch with a fella... Maybe... " Brigitte looked again at the first picture. "Yep. I bet's that's him — without eye glasses. Sure. They stopped here because of some car trouble."

"Car trouble?"

"Their radiator blew. Steamin' like an old locomotive. They had to hitch a ride with one of the truckers."

Agent Clanton was visibly excited. He started writing notes. "Did they mention where they were headed?"

"Tahoe, they said. That hussy said they was goin' to a weddin' in Lake Tahoe. That's why she couldn't wait around to have the car fixed. She was a real bitch about it. The poor guy... I felt sorry for him. She was a doll, though, otherwise."

"The car wasn't fixed? What did they do with it?"

"They pushed it out back." Brigitte gestured over her broad shoulder. "Uh... You come all the way out here from Sacramento? What did those folks do? Rob a bank?"

Clanton shook his head. "It's government business. Don't ask me what — I'm only supposed to help locate them. Do you happen to know who the trucker was?"

"Guy named Jim Mitchell. Comes in about once a week. Husky fella."

"What company does he work for?"

The woman fingered the cleft in her chin. "I ain't exactly sure. I think he's independent — has his own truck. It's a big silver rig."

"Where's it registered? Do you know?"

Brigitte looked surprised. "Hell, I don't know. You might find his card on the bulletin board by the cash register. You work alone? There's a lot of territory around here."

"Not too many stops, though. And there's two of us," Clanton said. "If you think of anything else, give me a call." He gave the woman his FBI card.

"You want coffee or anything? On the house."

Clanton shook his head. "No, thanks. I'm going to take a look at that car, then I have to report in. The government of the United States appreciates your help. Thanks."

Clanton waved, paused at the bulletin board, found Mitchell's card, then went to his car for a flashlight.

Behind the building, he saw the car parked in the darkness, out of range of the lights in front. He had been wondering about it since reading the description: A Mercedes-Benz 500SL; color gray, brown, or dull red; probably a crude paint job; fabric top; Illinois plates that spelled either "HIS OWN" or "NMO SIH" — which his prior law enforcement gig made him think of L.A. street code for "no mo' shit."

As he strutted around the vehicle, he realized he never would have recognized it as a late model 500SL. It looked like it had been around the world a few times, dented and rusted with some sections coated with auto primer.

Looking closely at the plates, he saw how they had been doctored and inverted, explaining the dual identification.

"Clever dude," he muttered.

He looked again at Mitchell's card and went to his own car to call Sacramento. He felt a sense of urgency. He liked that feeling.

Chapter 34

IMMERSED in the hot tub, they sat at a diagonal to each other — neither close nor opposite; simply neutral. Now and then while shifting positions, their feet or ankles made contact. Occasionally Grey Harper's eyes followed the bubbling water as it lapped along Elissa's breasts. At intervals, Elissa took sideways peeks at the firmness of Harper's bare chest. Mostly, though, they observed the emergence of stars, the reflections of lights bouncing on the ripples of the lake.

Smiling, relaxed, Elissa rubbed her shoulders and said, "I've been thinking about all the clothes I bought. You probably think I went overboard on spending, and you haven't even seen the hottest item yet, but..."

He frowned. "That's simply your business, Mrs. Pope."

"But my spending decisions can directly affect you. You see, I've been concerned about how we're using a charge card that's been dormant for a long time. Suddenly we hit the road with over a thousand miles of gasoline charges. Real hurry-up charges. Wouldn't that raise a flag? But then, several gift shop purchases in a resort town would seem more typical of vacation travel. Maybe less suspicious. You think?"

"Possibly," he said. "But it's all your money. You're the one who earned it and decides how to use it. Why ask me?"

"All right. I'm sorry I bothered you. Forget it."

Harper thought, *uh-oh.* He said, "I'm sorry. You weren't bothering me. Something's bothering you. How can I help?"

Tapping the glittering oval between the cups of her bikini bra, Elissa said, "This jewelry is expensive and not what I'd flash at the Onwentsia Country Club or even at the Lake Forest beach. So what reason did I have for *wanting* it?"

"To assert your own rebellion? Against social traditions?"

"Maybe that's it. I had been saving most of my earnings for the proverbial rainy day. And now we're in a *typhoon,* and I'm spending money like it's going out of style!"

Harper nodded. "Well, it would be a shame to come through this safely and discover you've got nothing left."

"It would be a worse shame to die without spending it."

Harper said, "I hope you're not serious."

She said, "Everything now is either serious or cockeyed."

"But I thought you'd gotten past such fatalistic notions."

"Almost. But you mentioned rebellion. Lake Forest is a charming community, for people with charmed lives. I had a swift rise in esteem, a swifter kick down, a tedious recovery. My second rise had none of the glitter of the first. When a whole village turns sour, it gets miserable to hang around. I yearned for any kind of escape, to simply breathe fresh air."

Harper said, "I also had the impression you found plenty of diversion in your theatrical troupe. Not true?"

A sad grin. "That was true. Those people are delightful. But they haven't quite grown up, and I doubt they ever will. They thrive on fantasies — and I did, too. But they also fuss and quarrel like spoiled children." She lowered her eyes. "That's where I picked up my salty language, by the way."

She sighed. "Now I'm getting too old to pursue acting seriously as a career. I want to junk all my fears, go splurging in boutiques, and start *living my life* — whatever is left of it."

Harper did not respond. This caused Elissa to study him until she noticed a jagged mark on his shoulder. She inquired, "Where did you get that scar? It looks very serious."

Harper glanced down briefly, seemed momentarily disturbed. He said, "It's from a scissors — a minor thing. Look, I'm sorry to change the subject. But there's tomorrow."

"Yes, there is," she said stiffly. "What about it?"

He turned toward the lake and its dancing lights. "I need to decide how to reach Carmel from here. I can't even begin to relax until I reach a definite decision."

"Okay," Elissa said. "What options do we have?"

"Normally, I could fly from Reno to San Francisco or San Jose, rent a car and arrive home in six hours. Or I could rent a car here and drive home in less than six hours. Or I could take a train to Oakland and rent a car. In each case, my driver's license is a dead giveaway. How do I avoid that?"

Elissa stretched her arms along the tub's rim and gazed at the sky. "You keep saying, '*I.*' Whatever happened to '*we*'?"

"Well, let's look at facts. First, I doubt the FBI can trace us here unless they know about our independent trucker. And how could they? So we're safe until tomorrow, until our hosts run your Gold Card. Before then, you should taxi out of here and fly home from Reno. They won't expect you in Lake Forest after all this time. You can get a lawyer — "

"*Oh hell!* We've had that discussion! *Twice!* I thought we settled that! This makes the *third time* you've whacked me with that kind of blow to my guts."

"Mrs. Pope, we've reached the narrow end of the funnel."
She said, "We've also come so *far!* Surely, one final day... "
"Could be final. I'm sorry you take this as a whack."
"I meant figuratively. Even so, it does hurt like a fist."

Recalling her attitude on life expectancy, Harper said: "I *can't* take you. Alone, I could slip through that funnel. But with you along, I'd be terrified of losing you. It's no good."

"So now I'm a *burden* to you! I can't say *damn you* because I think too highly of you! I'd say *go to hell* if I didn't love you! But I *do* offer my *suggestion* you go jump in that *lake!*"

She stood quickly. "I feel all sick inside." She hopped from the tub, grabbed a towel and energetically dried off with her back to him. He watched her shoulders tightening, a tremor running through her torso. She stepped clumsily into her sandals, wobbled to the low terrace wall and threw open its gate to the shore pathway. Beyond her, the mountain peaks were aglow from a rising moon. The deep water reflected lights from the far shore and stars from the sky.

She draped her towel on the gate and leaned back against a lamppost. Her right hand went above her head to grasp the post, and her left knee came up as she rested the sandal's heel against the stones of the wall behind her.

Turning slowly, her eyes glistening in the lamplight, she said, "You will *not* get away from me until we've made love."

Her languid pose impressed Harper as both submissive and defiant. He responded with a gentle nod.

She dropped her foot to the deck and marched past him. "Stay where you are. I need the facilities; then I'm back."

He called, "Instead, let's meet in my bedroom."

She halted. She tried not to smile. "Whose bedroom?"

"Our bedroom," he conceded.

Her lips parted. "Why are you looking at me like that?"

"You have a gorgeous gleam about you when you're livid. You must have known that from others."

"No. You're really the first — because that *livid* reaction is wholly different from how I've ever felt with anyone else. So, damn it... give more thought to our working together."

"Okay."

Sliding the door open, she released a perfervid smile. Her chest swelled as she slipped into the house.

***

Punching the mysterious buttons on the bed's console, Harper discovered the first one controlled the curtains at the lakeside windows. He kept them open for the glow.

The second button activated lights on the deck. With illumination from stars and shore, they didn't need that.

The next button triggered a vibrating action in the bed. He shut it off immediately.

The fourth brought up the stereo, the fifth advanced the music tracks. He paused at Ravel's *Bolero*, decided it was too blatant and continued until the music became more gently romantic, a mellow background of guitars and flutes that evoked soft images of wind-rustled trees and falling water.

The sixth button had no apparent effect with repeated jabs — until Elissa poked her head from the bathroom and said, "What are you doing with the *lights?*"

"Oh. Sorry," he said. "I'm testing this panel of buttons."

The seventh and final button produced a laser show on the ceiling — beams and points of colored lights, swirling with the music. *Not bad*, he thought. *But distracting.*

He tapped off the seventh button and stretched out. He listened to the music and waited.

***

In the bathroom, Elissa leaned over the counter, drawing deep breaths. She reminded herself it was not Patrick Pope snapping bathroom lights from a switch by his bed, demanding that she *hurry up and perform!* No, Grey had said he was only testing buttons. It was no cause to suffer shame or fear. Even so, she crossed her heart and silently prayed he would be gentle with her...

***

While Harper watched, the bathroom door came ajar, releasing a shaft of light. Elissa's hand swept across a switch, and the light winked out. Her gossamer shape drifted into the bedroom and paused. She proceeded toward him one slow step at a time. Partially illuminated by lights around the lake, partially concealed in the shadows of the room, she approached like the patter of rain in a forest — slowly, steadily, inevitably. Four feet away, Elissa stopped. She remained perfectly still. "The show continues, my Darling... and I'm calling you that, like it or not. This is Act Three."

She wore bright white satin cut low on top, high at the bottom, with very little in the middle. There was a drama of sheer stockings on her stately legs. "I now present my final purchase from Estes Park," she said softly. "I couldn't resist it, and I hope you can't, either." She crept onto the bed. "Feel this satin, the luxury of it." She drew his hand alongside her breast. "Whenever I touch it — the satin — I'll be reminded of this night. Is that corny? I don't care. It's true."

"It isn't corny," he said quietly. "I'll remember, too."

She traced her fingertips across his throat and shoulder, lightly circling the scar. "Do you enjoy *le parfum?*"

Harper's slow reply surprised her. "Remember the morning in Estes Park — when I brought a breakfast to you?"

She wrinkled her brow. "Yes. Of course, I remember."

"I had come in from the clean smell of Rocky Mountain air that morning — and I found you fresh from your shower, your hair and skin smelling naturally sweet to my senses."

He raised his forearm and stroked her hair. "It reminded me, after I had quit smoking years ago, of many smells I had forgotten since childhood — and how they all came back."

Elissa smiled gently. "I only asked if you liked *le parfum.*"

"I was getting to that. Imagine the purity of Rocky Mountain air in the morning, your freshness after a shower, then add the mystery of a totally new olfactory discovery. I don't just like *le parfum*, Elissa. I'm enthralled by it."

"Wow! I love that! I'm sorry if I seemed a bit impatient."

"I didn't mean to hold you off," he said.

"I'm actually glad you're not in a big rush. This is foreplay. It warms me up deliciously; and then it stokes my fire."

He smiled. "What *is* that fine perfume, anyway?"

"Ah, it's from *la* new designer, *Étienne*, from Lyon, now at Grasse in south of *Fraunce*. Not France. *Fraunce*. In *tribut* to *Étienne's* home town, he's named *la aróme...* the *Lioness!*"

She attacked him with little growls, and nibbled at his neck with little bites, mumbling, "I love the taste of you."

"I love the feel of your skin," he said. "You're sleek as a satin doll. How do you achieve such elegance?"

(*Should I tell him?*) She whispered: *"Old-fashioned cosmetics. Soft puffs of French powder after showers or hot tubs. Tell no one."*

He whispered, *"The secret is safe. Do you truly speak French?"*

She whispered, *"Only a teeny bit... from a high school class, and I have forgotten most of it. I just fake the nuances."*

He smiled. "You do have excellent nuances. But be careful how you apply them. I have nothing for your protection."

She smiled back. "Unprepared again? No problem. My monthly fertility cycle is dependably regular. In fact, your Rolex should be so precise. You've got free sailing, sailor."

Her knee dipped between his legs, and her nylons raised a sensation along his thighs. Playfully, she licked her lips to moisten them, then softly pressed her mouth to his. Her tongue entered and circulated. Her nostrils expelled warmth onto his cheeks. Her furry thick hair engulfed his face. She whispered into his ear, "Would *you* say I'm a frigid woman, my Darling?"

"Lord, no!" he said. Harper's hands moved with feathery lightness across her satin skin, sending Elissa into bodily shivers. Her prayer had indeed produced heavenly results.

At the edges of his vision, Harper was aware of lights around the lake, of lights in outer space. Within the limits of his hearing, he felt stereophonic melodies of wind and rippling water. Beyond these faint external signals, all else in his universe was Elissa — her hair, hands, fingernails, her breasts, teeth, eyelashes, tongue, thighs, lips, her tantalizing *parfum*, her intimate moisture... and finally...

"I think I have found Heavenly Valley," he murmured.

"Uh! Indeed you have," she whispered. "Welcome home."

Her hips led him on tour, and his explorations were delicious. She was electrified when he arrived at their destination, and she quickly joined him, releasing teardrops of joy that fell like warm dew onto his chest. She had been so starved for romance, and now... this! At last. At *long* last!

Rolling onto her back, Elissa put her fingers over her lips, intending to keep her surge of gratitude within herself — a precious little personal secret. But there was no way to suppress a smile that brightened her whole face.

Soon, wondering about an encore, Elissa flipped onto her side and propped her chin on her hands. Her soft eyes traced Harper's profile as he breathed quietly, steadily, his eyes closed. Quiet minutes ticked by as Elissa gazed lovingly at his handsome, beautiful, noble features.

Earlier, she had playfully mussed his hair and had left smears of her lipstick on his lips, and he looked so adorable. She knew he knew the lipstick was there and he didn't care, because he also knew how such little larks made her happy.

Now here is a man, she thought, who possesses unshakable self-confidence. She was so deeply proud of him!

Gradually, with his eyes still closed, he smiled.

Elissa sighed happily. "Darling, you're awake."

"Yes I am, Mrs. Pope."

Whoa! She couldn't believe it! She scooted to her knees. "Don't you think, after all this, you might call me *Elissa?*"

His eyes came open. "Yes, of course, Mrs. Pope."

She stared down at him. "Not very swift, are you?"

"Force of habit," he said. "I meant to say — yes, *Elissa.*"

Grabbing his hair, she firmly kissed his neck, nose, mouth. "Well," she whispered, "— it's darn well about time!"

"You are right, Mrs. Pope... Oh, no! I've done it again!"

"Am I going to have to work on you *all night*, Grey?"

He grinned. "Quite possibly."

Intermezzo

ON A HOLLYWOOD SET, on a glossy marble terrace beneath shining stars, Elissa Bennett Pope swayed to Sinatra's rendition of *My Kind of Town* — the jazzy tribute to the windy city where Elissa had enjoyed cruising just for the lights and the sights. Oddly, a Chicago skyline shimmered beyond the California palms, while in Capezio's highest and sexiest silver heels, Elissa performed a finger-snapping, high-stepping, hip-slinging, hair-tossing, head-rocking, beat-thumping dance while Grey Harper leaned against a vintage lamppost and watched. She swiveled towards him in her clinging cocktail dress, peering over a raised shoulder, and stopped suddenly face-to-face, her curvy leg extended. With her eyes focusing on him like a laser, she synchronized her lips with Sinatra's voice on *"my kind of razzmatazz!"* It brought Harper's hand to the small of her back, his knee inside her thighs, lifting her into a whirl that sent the Chicago skyline into a sweeping orbit that took her breath away.

***

"Whoosh!" Elissa bolted straight up in bed, instantly awake. In the Lake Tahoe moonlight, she saw a vacancy in the space alongside her. A strip of light shone under the bedroom door. She stood and walked cautiously toward the light, turned the door handle, and looked up to the living room. Grey sat at the bar, his back to her, wearing shorts.

Naked, Elissa closed the door soundlessly and returned to bedside. She sat, tapping her fingernails on the console.

The dream had seemed so real, especially Grey's role in it. Instinctively, she felt Grey Harper could dance exactly as in her dream. It was another secret wish. She herself was an accomplished dancer; but when she had asked whether Grey liked to dance, he had said, "It's been years." Nothing more.

Despite her deep affection — her burgeoning love for this man — Elissa felt an urgent need for more... much more. She had shamelessly revealed so much about herself; yet Harper had somehow managed to evade her curiosity about any of his personal intimacies.

To this day, Grey still had said little about Heather. Had he thought of Heather tonight, while making love to Elissa? Was he thinking of Heather now, while sitting alone at the bar? Lowering her hand to the top sheet, she found the satin lingerie she had worn earlier — and had discarded so easily.

She released the lingerie and looked at the clock, wondering what *would* she do, what *should* she do.

And then she thought of that delicious moment when he had gently turned her over, brushed her hair aside and so sweetly kissed the back of her neck. *Oh, that was so exquisite!*

But in two hours they would part. It wrenched her heart.

With her mind and emotions at such terribly aching odds, her love and trust in a maddening fog, Elissa wrapped herself in a terry bathrobe and marched bravely to the door.

Grey immediately got up from the stool, revealing a stack of documents and a phone on the bartop. He looked down to her with a concerned smile and said, "I'm sorry if I woke you. But I'm glad you're here, Elissa. We need to talk."

Chapter 35

THE Hartmann luggage beside the front door contained all the clothes Elissa had bought or borrowed for their escape.

On the occasion of this Final Day, she had reverted to her own businesslike ensemble — the powder blue cashmere turtleneck and black silk skirt she had worn to Grey's Lake Bluff cottage; her single-strand pearl necklace and a plain white shell bracelet; her black onyx ring; and her glossy high heels, one of which Grey had broken and then repaired.

These garments were comfortable for mountain air or commercial travel. More importantly, if she were going to die, she didn't want it to happen in someone else's clothing.

Now, lingering before calling a taxi, she stared wistfully at the lake from a comfortable chair in the living room.

Remembering the night, reliving the ecstasy, she sipped orange juice and watched the early morning activities along the shore. The sun had not yet scaled over the mountains, and the water appeared cold and silvery. Even so, boaters were shoving their crafts away from the docks, stashing gear, and rigging sails.

Abruptly, she was startled by the dark shadow of a man — a man who sprang in front of the sliding door.

Elissa gasped and dropped her juice glass onto the carpet. Before she could reach the door handle and lock it, the man had slammed it open. *"Hold it there, Mrs. Pope!"* At the same instant, Elissa heard sharp gunshots and a splintering crash at the front entrance behind her.

The man at the rear sliding door came through, holding a gun in both hands, its barrel at her chest. *"Where's Harper?"*

That man was Officer Baker.

"Oh God!" Elissa moaned.

Someone stepped behind her, but she couldn't take her eyes off that hideous gun — a gun she wildly imagined blazing at her eyes and hammering her head with blows of lead.

"Don't shoot me! Please don't."

The hard voice behind her said, "You're dead in two seconds, if you don't tell us where he is right now... One..."

"Gone!" Elissa screamed, her whole body in shivers. "He isn't here! He left an hour ago! Please don't kill me!"

"Turn around!" Baker yelled at her.

Elissa turned, encountering the husky cop she had seen in Salt Lake City. He, too, was thrusting a gun at her.

"What do you want with me?" she cried.

"I want Grey Harper," the man said.

Elissa's arms were grabbed from behind by Baker. He jerked her wrists viciously and painfully and clamped them in bands of cold metal. "Oh, no!" she begged, too late.

The big man nodded to Baker. "Watch that door," he said, pointing toward the kitchen. He then scampered toward the bedroom door and kicked it wide open. He hesitated for a moment, then barged through the opening. Elissa heard his feet shuffling about, heard his big shoes bashing the door to the bathroom. After a brief silence, the man reappeared. He nodded at Baker.

Baker pushed Elissa toward the kitchen, causing her to rock and stumble in her high heels. Grabbing her neck, he thrust her forehead against the door, knocking it open. She toppled to the floor, striking it with knees and shoulders. Her vision swarmed into a black hole. She thought she heard pistol barks at other rooms... or perhaps the echoes of shots entering her brain... and...

Deadly silence.

***

Then came gradual light, sorrowful awakening.

Sharp pain at her shackled wrists.

Dull, throbbing pain in her head and shoulders.

As her eyes focused, she noticed her left knee — stocking torn, skin bruised, a bloody smear on the ceramic tile.

"Oh, *damn,*" she groaned. She shut her eyes and clenched her teeth. She struggled for self-control, against her lonely fear of being murdered with hot bullets on a cold tile floor.

Then gradually came a spark of anger, rising inside.

Huge shoes thumped down hard on the tile near her face, and Elissa raised her eyelids. She saw a pair of large wingtips coated with dust and scuffs.

"Mrs. Pope?"

The voice belonged to the big man.

"Take it easy, Mrs. Pope. We're going to help you now. We apologize for getting rough, but we couldn't take any chances... Do you hear me, Mrs. Pope?"

Elissa sucked up a deep breath.

"Take off the cuffs," the voice said.

Elissa felt Baker's hands, heard the snaps, felt her arms fall free, flopping to her sides.

"Help her up," the big man said.

Baker lifted her up and sat her down on a chair.

The voice said, "Are you all right, Mrs. Pope?"

Good grief — they've got to be stupid!

"Mrs. Pope. I am Inspector George Carlisle of the FBI. This man is John Baker. You thought he was a policeman, but that was something we arranged. We needed to get you away from Grey Harper, you see. We didn't know if you were a conspirator or a hostage, and so we had to be careful about protecting you... Are you listening, Mrs. Pope?"

Elissa felt the tingle of circulation returning to her arms and hands. She also felt dull stabs throughout her upper body and on her knees. The pain merged with her anger.

"What do you want?" she said bitterly. "I haven't done anything. What do you want from me?"

"We had to be rough," the Inspector said. "We didn't know whether Harper had deceived you. I mean to say, he might've convinced you he was the victim of a conspiracy of some kind. He could have won your loyalty and your help. We didn't know what you believed. We couldn't take any chances, you see — for your sake, or ours. That's why I shot the locks off some doors here and went in hard. You understand? Do I make any sense, Mrs. Pope?"

"No," Elissa said.

The big man sighed. "I was afraid of this." The Inspector stood up and motioned at Baker. "Bring her some water."

Elissa, shivering again, stared at the Inspector's wingtip shoes. She hugged herself and continued shivering.

"Take it, Mrs. Pope." Baker held forth a lucid glass of shimmering water.

Elissa *slashed* at the glass, knocking it away from Baker's hand. Water sprayed onto his dark suit and onto the carpet. The glass sailed brightly end-over-end, shattering against the fireplace.

Elissa heard the sprinkle of broken glass. She also heard the chirping of birds outside, the sounds of the lake sucking against rocks and sand, the chime of a clock somewhere in the house.

"That was uncalled for," the Inspector said. "We just wanted to help you."

"Yeah, help you," Baker said.

Elissa hugged her arms around her torso and allowed her reluctant lips to frame the only appropriate word:

"Bullshit."

***

It was Baker's turn to convince her.

Elissa sat stiffly on the living room couch, hands in her lap. The Inspector was in the bedroom, using the phone. Baker had removed his jacket and sat across from her, his hideous black handgun embedded in his shoulder holster.

"What made you think we wanted to kill him?"

"Are you joking?" she said. "Give me a break!"

"No, really. What motive did you imagine?"

"It's about the radon on the Fort Sheridan property," Elissa answered.

Baker shrugged. "Is that what he told you? And you believed him? That's a hoot. Look, if he found radon, so what? The United States government has no more interest in that land, Mrs. Pope. It belongs to private developers. There is no reason in the world that we'd give a damn about some little environmental problem like that."

"I saw soldiers attacking the house where we stayed in Lake Forest. They weren't private developers, Mr. Baker. They were soldiers!"

"Yes, they were, Mrs. Pope," Baker said. "They were, in fact, a hostage rescue team. I rounded them up to save you. Can't you understand that?"

"*You* rounded them up? You're not FBI," Elissa said. "Real FBI agents do not point guns at innocent women and threaten to kill them. Real agents wouldn't handcuff me and mop the floor with me the way you did."

"How do you know that, Mrs. Pope? From watching TV? What in hell do you know about real police procedure?"

"I know *that* much," Elissa insisted. "I just know that much about the FBI, and every American knows — they've always been the good guys, protecting us."

Baker stared at her, stared directly and sternly. "Jeez, you're a sad wretch."

He gestured outward, far beyond the house. "You may not know it, but there's a real world out there, Mrs. Pope, and it's filled with mean and crazy sons-of-bitches. Hell, Harper's one of 'em. He faked that cover-up story to hide his own failure to run tests for radon. He killed Munro because Munro knew it was Harper's blunder, not the military's, not the government's." Baker paused and looked to Elissa for reaction. None.

"So Munro went to the site to fire Harper. He threatened to sue Harper for delays and damages. That's why

Harper never told the workers why he was shutting them down. In order to blame Munro, he had to kill him first."

Elissa seemed in a trance. Baker continued:

"But Harper made another mistake, a real huge one. He left Munro's body on federal property, Mrs. Pope. And that's how the FBI got involved — how *we* got involved. It's why Inspector Carlisle was assigned to the case. That's the whole reason. And no matter what Harper told you, there is no kind of conspiracy happening here."

"How do you explain the reporter?" Elissa said.

"What?"

"Somebody killed a *Tribune* reporter and blamed Grey Harper for it," Elissa said. "I know he didn't do it, because I was with him. He couldn't have done it, and I think you did it, and you tried to frame both of us."

"Mrs. Pope," Baker said, "are you referring to a woman named Rita Chan?"

"Yes," Elissa said.

Baker grunted. "Mrs. Pope... Chan's killing was solved by the Chicago police yesterday. Had nothing to do with this case. She was killed by a junkie at the airport while she was waiting in the garage — waiting for the interview we promised her with Harper. That's all it was. A junkie, a bad trip or foul-up, because of all the drug trafficking around airports."

Elissa remembered Harper's story about witnessing a drug bust near SFO. That didn't necessarily add credence to Baker's story. "But you accused *Grey* of killing Rita Chan. It was in all the newspapers."

"At the time, that's what we thought. We figured you two ran into her while escaping in the garage. She recognized you from the pictures; so you killed her. Instead, some junkie showed up, thought Chan was there alone in the dark to deal drugs. He finds out she's a reporter and kills her for her cash or whatever. Who knows? Who cares? It wasn't us."

Elissa stared quietly at Baker. Finally she said, "I don't believe you. There were two Rita Chans, and I think you killed the real one. Your guys said Grey used the gun that killed Munro — which he didn't have!"

"Okay, we didn't want the world to know Harper got my gun; so we told the press it was the other one. It was neither -- just a street rod. So what? Why should we kill her?"

"To hang another frame on Grey... Or to shut up Rita because she learned too much. Or all of the above. I don't know what the hell you guys do. I don't believe any of it."

"Well, that's too bad. For you."

Baker stood up in front of her. "I'll tell you what. One last chance. I'll give you the number for the Chicago police, and you can call them. Verify what I just told you. Would you want to do that?"

Elissa shook her head. "No thanks. Last time Grey and I called the police, we got you."

Baker smirked at her. "Fine. Suit yourself. I can see Harper did one real big number on you, babe. He must've shagged your brains out, and now you're all in love with that bastard, despite everything he did to ruin you."

"You...bloody heel!" Elissa sputtered. "You...bag of scum!" She jumped up and threw a slap at him.

Baker caught her wrist and twisted it. "Hot damn! You got one hell of a temper, babe! Did I just happen to pinch a nerve?"

Chapter 36

OF MANY WAYS that Harper could have traveled on this final day, he hoped his choice was a shrewd one.

As he sipped coffee and stared at scenery, a white-haired chauffeur smoothly transported Harper in a stretch limousine down the long grade from Donner Pass to Sacramento.

The car seemed to crawl, though, often passed by monstrous trucks that careened down Interstate 80, building momentum for the next upgrade.

Advisory signs along the route alerted truckers when to downshift, when to cool their brakes, when to "Crank Up" or "Let 'er Drift." Harper's driver seemed to like "drifting" best. He drove as if he were captain of an oil tanker.

Harper had found him in a local directory among several independent limo services. The name, *"Escape Limousines,"* had seemed neatly appropriate. Also, Charles P. Dugan, owner and driver of this Cadillac submarine, had unblinkingly accepted hundred dollar bills for payment and a business card for identification — the business card of District Sales Manager Steve Downey, representing the Travel Club of America, from Salt Lake City, Utah.

Along the way, gazing through the left windows, Harper had observed an eastbound freight train snaking through the snowsheds above Donner Lake — a train destined to backtrack the entire route he and Elissa Pope had taken from Chicago.

The sight of that train had fired an emotion. He suddenly had missed Elissa Pope's company, and now he was increasingly concerned about her safety and comfort.

It didn't matter that they had spent an hour before dawn discussing and finally agreeing upon a plan that required them to separate and take chances. They were miles apart for the first time since their escapade had begun. And he had no way to know if they were getting closer or farther.

Harper reached forward, across the champagne bucket, and tapped the driver's shoulder. "Charles," he said, tapping.

The driver's head shifted a few degrees. "Yes, sire?"

"Could we manage a little more haste?"

"Are we in a hurry, Mr. Downey?"

"Yes, Charles. We are somewhat in a hurry."

The driver nodded. "Very well, sire."

The limo moved ahead. The speedometer needle climbed several notches up the scale.

Charles said, "We have now obtained the legal speed limit, Mr. Downey."

Harper knew Charles was being meticulously proper, hoping for a favorable mention in the Travel Club magazine.

"Good for you, Charles. If you would be so kind, please keep this monster cranked up there for the whole trip."

He eased back against the leather and crossed his legs. When all this was over, Harper decided, he would indeed make an effort to sponsor an advertisement for Charles in the Travel Club magazine.

***

SHE OFFERED no resistance. Baker snapped the cuffs onto her wrists again, then attached a second pair to her ankles. "Sorry, Elissa. We had hoped you'd cooperate, but since you won't..."

"The name is Mrs. Pope!" Elissa said.

"Well ex-*cuse me!*" Baker grinned. He thought she was damned good-looking, and it was going to be almost a dirty rotten shame to recycle her. He shrugged and went to the bedroom where Inspector Carlisle was still on the phone.

Standing, the Inspector said a few words, hung up, and turned to Baker. "What's she doing?" the Inspector asked.

Baker peeked out. "Yawning," he said.

"Yawning? What, she's bored?"

"Scared," Baker said. "You get really scared, you need more oxygen. It's a reflex."

"You put cuffs on her again?"

"Wrists and ankles. She's not going anywhere."

Inspector Carlisle nodded. "Wish it was true. But we gotta bring her along with us."

"What? Why?"

"You know, while I was on the phone, I was thumbing through a guidebook over there — it says this lake has enough water to lay fourteen inches over the whole state of California. It must be one hell of a *deep* lake. We could sink that woman to the bottom and nobody would find her in a thousand years."

"Sounds like a plan," Baker said.

"Even so — Rogers and the General, they have a better idea." He shrugged. "They say, bring the lady with us."

"Why?" Baker demanded again.

The Inspector flapped his arms at his sides. "They want to talk to her — personally."

"No kidding?"

"No kidding."

"Where?"

"Where this whole thing finally goes down... at Harper's house, in Carmel-by-the-Sea."

Baker looked doubtful. He said, "Okay, that's what the broad's been trying *not* to tell us. But, you really think we'll catch Harper at his own digs? You think he's that dumb?"

The Inspector shook his head. "Not dumb. Desperate. He's on a desperate journey, and that's where it ends."

***

With her hands cuffed, Elissa endured Baker's thick arm between her elbows and backbone as he forced her into the back seat of a plain white two-door Thunderbird sedan.

The car rocked as the men got in and slammed its doors.

Her mind went numb. Her whole body felt like a bowl of jelly, quivering in fear of these cruel men, wherever they were taking her, for whatever cold and horrible purpose.

In the rearview mirror, Baker's snaky eyes watched her.

She held one spark of hope: her captors had brought her luggage along, in the trunk. It contained her intimate things — her only tangible connections to her life on this earth.

She focused her thoughts on Grey Harper, wondering if she would ever see him, ever hold him, at least once more.

Chapter 37

WHEN SHE FINALLY SAW THE OCEAN HOUSE... it did not fit Grey Harper's description at all!

As Baker cruised slowly past the driveway's wide-open gate, Elissa gazed at the dwelling from her back seat. It was a huge modern mansion built on many levels, with numerous cars parked along the drive. It looked as though a dozen people lived there and partied around the clock.

She also witnessed the confusion of her captors.

Inspector Carlisle had the antenna fully extended on a handheld radio, communicating with one of the agents who had been sent in advance from San Francisco to stake out the residence.

"Uh-huh.... yeah.... uh-huh.... What? You're kidding! You're *not* kidding! You're sure about that? Well, then, what *is* the address?" (He wagged his head at Baker.) "Then get back to me as soon as you find out, and make it damn quick. I don't care how busy they are up there! Damn!" He shot the antenna into its receptacle and stared at Baker.

Baker said, "What's going on?"

"That's not Harper's house."

"It's the address he gave me! It's in my notebook. Look for yourself."

"Baker, look at that place. Does it maybe seem a little bit familiar to you?"

Baker shrugged. "No. Well... Maybe a little. Why?"

"You like sexy movies, right?"

"Yeah. So?"

"Our agents found out, to *our* embarrassment, this place is famous around here. It was in the movie, '*Basic Instinct!*'"

Baker stared hard at it. "Harper lied to me! That bastard! He broke the law! I told him I was a cop, and he lied!"

"Shut up." Carlisle nudged Baker to remind him of Elissa in the back seat. He said, "We'll talk about the blame later. Now, we got a problem tracking down Harper's real address. With the Special Agents down here, the San Francisco office is juggling priorities. It means you and I have to rethink real hard how we're gonna surprise the shit out of Harper."

For the first time in hours, Elissa had something to hope for — better than a quick and painless death...

***

THE SILVER MERCEDES had sped through the Santa Cruz mountains, flying toward the house in Carmel.

Grey Harper had held the steering wheel in both hands, his mind and vision a thousand yards in front, anticipating every treacherous curve of Highway 17, a road heavily dappled in shadows from the surrounding pines.

This Mercedes, silver like the one he had leased in Chicago, was — he had smiled — "his own." He had picked it up where the limo had dropped him, in the long-term parking lot at the San Jose airport. He had avoided disclosing the location to Elissa, deciding such vital knowledge was too dangerous a burden to impose on her.

But it had taken half an hour to settle the airport parking charges and clear the lot. Then he had stopped at a Silicon Valley electronics outlet where he had an account. And there had been traffic on all the roads.

But the Mercedes had slipped through traffic like a phantom. A California Highway Patrol cruiser had swept past in opposite lanes, and the officer just didn't notice the low-slung sports car as it flitted behind a truck, then shot forward again after rounding a curve.

Harper had known he would reach his house.

He had been far less confident of getting there soon enough to accomplish everything he had to do.

Especially worrisome was his remote check of his home answering machine. There had been no call from Elissa.

Chapter 38

NOW THIS HOUSE fit Harper's description, yet somehow exceeded it in a way Elissa could not define.

Up the road from the movie mansion, this smaller home leaned into the wind and surf in bold defiance, as if alive and confident of its solid footing. Its angles matched the vertical cliffs beneath it and the horizontal branches of cypress trees around it. It seemed both man-made and natural at the same time, as though Harper had used wind, rain, and lightning for his tools.

It was, Elissa felt, breathtaking!

"Move it," the Inspector said, pushing Elissa forward.

After finding Harper's house thirty minutes ago, Carlisle had split the team. Baker had gone inside to scout the place, while the Inspector stayed outside, holding Elissa as a handcuffed hostage — in case Harper was on site with a gun.

Now Baker came out the front door and motioned them to enter the house.

With her cuffed wrists, Elissa felt a bit off balance as she stepped along a flagstone path in her high heels, ahead of the Inspector. While observing their approach, Baker said, "He hasn't been here for a while. There aren't any fresh signs of a person or vehicle anywhere on the property."

"You're probably right," the Inspector said, pushing Elissa through the doorway. He dropped her luggage in the foyer. "It's not that far from the other house; and the agents were watching the whole area. Nothing. So, you can get rid of those guys now — tell 'em we'll take it from here."

"Right." Baker raised the hand-held transmitter to his mouth and relayed the orders. Somewhere in the vicinity, the San Francisco agents acknowledged and faded away.

Elissa followed Baker across the foyer and stepped down into a sunken living room. Her eyes surveyed its quiet splendor. *So this is Harper's home. This is where he lives, alone, day after day...*

Although the room wasn't immense, it had a sense of depth, as though it reached beyond its western wall of glass and encompassed the entire Pacific Ocean. Overhead, solid redwood beams seemed to cut right through the glass and stone, supporting wing-shaped sections of roof that extended over a terrace. To the left and right, the room had no clear boundaries. In place of walls, there was the largest contemporary fireplace she had ever seen — inspired by a "medieval castle," Harper had said. Beyond it were staggered ledges of stone, interspersed with ferns and alcoves.

In fact, Elissa realized, this was not an ordinary "living room" at all. It was more like a sheltered cove carved among the ocean cliffs by the surf — a surf she could hear whooshing softly beyond the glass...

Her reverie did not last. "Sit," the Inspector ordered.

As she sat, Elissa felt immediately more comfortable despite the handcuffs. This chair was not purchased from any collection she had ever seen, and it felt like none she had ever tried. She noticed all the furnishings were like this — low, simple, with textured fabrics and invisible framework. The couch across from her seemed to float.

When the Inspector sat in that couch, she thought he defiled it. "You really belong on a cot," she said. "A jail cot."

Inspector Carlisle looked at her in surprise. "Hoo!" he said. "Big talk from the little tart." He leaned toward her and pointed a beefy finger. "You should say something, will get you out of this crap instead of deeper into it!"

Elissa dismissed that. Then Baker crossed between them and dropped onto another chair. He stretched his legs out and pulled back the lapels of his jacket, again exposing his holster and the handgrip of his gun. "Damn, this is comfortable, Inspector. Harper has a swank layout here. What's the chances of attaching this place, using it as a safe house?"

"Interesting idea," the Inspector said. "I'll look into it."

The idea shocked Elissa. "You're both disgusting!"

Carlisle ignored her, asking Baker, "What's the time?"

"Seven thirty-three," Baker answered.

"Almost that time," the Inspector said.

"Time for what?" Elissa asked.

"Time for you to face the music and dance," the Inspector said. He stood, and Baker stood, and they each grabbed Elissa's arms and dragged her to a door. They kicked open the door, pulled her into a bedroom and then heaved her onto a bed.

Elissa closed her eyes tightly. She felt cold and shivery as she wondered where Harper was, and waited — waited to endure whatever these men intended for her.

Chapter 39

ELISSA opened her eyes. To her relief, Baker and Carlisle had left the room without harming her. The door was closed and the bedroom was becoming dark. The only sound she heard was the surf.

Squirming to the edge of the bed, she dropped her legs over the side and managed to sit up. She was facing a glass wall that framed a view of windswept cypress trees and, beyond, the heavy swells of the ocean. There was fog moving in, and the horizon was obscured.

Turning to the left, she saw an ergonomic recliner facing the ocean. Beside it was a low table with several books. On the floor was a pair of moccasins.

This is Harper's bedroom, she realized.

She stood and stepped carefully in semi-darkness to the table. She gazed at the books: well-worn copies of *Pieces of My Mind* by Andy Rooney; *Inside, Outside* by Herman Wouk; the thick *Time-Saver Standards for Architectural Design Data*.

On the other side of the chair were shelves full of books — all kinds of books — stacked in no apparent order. Beyond the bed was a mirrored closet wall that reflected the ocean view. It made the room seem like a small island or peninsula, with ocean on both sides.

Stepping out of her shoes, Elissa walked toward the closet and used her stockinged toes to slide open one of the mirrored doors. She gasped at what she saw inside — a huge organized display of women's clothes, all stylishly luxurious, and a wall of shoes and accessories. This had to be Heather's closet, with Harper's through an opening in the stone wall beyond the bed. That closet was smaller, and then she found herself in Harper's bathroom. It wasn't actually a room, but another undefined space of glass, redwood, and stone ledges. A long window spanned a countertop facing the sea, and there was a glass enclosed shower stall and a whirlpool bath tucked among hanging ferns.

Appraising what she had seen of Harper's house, Elissa felt briefly like her old self — a real estate broker and property manager — and forgot, for a moment, that she was a prisoner. A desire to touch the stonework jarred her back to reality — she couldn't bring her hands from behind her.

She turned toward the bedroom — and froze. Baker was standing there, holding her shoes, staring at her.

"Don't even think about escaping," he said. "Outside, it's a good two-hundred-foot drop to the ocean."

"I wasn't..."

He dropped her shoes. "Never mind. Just turn around."

Elissa obeyed, and Baker removed the cuffs. "Now, get your shoes on," he said. "You got visitors."

***

"There's fog moving in," General Norgan said to the Inspector. He shut the front door and clapped his hands. "It's getting damned chilly out there."

Attorney Donald Rogers shook off his topcoat and draped it over a chair. "It seems cold inside here, too," he said, sniffing. "Inspector, why don't we start up that big fireplace? It looks ready to go."

"We can't do that, Counselor," the Inspector said to Rogers. "Harper approaches, senses heat or smells smoke, or sees a light, he'll know somebody's here."

"Our rental car..." Rogers said. "We parked in front."

"Give the keys to Baker. He'll park it down the road."

"Where *is* Baker?"

"He's with Pope. He'll bring her out whenever you want."

"Bring her out now," the General said.

***

Elissa stepped into the darkened living room, massaging her wrists, and saw three men in shadows. One appeared to be Inspector Carlisle, but the other two were tall and sinister, obscured in shadows cast by the cypress trees outside.

"Who are you?" she asked, a tremble in her voice.

The voice that responded was familiar: "Hello, Elissa."

"Who..."

"It's me, Elissa — Donald Rogers. I'm here to help you."

"*Don?* Good Lord!" Elissa was relieved but stunned. She didn't know whether to rush forward and hug him — or not.

Something held her. With a raised brow and a choked voice, she asked, "What is your... *interest* in this, Donald?"

Rogers moved from the shadows and grasped Elissa's arm, frightening her more. "I came to help you out of this trouble, Elissa. I also brought along someone else who can help you." He turned. "General?"

The other man emerged from the shadows. Elissa saw his face come into view slowly, a face like the stone behind him — hard, coarse, ridged in an ugly-handsome way.

"Elissa, I'd like you to meet my old friend, General Lyman P. Norgan, U.S. Army. And, General, meet Elissa Bennett Pope, another old friend."

"My pleasure, Mrs. Pope," the General said.

Elissa stared anxiously at both men. She glanced at the Inspector and Baker, who stood aside, their expressions invisible in the dim light. To Rogers, she said, "How... how can you help me?"

"Please sit down," Rogers said. "And let's talk."

As Elissa settled gingerly, Rogers spoke to Baker and then gave him a set of car keys. He turned to the Inspector. "The General and I will appreciate being left alone with Mrs. Pope — if that's okay, Inspector. Legalities, you know."

The Inspector nodded and led Baker out of the room.

Elissa grasped her hands together, moist and trembling.

Rogers rubbed his hands, dry and hard. The General sat on the couch facing Elissa. His narrow eyes peered at her.

The room was getting darker, and the surf seemed a bit noisier. No one spoke. Elissa tried hard not to shed a tear.

She heard a car engine starting up. The sound became a rumble that faded away. Breathing in, finding strength, she said, "Am I supposed to hire you, Donald? As a lawyer? Excuse me, but I'm... puzzled why you're here."

"It's because of the Fort," Rogers said. "Elissa — do you know the trouble you're in?"

"Trouble?" Here eyes flared. "Do you mean being chased and shot at? Do you mean being pushed and jabbed and knocked to the floor? Do you mean being kidnapped, and being handcuffed all day? Is *that* the trouble you mean?"

Rogers sighed. "No, Elissa. I mean the trouble you got yourself into. You are under arrest for aiding a fugitive, a man wanted for suspicion of murder. *That's* what I mean by trouble, Elissa, and you're buried to your neck in it. You could spend the rest of your life in a federal prison."

His words abruptly changed Elissa's whole concept of Donald Rogers. Defiantly, now, she leaned back in her chair, deftly crossed her legs and raised an eyebrow. "Excuse me, Donald, but that's horsepucky!"

Rogers looked stunned. He selected a chair that placed him at a diagonal between Elissa and the General and sat down. "In our social circles, Elissa, I've never heard you talk like that. Perhaps you'd better explain what you mean."

"Perhaps you're more familiar with the term horse *shit?* I mean that Grey Harper didn't shoot anybody, Donald. He's being framed. And those two so-called FBI agents have no intention of taking me back for any kind of legal process. If they find Harper, they'll just... kill him. And then..." she held her breath "...they'll do the same to me."

"How can you believe that?" Rogers asked. "Did Harper *brainwash* you?"

Elissa shook her head.

Rogers said, "May I ask some questions, Elissa?"

"Do as you please."

"Okay. From what I understand, you believe Harper is being, um, framed, because he said he found a radon cover-up, or some such thing, at Fort Sheridan. Correct?"

"Yes. That's correct."

Rogers turned to the General. "General Norgan, I believe you have something to say about this?"

The General cleared his throat and leaned forward, placing his hands on his knees. "Yes. Um, Mrs. Pope, at one time in my career, I was commandant of Fort Sheridan. I held the post for about four years, and I can tell you everything that anyone knows about that property. There are ravines used for landfill, some of it toxic, perhaps even a bit radioactive. But it's all been dealt with, Mrs. Pope. There's nothing there to hide." He stared at her with stern but hopeful eyes.

Elissa stared back at the General. Her dark eyes became intense as they searched for sincerity in his expression. "How do I know you're telling me the truth?" she asked. "How do I even know you're the person you say you are?"

The General reached into his jacket pocket and extracted a folded sheet of paper. "Take a look at this," he said, passing it across. "I believe there's enough light to see it."

Elissa did not reach out. "Identification? It could be a fake," she said. "How would I know?"

"If you're not afraid of the truth, Mrs. Pope, you will, at least, take a look at this." The General fluttered the paper.

Snatching it, Elissa unfolded what appeared to be a... a book jacket! On glossy paper, clearly visible even in dim light, was the title, *The U.S. Military in Transition: Da Nang to Desert Storm — by General Lyman P. Norgan, US Army, Pentagon.*

"It's a treatise on the need for military strength in times of supposed peace — disguised as memoirs," the General said, smiling. "Still working on the final draft. But the publisher went ahead with the jacket, and that's a press proof. Take a look at the other side."

Elissa turned it over. On the inside back flap was a picture of Norgan in dress uniform. Beneath it was a brief biography, describing him as a thirty-year career soldier who had served in U.S. Army Intelligence in Vietnam, then as commandant of Fort Sheridan, and now as a senior logistics officer in the Pentagon.

"Okay," Elissa said, dropping the book jacket on the table beside her chair. "The title's long, but I'm impressed."

Attorney Rogers brought his hands together and said, "Now then. It should be perfectly obvious that Harper lied when he told you there was some secret radon conspiracy at the construction site. That means..."

"Excuse me, Donald," Elissa said. "I told you I was impressed. That does not mean I am fooled."

Rogers unclasped his hands and threw them wide. "Elissa, do you know the General is an adviser to the Army Chief of Staff, who reports directly to the President of the United States? Why on earth would a man of his rank try to fool you? Don't you see? We're on your *side!*"

"No. You're on my *back*, and I wish you'd get off."

"Good Lord," Rogers said. "This is worse than I thought." He shook his head at the General. "It must be the Stockholm Syndrome. I'm afraid Elissa has been completely manipulated by Harper — twisted to the point that she has lost all touch with reality. I really don't know if I can help her in this state."

The General gave Elissa a rather pained expression. He raised his brows and sighed. "Quite sad, really."

Elissa clapped her hands. "Cut! Can we try all that once more with feeling?"

Rogers bent his head toward her. "Stop it, Elissa. I have more questions."

"I'm sure. Go right ahead." She was bristling now.

"Do you honestly believe that FBI Inspector Carlisle, and Agent Baker, have a desire to kill you?" Rogers asked.

"Absolutely," Elissa said. "As much as I don't like the idea, I am convinced they fully intend to do away with me!" She smartly re-crossed her legs and wagged her foot.

"Hmm." Her leg action had momentarily distracted him. "And just what have they done to make you suspect that?"

"They... I've told you! They pointed their guns at me and threatened to shoot me. They roughed me up and knocked me down. Without any basis for arresting me, they handcuffed me and they *kidnapped* me."

"Did they actually strike you? Did they punch you?"

"No... not *actually*," Elissa said flatly. "They..."

"Did they rape you, Elissa?"

She shuddered. "No..."

"Did they fondle your breasts or squeeze your bottom?"

"God, this is..."

"Did they?"

"No!"

"But Harper did," Attorney Rogers said, knowingly.

"He did not! He did none of those things!" Elissa was outraged, and her face was flushed and her eyes were afire.

Rogers shifted in his chair and looked straight into her eyes. He pointed a finger and said, "Harper never touched you *here* — or *there? Never* got in bed with you?"

Elissa gazed at the Attorney's face and her lips quivered. Her body shook and tears welled from her eyes. "My God,

Donald... You're.. *defiling* me. And *him*." She sank her face into her hands. Trembles rippled across her back.

Rogers got up and stepped in front of her, placing his hands on her throbbing shoulders. "I know," he said. "It didn't seem like rape at the time. But Harper was very clever about the way he kidnapped you and used you. He told you a story that was so fantastic you believed him. And he dragged you through hell and turmoil, making you fear for your life. You became vulnerable, and you started clinging to him for your own protection. Don't you see? You lost touch with reality. And he embraced you, and you thought it was kindness. All the while, you were nothing but his shield."

Elissa sobbed quietly and felt she was going to be sick.

The General, hands on his knees, just stared at her.

Rogers straightened up and cocked his head at the General. "So much like Stockholm," he said sadly. "I don't think all the charges against her are justified. What do you think, General?"

Norgan shrugged. "I'm just a bystander," he said, "coming here as a personal favor to you. But it does seem the lady is a victim, not a criminal."

Elissa raised her head from her hands and aimed her reddened eyes at Rogers. "Donald," she said in a low and scratchy voice. "You are so wrong. You weren't there. You have no idea what has happened."

"To the contrary," Rogers said, standing back and unfolding a newspaper clipping from his pocket. "From the moment you disappeared with Harper, I have been extremely concerned. This story appeared in the *Sun-Times* and went national. In a direct quote, I'm saying, *'Elissa is much too smart to pull anything that foolish. It's more likely she has been taken against her will.'* Here. Look at this..."

"I saw it in Colorado. It was in *The Denver Post.*"

"There, you see? I was on your side from the very beginning." He pocketed the clipping. "You have to realize, police treatment can seem pretty rough. But they have good reasons for trying to frighten you and protect themselves. It doesn't mean they're murderers!"

He squatted in front of her. He tried to look consoling.

"Meanwhile, Elissa, I have followed every single report of your movements. And I have had my entire office — every member of the staff — doing extensive research and investigation on your behalf. And believe me, I know a lot more about F. Graham Harper than you do."

"Good grief, Donald," Elissa said. "That's impossible."

"Is it? Let's compare. What do you know of... *Heather?*"

A cold wave hit Elissa, and she hesitated before answering. "Heather was Harper's former wife," she said softly.

Rogers nodded. He asked, "What *happened* to Heather?"

Another cold wave. "She... she died."

"Yes," Rogers said. "And *how* did she die?"

Elissa did not answer.

She did not know the answer.

Chapter 40

BAKER SLAMMED the loaded magazine into the butt of his automatic and cocked it. "Shoot on sight?" he asked.

"Don't be so eager," the Inspector said. "The General wants to interrogate Harper, followed by a murder-suicide scenario off the cliff. If you gotta shoot, just whack a knee, like it got slammed against the rocks down in the surf."

"Cool." Baker tossed the handgun into the car trunk and grabbed a long-barreled revolver. "Then I got just what you need. It's an S and W 686. I can switch its Magnum rounds to low-power, hollow-point .38 Specials. Not much recoil or penetration, but it'll crack his knee like a sledgehammer."

"Fine," the Inspector said. "But what about accuracy? Can you even hit a knee in this dark and fog?"

"Hey. With its easy trigger pull and the way I'm setting it up, even a *woman* can cripple a guy with this revolver."

The Inspector wagged his head. "But what makes you so sure you'll even see Harper before he sees you? Even if you have a starlight scope in your bag, there's no damn starlight."

Baker grinned. "With a laser illuminator, my night scope don't need any starlight. And *I* don't need it. I use expert hearing — tracking a guy by the tiniest sounds he makes. I'll step right in his face before he suspects anything. Then pop goes the knee. Both knees if you want."

"Yeah, well," the Inspector said. "Just don't forget he's the guy that kicked you down a flight of stairs and took your gun and locked you in a closet wearing your own handcuffs."

"That," Baker said, "I'm never gonna forget."

***

THE COLD and heavy air hit Elissa like an avalanche.

"Come along," the Attorney said, pulling at her elbow. "You won't fall. We've got you." He nodded at the General, who grasped Elissa's other elbow, and together they yanked her onto Harper's terrace toward a hip-level stone wall.

"It's freezing here," Elissa protested. "What's the purpose of this?"

"There's something you must see," Rogers said. "It won't take but a minute. Come along."

They easily overcame her resistance, and they hauled her to the low wall and held her there, facing over the edge. Her heart was thumping, and she twisted her arms, only to feel pinches and pains as they tightened their grips.

"What are you doing!" she demanded.

"We're showing you," the Attorney said. "Look down."

Elissa looked over the wall, down through layers of dark fog, and she saw a smoky cauldron of surf smashing against the rocks far below.

As she stared, she felt a deep rumble as another huge swell rolled in, then a heavy boom as the sea exploded against the cliff. The power of that surf was riveting. It came across thousands of miles of raw ocean, building tremendous momentum, and it slammed the rocks with megatons of energy.

"My God," she whispered. "It's... magnificent."

The two men held her but did not move or speak.

After a moment, Elissa said, "It's also very frightening. Can we go back inside — now?"

"I'm afraid not," the Attorney said. He cued the General, and together they tightened their grips, and they pushed Elissa out and over the wall.

***

"WHAT'S that?" The Inspector waved toward the sound.

"A scream," Baker said, "— from behind the house."

"The Pope woman?"

"Had to be," Baker said. "Damn, I hope they didn't toss her over the cliff already. I wanted a nice piece of her before they did that."

The Inspector frowned at Baker. "I'll check it out and let you know. You get on patrol."

"Inspector...?"

"Yeah — what?"

"If they killed the lady..."

"Yeah?"

"Hell, never mind. They can always get me another one."

***

THEY lowered Elissa back onto the terrace.

Rogers said, "And *that*, Elissa, is how Heather died."

She was shivering and sobbing and unable to speak. She was barely able to stand.

"Okay," the Attorney said to the General. "Let's get her back inside."

As dead weight, Elissa created a struggle for the two men. Coming through the terrace door, she collapsed, and they lost their grips. She splayed onto the carpet, her eyes in a trance-like state, horrified by the vision of that deadly surf.

***

Half an hour later, Elissa stared at an untouched glass of brandy and sat curled up inside a cocoon of blankets on the couch in Harper's living room. She still felt a sickness inside.

All her life, she had feared the "unknown" more than the "known." A man in a dark hallway would frighten her until she saw his face; then she was okay. But now she *knew* she was *falling, falling* down to rocks and surf, *knew* she was *dead* and *broken* by the impacts! It was far more horrifying than all fears of the unknown she had felt during her years of life.

The shadow of Donald Rogers loomed in a nearby chair.

From that shadow came her name: "Elissa?"

She did not answer.

"Have you regained any of your senses?" Rogers asked.

"There are no senses to any of this," she murmured.

"That's true," Rogers agreed. "If you hadn't stood in the way, we would have caught that criminal on the second day, and none of this would have touched you. If you would only cooperate now, I could put you on a plane and have you home by noon tomorrow. All this would go away, Elissa. You would return to your normal life, and you might even pre-tend that none of this ever happened to you. It would be no more than a bad dream. And you only need to... *cooperate!*"

Elissa remained silent.

"Would you like another brandy?" Rogers asked. Then, "Oh, but you haven't touched it."

"It's not yours to offer, Donald."

Rogers smirked. "Oh, nonsense, Elissa. The bottles and the glasses in the liquor cabinet have dust on them. Harper must keep them for guests. I doubt very much he'd object. And certainly not to you, for all that he put you through."

She held herself still in the shadows. "I said no."

"Very well," he said. "Let me repeat what I told you, while you were in such a panic, you may not have heard it all. My investigation of Harper's background..."

"Don't, please," Elissa murmured. "I've had enough."

"...discovered that his former wife, Heather, had died under mysterious circumstances. She was an heiress, you see. Worth not a large fortune, but by no means a small fortune. Her father had been a San Francisco electronics engineer — a clever fellow — who held private patents on fiber optic devices used in the telecommunications industry. At the time of his death, those patents were worth a few million dollars. Well, Heather sold them — sold them off at about the same time Grey Harper felt an urge to leave his faltering career with the architectural firm of Adler, Brown, Kiening and strike out on his own."

Elissa remained perfectly still and listened to the surf.

"Harper may have thought Carmel was a place where he could make his mark. But Heather just wasn't happy here. She had money now. She missed all her friends and associates in San Francisco. She resented living in a village that offered nothing more than tourist shops and a minor population of artists and poets. Matter of fact, she told Harper — bluntly — that they must return to the city. Otherwise, she would divorce him... and take all her money with her."

Elissa turned her face away, toward the ocean.

Beyond the glass wall, the fog formed ghostly images of strange beings, groping for admittance to the dark house.

"At first, Harper didn't fight it. He agreed to the divorce, and he pursued whatever projects he could find here in Carmel-by-the-Sea — a small shopping mall, a store remodeling, a custom home. But then Heather came after the house — *this* house — insisting that half belonged to her. Harper refused to sell and divide the proceeds...

"Finally one night, in exasperation, Heather came here, into this house, to speak to him personally. She was ready to deal. She would take this house, and she would give Harper a half-million-dollar check to vacate. We know that, because her attorneys drew up an agreement, and those attorneys agreed to disclose the details in the interests of justice — especially since they no longer had Heather to protect as a client... because Heather is dead!"

The room, or cove, as she had imagined it, was now a dark cave. There was no light except for glowing pinpoints in the fog that swirled across the glass. There was no clear sight of Attorney Rogers — only the deep and authoritative sound of his voice.

"Of course, nothing could be proved," Rogers said. "After all, Heather had fallen to the rocks! And her remains were totally bashed by the surf into... well, *pulp*. There was no forensic evidence. No witnesses. Harper claimed it had been an accident — that during a temper tantrum, Heather had run onto the terrace and just toppled over the wall to her death. Nobody believed that, obviously, but there wasn't sufficient evidence to bring him to trial."

Elissa gazed in the direction of the Attorney's voice and said, weakly, "If there was no evidence of guilt, he must be presumed innocent. Isn't that the law?"

"Well, technically, yes," Rogers said with a sigh. "But they'd been *fighting*, Elissa. There was a trail of blood on the terrace. Can't you imagine the rest?"

Elissa sat still again, and she gazed at the fog.

She could visualize Heather — tall, blonde, and misty — backing toward the wall as Harper approached her. There was fog and darkness all around them, the roaring ocean, and then... Suddenly she felt *like* Heather, except she was standing against a wall on Trail Ridge Road in Rocky Mountain National Park. She was staring into a black hole, feeling Harper's hands gripping her hard, then the strange look in his eyes, a frightful sensation of careening over the edge...

"Oh God."

She heard another breaker rolling in, and she imagined a trembling of the house in the ocean's fury, much as her own mind was trembling in fury and fear. She shuddered.

"I think," Rogers said quietly, "that it's time for you to forget about defending Harper and start telling us a few of the things we need to know. And then you can go home, Elissa. You can go home and sleep in your own bed. And go back to living your own life."

The Pacific Ocean crashed against the rocks.

Rogers stared at her intently, waiting.

With a dim sparkle of a tear showing in the dark light, Elissa looked away for a long moment, and then in a voice barely audible above the sound of surf, she said:

"What kind of things do you need to know?"

Chapter 41

THE INSPECTOR rejoined the little group in the darkened room and sat down quietly.

Attorney Rogers glanced at him, then returned his full attention to Elissa. "Where is Harper now?"

"He's..." She hesitated. "He's probably very close."

"Did he intend to come into this house?" Rogers asked.

"Yes," Elissa said weakly.

"When did he plan to arrive here?"

"Soon, I suppose."

"*Soon?* Does that mean tonight? Tomorrow? Next week? Come on, Elissa, be specific. Vague answers won't help you."

Elissa held her hands together in her lap and said, "I can't be specific if I don't know the specifics, Donald."

"Then tell us whatever Harper said he *intended* to do. He must have told you that. He wouldn't just leave you at Lake Tahoe and run off without a hint of his plans."

"Well, he thought about renting a car and driving down here, or even flying to San Jose and renting a car there..."

"No good, Elissa. The FBI checked all the rental agencies against his driver's license. Nothing."

"He considered you might do that," Elissa said sadly, "and the airports, of course. So then, he planned to hitch a ride and work his way down, but he had no idea how long it would take. If he got lucky, he thought he could get here by tomorrow. But it could take another day. Even two."

"Let me get this straight," Rogers said. "Harper planned to hitchhike — all the way from Lake Tahoe to Carmel-by-the Sea?"

"Yes, that's right," Elissa said. "He had no other option."

Rogers looked at the Inspector. "What do you think?"

"I think she's lying," the Inspector said from his chair. "Harper would be too exposed hiking along the road with his thumb in the air. He can't be that stupid."

Rogers turned back to Elissa. "Well, Elissa?"

"That's not the way he would hitchhike," she said. "He would sit in a coffee shop, someplace where there'd be truck drivers, and he would negotiate a ride with cash. That's exactly how we got to Lake Tahoe, from Frenchman, Nevada."

"Hmm," Rogers mused, raising a brow at the Inspector, who nodded his silent affirmation. "Okay, but why all that trouble? What did he plan to do when he got here?"

"He was going to get his hands on some cash — enough to get us out of the country for a year or so."

"A whole year? Or *two?* Did he say where he'd get all that money?"

Elissa hesitated before answering. "He said... he said he knew where to get it."

"Ah-ha," Rogers said. He again turned to the Inspector. "His wife's money, no doubt, hidden somewhere." He turned to Elissa. "What about a gun?"

"What gun?"

"Does Harper have a gun? Any gun?"

"No," Elissa said.

"Then what did he do with it?" Inspector Carlisle asked.

"With what?"

"With the gun he stole from John Baker!"

"Oh... that gun. That's long gone."

"You mean to tell me... he threw it away?" Rogers asked. "While people were chasing after him? People with guns?"

"He didn't have a choice," Elissa said, raising her eyes to the Attorney's. "We took an airliner to Detroit and back, you see, and he couldn't smuggle a gun aboard."

"Then tell me, Elissa — where did he discard the gun?"

"As I remember, he dropped it in a trash barrel at the airport — at O'Hare."

Inspector Carlisle stood. "As you remember?" He approached her. "Elissa, you better be sure, because we're going to check it out. We'll have a hundred men going through trash barrels, garbage trucks and dumps, looking for that gun. If we don't find it, we'll know you lied to us, and you will not go free."

"It was a trash barrel. Beside the elevators in the parking garage, near the American Airlines terminal. Check it out, but don't blame me if you can't find it. That was days ago."

"Okay." The Inspector nodded at Rogers and said, "I'll get the bedroom phone and bring it out here and make the calls. Wait for me."

Rogers used the break to light a cigarette with an old Zippo. Then he snapped the lighter's lid shut, snapped it open again, snapped it shut...

The Inspector brought a cordless phone into the room and sat down. He poked at the buttons, and the dial tone was distinct in the silent room — silent except for the snapping of the Attorney's lighter.

The Inspector punched more numbers and, within a minute, began speaking quietly to his Chicago field office. Elissa heard him say, "Start with airport security — they might scan the trash barrels as a matter of routine... Yeah, and then get the administrator's office to give you the contractor that collects the trash — and you know where to go from there... What? Yeah, sure it's late, but security works all night. Start with them... Yeah, you too. G'night."

The inspector switched off the phone.

Rogers pocketed his lighter and stuffed his cigarette butt into a potted plant. "Back to you, Elissa. Tell us what people Harper had planned to contact."

"Well, he wanted to start with the newspapers. You know about his attempt to reach the Chicago *Tribune*..."

"That was a perfectly rash idea that backfired," Rogers interrupted. "I don't know whether he believed he actually could fool the *Trib*, or if it was just a stunt for your benefit. Anyway, have you noticed he never tried that again?"

"Yes. In fact, I had urged him to try another newspaper, even a small one, in any town we passed through."

"How did he reply to that suggestion?"

Elissa touched a hand to her mouth and yawned. "He, um... He said the small papers wouldn't care. They do only local news. He said they'd be suspicious of his story and might even call the authorities — and they'd give us away."

"Of course, that made sense to you."

"Yes, at the time."

"Anyway," Rogers continued, "I'm not interested in the contacts that failed. I want you to tell me whom he planned to call when he reached Carmel. Who is here that we don't already know about?"

"I don't believe there's *anybody*," Elissa said. "He just wanted to get the money to buy our way out of the country."

"Where did he plan to get the money from?"

Elissa took a deep breath.

"Elissa?"

She shook her head. "From..."

"Yes? Go on."

"Donald, after I tell you this, can I be released? There is nothing else I can tell you about him except this last thing."

"Yes, you probably can be released and sent home. We may need your deposition later, but we know he kept secrets from you. That's the only reason you're not under arrest."

"But you will release me tonight?"

"I will drive you to the airport myself, and General Norgan will escort you on his way to Washington."

"Is that a promise? No more questions?"

"Elissa, you are trying my patience. I already told you the deal. Quit stalling."

"Yes, well..." Elissa inhaled again. The deep silence in the room filled her head with ambient creaks and rustles. Then, as if suddenly coming to grips, she said, "He didn't need to go *anywhere* to get his hands on a bundle of cash. He has it tucked away right here, in this house."

Both the General and the Inspector stood, joining the Attorney, and the three of them gathered around Elissa.

"Where in this house?" Rogers asked.

"He has a special kind of room, like a vault room, where he keeps important architectural drawings and documents. The money is in there somewhere. I presume it would be kept in some sort of a safe."

All three men exchanged looks.

The Inspector grunted. "Did he say how much cash he keeps there? Did he say where he got it? Did he say why it's not in a bank, for Christ's sake?"

"He just said a lot of cash. He had put it aside to avoid splitting it with Heather when they got divorced. Whatever he kept in a bank that might be considered joint property would be split fifty-fifty under California divorce law."

The Attorney said, "I think we should check out this story, gentlemen."

"I agree," the General said. "Inspector, did you and Baker see anything like a vault room when you searched the house?"

"I didn't," Carlisle said. "Baker — he didn't mention it."

"Call him in," the General said.

"He's watching for Harper," the Inspector said.

"*Screw* that," the General said. "If Harper's hitchhiking with truck drivers from Tahoe, he won't get here for hours."

"If the lady's telling the truth," the Inspector said.

"If we find a stash of cash," Rogers said, "we'll know she's telling the truth. If we don't find it, we'll know she's lying. That's a lot faster than waiting for your agents in Chicago to search through sixteen tons of rubbish!"

The Inspector nodded. He lifted his radio and tapped a button. "Baker," he said. "Get in here. Now!"

Chapter 42

BAKER LISTENED intently as Inspector Carlisle described the room they were looking for, and Baker nodded and said, "Oh, yeah, that room...

"...I wouldn't call it a vault, but there's a room with a bunch of junk and files, and it's down past the utilities. You go through the kitchen and laundry, and there's a photographic lab. Then from there, you go through the utilities. It has some kind of small furnace that's labeled a 'heat pump,' whatever the hell that is, and then there's a U-shaped stairway to a lower level hallway and a door that opens into a small room with lots of shelves and file cabinets. I didn't go inside, because I didn't see anywhere a guy could hide. But I guess that must be the room you're looking for." He raised an arm and pointed. "Down that way."

"We'll check it out," Inspector Carlisle said. "Stay here and keep an eye on Mrs. Pope."

"What are you looking for?" Baker asked.

"I'll explain later," the Inspector said.

"What about Harper?" Baker asked.

"He'll be late. But if he shows up while we're downstairs — do you think you can detain him?"

"With pleasure," Baker said.

When the others had left, Baker ambled to a window area where Elissa was sitting on a couch. A swath of moonlight touched her through a break in the fog. She had wrapped herself in a blanket, her legs tucked beneath her.

He stared at her vague form. "Nice and cozy?"

She raised her head, and her eyes flashed as though lighted from within. "Buzz off," she said.

"Buzz off?" Baker thought this was hilarious, and he bent over with his hands on his knees, his torso quivering in spasms of mirth. "Jesus, that's amusing," he said.

***

THE INSPECTOR aimed a penlight at a laundry tub. "This must be the laundry," he said.

"Hell with laundry," Norgan said. "Find the photo lab."

The penlight picked out a door knob. "That's gotta be it." His pudgy hand grasped the knob and gave it a twist.

Probing through the door crack, the miniature beam of light swept across a steel sink and a stack of plastic trays. As the Inspector flicked his wrist, the light picked out other photographic items — bottles, film reels, enlarger, easel...

"It's the photo lab," the Inspector announced.

"What's next?" the General asked.

"Utilities," the Attorney said.

The penlight beam found another door. "Over there," the Inspector said.

The three figures moved hurriedly through the dark photo lab toward the utility room, and all three hit the door with a simultaneous *whump!*

"Holy cripes!" the Inspector bellowed. "Back off! Give me some god-damn room!"

"Sorry," Rogers said.

"It's god-damn dark in here!" the General said.

"Never mind," the Inspector said. "Just... concentrate on taking one step at a time. We go through here, then down some stairs, and then we'll reach the god-damn vault. It ain't going anywhere, so just take your time."

"Right," Rogers said. "There's no hurry."

"It's just god-damn dark," the General said.

Grouped closely together, they crossed the utility room and found the stairwell.

The Inspector's shoe slipped on the first step. "Shit!"

"This is like a tomb," Rogers said. "There are no windows. There's really no way any light from here can be seen outside. Harper's still far away. So why in hell don't we flip on a light instead of trying to follow an itsy-bitsy penlight?"

The Inspector hesitated. "Uh... I don't see nothing wrong with that. General — what do you say?"

"I say it's god-damn dark. I say turn on some god-damn lights before one of us busts a god-damn leg!"

Rogers found a switch, and they walked down the stairway in ample light and along a corridor to the next door.

"Okay," the Inspector said. "This must be the vault. I don't see any kind of alarm or even a lock. Do you?"

"Nothing," Rogers said.

"It's just a door!" Norgan insisted. "Open it!"

The Inspector turned the knob, and the door swung open with slight resistance. He brushed his hand along the wall and found another light switch. He flicked it.

Overhead, a pair of fluorescent bulbs glimmered briefly and then snapped into brilliance. These lights exposed a room about twelve feet square with concrete walls and no windows. The walls were lined with file cabinets and stacks of drawers made for large drawings. "All right!" the Inspector said. "This is it. This is the place. Let's tear it apart and find Harper's little fortune."

The three men spilled into the room and assaulted the drawers and file cabinets. They yanked drawers out of their recesses and dumped the contents onto the floor. They rummaged through folders and envelopes and ripped apart boxes. They flipped through ledgers and stripped covers off bound volumes. They worked for ten or fifteen minutes and built up layers of perspiration.

And they found no cash.

"The hell is this?" the Inspector wondered aloud as all three drooped in frustration. "There's no cash down here!"

"I'm afraid you're right," Rogers said. "It's just all worthless paper shit."

"I think we ought to go and have a few more words with the Pope woman," the General said.

"I think we oughta go and have a lot more than words with that broad," the Inspector said.

"I think you're both right," the Attorney said. He turned and reached for the door handle.

He reached *again* for the door handle.

"God-damn sonabitch!" Rogers blurted.

"What the hell is the matter?" the General asked.

"There's no god-damn door handle!" Rogers yelled.

Chapter 43

ELISSA GLARED furiously at Baker while he laughed at her, and when he finally stopped she said, "I'll be so glad when you're out of my life."

"You going somewhere?" Baker's expression was thoroughly amused. He placed his handheld radio on a chair.

"In twenty minutes, I'll be on my way home," she said.

"Who told you that fairytale?" He looked at his watch.

"*They* did," Elissa said. "Inspector Carlisle, the General, and Donald Rogers."

"Uh-huh." Baker cracked a sly grin. He lifted his huge revolver from its belt clip and placed it on a side table.

"Look, I told them everything they wanted to know, absolutely everything, and they all agreed to put me on a plane — tonight! Bye-bye, Baker."

He tossed his suit jacket on a chair. He reached down and yanked away her blanket, discovering that Elissa's silk skirt had bunched up near her hips, exposing the full length of her legs. She grabbed at the hem to pull the skirt down. Baker's hands caught her wrists and held them.

"Don't be so modest!" he said. "You've got great legs — real sexy legs. You don't need to hide those sexy legs."

"Get away from me!" she blurted.

"Hey, sexy little pussycat, I'm supposed to guard you! I'm doing my duty for Uncle Sam."

"I'm going to *report* you," Elissa said.

"*Report* me?" Baker swayed with laughter. "Jeez, you sound like Lucille Ball! I'm halfway going to regret throwing you off the cliff. But we can play first. C'mon, pussy girl, gimme a kiss before we part." He puckered his pale lips and pressed his nose against hers.

Elissa twisted her face aside, narrowly escaping his mouth. "Get off me, you sick monster! I'll scream!"

"Please scream," Baker said. "That's really, *really* sexy."

Heatedly, she turned her face and spat onto Baker's nose.

He dropped her wrists and jerked away. "That wasn't polite, you miserable whore! I hate spit!"

"I hate miserable creeps."

"Yeah.... okay!" Baker wiped his face with his sleeve. "That does it bigtime, pussycat. Your playtime is over."

He pounced at Elissa and clutched her head in his hands and wrung her body off the couch and onto the floor. Dropping to his knees, he straddled Elissa and clamped one strong fist around her left wrist and pressed it against the carpet above her head. He used his other hand to yank her sweater up to her neck. He bent low and whispered, "Baby, trust me. Nobody here ever intended to send you home."

Elissa stared into his glassy eyes.

"Forget Harper," Baker said. "He's dead on arrival. As for Norgan, Carlisle, Rogers — whatever the hell they said, it's a fib. They're just my business clients. I'm their broker, and I work on commission. You're part of the deal, and I'm gonna collect my bonus right now."

Elissa worked her right forearm across her chest.

"Yeah, do that," Baker said. "Try and protect your nice boobs. Fight me real hard, the harder the better."

Elissa seemed to go numb. Her facial expression became complacent. Her mouth curled into a tiny smile. She said, "Your bodice-ripping assault is nothing new to me, Baker. I've been beaten and raped by an expert. Compared to my ex-husband — why, you're just a slimy little *stink* worm."

And she rammed her elbow hard into Baker's throat.

Wide-eyed, Baker toppled backwards onto the floor, kicking his legs and gagging, scrunching his eyes and sputtering. "You bitch!" he croaked. "You stinkin' *slut!* I'm gonna kill you... kill you right here and... (croak) and right now!"

"That's enough," came a deep voice from directly overhead. Opening his eyes, Baker saw the darkened face of Grey Harper looking down at him. And barely an inch away — the menacingly darker muzzle of Baker's trusty Beretta.

"It's your gun, Baker. It's loaded, cocked, safety off, a round in the chamber. If I were you, I wouldn't move much."

***

IN THE VAULT, Inspector Carlisle picked at the steel door with a pocket knife. "It's tight! Crap! So how come nobody saw the handle was gone when we all rushed in here?"

"Quit fooling with it," General Norgan said. "Get Baker down here."

"Yeah, yeah. But this is embarrassing." The Inspector withdrew the radio from his belt case and toggled the switch. "Baker!"

He waited for a reply. When none came, he tried again. "Baker — acknowledge."

Still nothing.

"Baker, the hell you doing? It's the Inspector! We need you at the vault! Pronto! Acknowledge!"

"A radio problem?" Rogers asked. "Maybe it's not penetrating the concrete."

"Nah. We use these things in skyscrapers — never have any problem. Baker!"

The General thumped his fist against a file cabinet. "This time, god-damn it... it's a *problem!*"

"Whattaya mean?" the Inspector asked.

"I mean we've been suckered into a trap!"

They looked at one another in disbelief.

"Hell with that," the General said. "Get out of the way." He drew out his Colt .45 and fired at the door.

The round clanged off the door and ricocheted twice past their heads before rattling onto the concrete floor.

"Holy shit," the Inspector said, "Don't try that again!"

Chapter 44

ELISSA emerged from the shadows, rearranging her disheveled clothing. She wandered a broad path around the sprawled-out John Baker and stopped at Harper's side. She stood still a moment, gazing up at him. Then she whispered:

"I'm so anxious for a big bear hug — but not with that beast *slouching there. What are you going to do with it?"*

Harper answered, "I'll want a few words, then we'll see. That was a whopper punch. Where did you learn that?"

"At a defensive Karate course with the Lake Forest Parks and Recreation Department. Back when I thought I might need it." She took a breath. "They cautioned me; so I never tried it on Patrick... only because he never really threatened to kill me." She flipped a thumb at Baker. "But *he did!*"

"You have a lot of courage. He's a seriously vicious thug."

"And I was seriously scared! Until I saw you behind him."

"In the darkness? How did you know it was me?"

She rolled her eyes. "It *had* to be you."

They were interrupted by a metallic voice coming from Baker's handheld radio: "Baker! ... Baker — acknowledge!"

Harper lifted the radio and flicked it off.

On the floor against the couch, Baker sat massaging his neck. "You heard the Inspector. If I don't pick up, they'll all know why. They'll come and blow your puking head off."

"Not anytime soon," Harper said. "Meanwhile, just relax. Rub your neck. Then you and I can get better acquainted."

They heard what sounded like a distant shot. "You hear that?" Baker said. "Must be checking weapons. You're next."

"But John, right now, you're the one looking into the muzzle of a loaded gun. Be nice."

"*Excuse me!*" Elissa said. She quickly approached Harper and whispered into his ear, *"Don't keep provoking him! And what about that shot?"*

He said quietly, "Not a problem. But we could use some light in here. There's a control panel at the entry door."

Elissa quickly lighted a cascade of ceiling spots and came back, saying, "Grey, I've been so *anxious* to hear whether you found... *Oh!*"

She had stopped. Harper was heavily covered with black soot. She said, "Good grief! What *happened* to you?"

Baker started laughing. "You look like a sewer rat! Is that how you got in here? Crawling up through a sewer?"

"No, John, nothing nearly so difficult. I arrived ahead of you fellows and parked with all the sporty vehicles at the *Basic Instinct* house. Then I came up here before you fellows figured out where *here* is."

"The hell you did," Baker said. "I searched this place, and we had stakeouts."

"Baker, the stakeouts were focused on the wrong house. And never did anyone consider the cliff side of this one."

"The cliff?" Baker frowned. "Why would we waste time back there? Nobody can get in that way!"

"Wrong again. During construction, I rigged pulleys and a sturdy rope ladder to recover fallen debris — as mandated by environmental regulations. I never got around to removing the ladder, because it's almost invisible from the house — unless you know just where to look."

"Wait a minute," Baker said. "You're saying... you were hanging on the cliff all this time? On a rope ladder?"

"My God," Elissa said. "Please tell me you weren't!"

"I weren't."

"Then... *what?*" She stared at him, a hand on her hip.

"It's cold out there. I had a much warmer hiding place."

Baker said, "Quit playing stupid games! Just say *where!*"

Harper waved at the hearth. "In the chimney, old chum! I knew you wouldn't think to look up there. My knowledge of this house, and your ignorance of it, is the big advantage I had over your whole vicious enterprise."

Harper smiled at Elissa. "Of course, I was relieved they decided against starting a fire. I hadn't prepared for that."

Baker said, "Maybe you should've stayed up there. Why such a big fireplace, anyway? I never saw one that big."

Harper asked Elissa. "What do you think of it?"

"It's gorgeous," she said. "Much better than I expected when you told me about it. But... is it practical?"

"Well...no. It's purely aesthetic."

Baker said, "Ass-*thetic?* What the hell's that mean?"

"John, you saw the heat pump in the utility room..."

"Hold on. You heard me say that?"

"Yes, of course. I was listening the whole time. Anyway, that heat pump heats and cools this house efficiently. But I wanted to assimilate the rugged coastline into the home's interior, while infusing an ambience of refuge for guests and for reading in comfort during storms. That's what it means."

"You're shitting me."

"No, John, I'm not. I had been intrigued by the huge fireplaces built to heat rooms in medieval castles. Now, when evenings along this coast get cold, damp, and foggy, a roaring blaze in that fireplace is especially cozy. I can look forward to those cold, damp, and foggy nights, reading by the fire."

Baker said, "I always figured you for a wimp. I was right. So how'd you squeeze up that chimney and get out of sight?"

Harper grinned at him. "Easy. The flue has a diameter of twenty-seven inches, and the smoke ledge is eighty-four inches wide — that's seven feet — with a sixty-degree taper in the chamber's sides. All I did was take apart the damper, and I had plenty of room to spread out on the ledge."

Baker slowly got up and flexed his arms. He cracked his knuckles. "Screw your damn damper," he said. "With these bare hands, I can take *you* apart!"

Harper leveled the gun. "John, do yourself a favor and sit down. We've only just begun getting acquainted."

Baker said, "Sure, why not? I got lots of time. Let's relax like you said, until you get droopy and I kill you." He sat.

Elissa drew Harper aside and whispered. *"Please, be more careful with him. He's been seething with hatred for you all the way from Lake Tahoe. He says he has all kinds of tricks up his sleeves, and he means it! He'll try anything. Please, please watch out."*

"It's mostly bluster," Harper whispered back. *"I'm trying to undermine his confidence. I think it's working. He's acting puzzled."*

Elissa briefly closed her eyes and stepped away.

She nodded. "Well, Grey, I'm glad you thought of everything. So now, can we move on? I've been waiting anxiously to find out... did you find whatever you came here for?"

"I did," he said. "It's another hefty tale, but I can try to give you something like an executive summary."

"Oh, please do. I'm going to sit down." She went to an upholstered swivel chair next to the table where Baker had placed his revolver. Sitting, crossing her legs, she felt a sharp twinge at the bruise on her left knee. It had been nine hours since Baker had thrown her onto the floor at Lake Tahoe.

Harper remained on his feet, crossing his arms, keeping the Beretta aimed at Baker.

"During early stages of the project, I became concerned over the public opposition to private development at Fort Sheridan. We had similar issues with Parcheski's redevelopment in Monterey. And from that, I knew how architectural designs of a project can inflame or appease its critics...

"So I hired a graduate student, at Northwestern's Medill School of Journalism, to research local newspapers regarding all the issues. She did a thorough job. What I studied today came from clippings she had assembled many months ago.

"By the way, I also wanted to include heritage features in the design; so I had looked up historical societies and found a book of Fort Sheridan photos. I went through that again today. In these files, some items that previously had seemed incidental now became important, all because of Munro's murder and everything related to it." He paused briefly.

"Okay, for example:

"Today, I saw an old photo just like a new one I had shot during surveys. Same viewpoint, same landmarks. The difference is the presence and disappearance of certain buildings, like 'before' and 'after' pictures, but in reverse order."

Harper noticed Elissa becoming restless.

"Bottom line," he said quickly. "My recent photo showed no buildings on this spot. But the older picture had several large buildings that looked like... modern barracks."

"Barracks?" Elissa shifted. "Do you mean in the same location where you found radon?"

"Yes." Harper cast an eye at Baker and said, "For years, troops were housed over that radon. Recently, the barracks were removed. And I don't mean simply torn down. I mean erased. No footings, no pipes, no cables — nothing."

Elissa said, "Okay. The photos themselves prove that someone knew about the radon well before you did."

"And the commandant was General Norgan. He kept it secret — from those exposed to it and everyone else."

"For God's sakes, *why?*"

"He must have realized he could be held professionally accountable for exposing his men to those hazards. It could lead to all kinds of complications. This General is about to retire. His pension is at stake. His fiscal future is at stake."

"Aw, hell," Baker said. "If there was radon, so what? The General didn't put it there!"

"He put the barracks there," Harper said.

"Also," Harper continued, "keep in mind, most of the Fort buildings are a century old, riddled with air gaps that ventilate the interiors. Radon wouldn't be seriously trapped in those older structures. But the new barracks were built after General Norgan returned from his Vietnam tour — assigned to expedite Fort Sheridan's major role in the war buildup. This was the period in the 1970s when the Fort's population hit five thousand, the highest in its history."

Harper paused a moment. "Where was I? Oh yes...

"According to a local news columnist, Norgan specified buildings that were tight for energy efficiency. But he skipped over slowdowns such as soil analyses. When a building inspector asked about his tests for hazards, the General told him, 'War is hazardous!' and kicked him out. By the time another inspector arrived, Norgan had produced a Clearance Certificate which made no mention of hazards other than the well-known wastes in the ravines. Those had predated Norgan's arrival, and that put a stop to further speculation, or gossip, on anything like radon."

Elissa said, "And *nobody* looked any further into it?"

"Not according to the columns in the Highwood section of the *Highland Park News*. Highwood enjoyed direct economic benefit from the Fort. As the Vietnam War reached its peak, local economic and political debates overwhelmed the ramblings of that columnist. It just wasn't newsworthy."

Elissa said, "I don't remember any of that. But I was only about fourteen years old back then."

"Same here," Baker said. "But none of you young Lake Forest girls set foot in *Highwood*. It was too *low* for you."

Elissa said, "That's not true. We often went for pizza."

Harper smiled at her and continued: "Well, as years went by, troop transfers and deployments made any health issues hard to trace back to Fort Sheridan. Norgan counted on that. He hadn't foreseen how the government would close the base someday and sell the property for civilian use."

Elissa stood and deliberately placed a hand on her hip, her elbow pointing right at Baker. With a modest smile, she said, "I see a connection with Donald Rogers. He was Judge

Advocate at Fort Sheridan back then, serving under the General. He still uses Zippo lighters with army insignia."

"Interesting," Harper said. "So, maybe when Congress started targeting bases for closure, the two of them saw the threat of a radon controversy upon both their careers. With Rogers at the local end, Norgan could take advantage of his logistics command in the Pentagon. He could set up the removal of the barracks as government salvage for use at other sites. At Fort Ord, I learned the U.S. military has huge storage facilities for all kinds of surplus, including furniture and building materials." He said to Elissa, "Why, it's the old *elephant in the room* trick — hiding big secrets in plain sight."

Elissa said, "The whole thing — I don't know if it's really diabolical, desperate, or just foolish!"

Harper shook his head. "It might have been foolish. The soldiers weren't housed there too long before being shipped out. Still, the concentration of radon could have been quite high. I guess they weren't willing to risk what a discovery could lead to. And if I hadn't done my own tests, they probably would've gotten away with all of it."

"What was their idea behind that fake certificate?"

"Probably to mislead Keith Munro. I found a copy of the certificate among the documents Norgan sent to Munro. It looks like something an attorney could have fabricated."

"Didn't Munro even suspect anything bogus about it?"

"No," Harper said. "It was outside his expertise. When I explained, he blamed the army. In hours, he was dead."

Elissa asked, "But why did they kill him? Couldn't the company just hire another project manager and keep going?"

"Only if the replacement and the company had no hint about radon. Even then, I doubt Pacific Empire would want to keep going with the project without knowing why its two main supervisors had met violent deaths. Delays are costly. They'd be more inclined to sell or drop the whole thing."

"Really?" Elissa asked.

"I think so. That company has too many big operations in the pipeline to put up with complications that could tie up its cash flow. And with unexplained murders or suicides, there would be a ton of complications."

Another thought occurred to Harper. "Elissa, wouldn't a retreat like that give Rogers and his people a lot more time, perhaps years, to bring home their public park concept?"

Elissa said, "Oh yes. I can easily picture Rogers trying to do just that. He's convinced himself that he has acquired major influence among all the barons of the North Shore."

She sighed, tired of standing, and sat down again. "That's quite a remarkable summary. Was all of that covered in the newspaper articles?"

"No, unfortunately. Much of what I said is supposition. But the articles did provide enough material to back it up, and then we have our own experience to add. It's enough to start an investigation, at least, of those guys downstairs."

Harper turned to Baker. "You've been quiet a long time, John. Don't you have something you can bring to the table?"

"Sure, I got something to bring: I gotta hand it to you, Harper. You really convinced me."

"Convinced you? Of what?"

"That you and Mrs. Pope will never get out of here alive."

Chapter 45

"GOD-DAMNIT Baker!" Inspector Carlisle shouted at his handset and turned to General Norgan. "His radio's still off! What's he doing! Where'd you dig up that asshole, anyway?"

"Don't belittle him, George," General Norgan said. "He's one of the very few in the establishment who has absolutely no conscience. He'll do whatever needs to be done under wraps, for ordinary pay and high-tech toys and the fun of it."

The three men sat perspiring on overturned file drawers. Rogers, elbows on his knees, stared at a bare patch of concrete floor among the heaps of crumpled papers.

The Inspector gazed at the General with sad eyes and rubbed his cheeks with a handkerchief. "Listen, General. I consented to your plan for hitting Munro on federal property, so I'd get the case and control the investigation. But I don't get why Baker had to mess with a dead rat in Harper's bathroom, or why he and his gang of goons shot up a million-dollar mansion. What the hell was all that about?"

The General folded his hands and shrugged. "I thought he had a pretty good scheme. Don and I handed him the murder weapon and said, go frame Harper, make it look like a suicide, and keep the details to himself. Anything *we* don't know can't hurt us. But as you know, John likes to create heat. Lots of it. That's the reason for the name 'Baker'."

"I thought 'Baker' was his real name."

"I'm the only one who knows his real name, and I'm not telling," the General said.

The Inspector sniffed at that. "Okay. So what *was* this big smart scheme?"

"It was simple, actually. I knew John when he was a bad boy with a hot mom at the Fort. He still knows his way and has connections there. Anyway, he thought of planting the gun in Harper's toilet tank, but he needed a way for the cops to find it. He had this pet rat; it was becoming a nuisance; and he decided to deploy it. That stunt would prompt anyone to call the cops. And whenever the cops arrived, they'd find Harper dead, O-D'd over a bag of heroin. They'd search for other drugs and find the gun. They'd most likely conclude Harper's rat report was a drug hallucination. Hell. For a spur-of-the-moment plan, I thought it was brilliant."

"Oh yeah? You said you didn't want to know the plan."

"I didn't — until it went wrong. Then Baker explained."

"So what did go wrong?"

"The woman," Norgan said. "She went marching up to the door with a valise, and Baker didn't know who she was. She arrived well before Harper called the cops. Baker knew this because he had Harper's telephone line routed through his black box. Harper and the woman were talking for a long time. When Harper dialed out, Baker answered. A bit later, he drove his car up front and went to the door. He has a whole collection of credentials. Some are authentic."

"What were his intentions?" the Inspector asked.

"First, he needed to find out who the woman was and what she knew. Based on that, he decided to kill them both. It was a perfect murder-suicide setup. First, he cleared the rat evidence. Then he planned to use the murder gun from the toilet tank, shoot them both, then lay out a drug scene. He'd phone an anonymous report of gunshots. All perfect! ...Except the gun was in a sealed plastic bag." Norgan sighed.

"...So John hesitated at the top of the stairs, figuring how to draw the weapon out of the bag without tipping off his victims. Alas, Harper thought faster than Baker did. When Baker made a move toward his own weapon, down he went."

Attorney Rogers spoke. "General, explain to George why Baker went through all that trouble — why he went with the whole rat scenario instead of just shooting the people."

The General grinned. "Good point, Donald. George, I wanted Harper dead before he could stir things up. I wanted local cops to find both his body and the weapon the same day you were releasing facts about the federal investigation of Munro's death. Those gunshot deaths in that community involving men who worked together would certainly indicate a connection. The two crimes would merge into your lap, and the whole matter could get buried with the bodies."

The Inspector said, "Okay, I see that. So explain Baker's shoot-up frenzy at the Lake Road mansion. That nearly blew the roof off the house — and my case."

The General raised both hands. "Okay, Baker got pissed and called his team. He is, at times, a loose cannon."

"He has a *team?*" The Inspector looked startled.

"He calls it that," General Norgan said. "They're just misfits he recruits for various assignments. This bunch was the result of prior work when I was posted back there. Like I said, his later operations were under wraps and off-budget, deep in the Pentagon. My department. We call it Logistics because it means everything and nothing. Donald here is aware of some domestic parts, but your FBI hasn't got a clue, and I need you to leave it that way, George."

"Of course. But where do we stand now, regarding that mansion? Last I heard, the owners are on the way home. I'll need an explanation for them, pretty damn quick."

"Tell them it's not related. It was vandalism. That's what Baker had decided to use for cover the minute he realized Harper and the woman had escaped. The team actually shot up the place even more. They dumped out the refrigerators, plugged the toilets, all that stuff. They even found some paint and sprayed the walls with swastikas."

"Why swastikas? What's the point of that?"

"Hell, I don't know. Baker just said it doesn't matter. The whole Nazi thing is regarded as lunacy, and the incident can go down as mistaken identity or a nut case — or whatever."

The General stood up and added, "Baker said he always wanted to do a job like that. The vandalism stuff. After what Harper did to him, the kicks he got from his five-man ballistic assault on a luxury mansion rescued his whole day."

"Jeez," the Inspector said. "So now where the hell is he, when we really need him?"

Chapter 46

IN THE LIVING ROOM, Grey Harper sat with his legs crossed, his gun-hand propped on his knee. He looked thoughtfully at Baker and said, "So tell me, John. What makes you so confident those *clients* of yours can get rid of me and Mrs. Pope?"

"It's so *easy!* Just count to four! There's four of us packin' guns. You got one gun and she's scared to death of guns. I don't think she ever held one in those hot little hands."

Harper suspected what Elissa thought of that remark without glancing at her, and he kept a straight face. "So, John, you're still expecting your *clients* to arrive and shoot me in the head? Aren't you wondering what's keeping them?"

"Hell, they're busy digging in your storage room. From what I saw with all those cabinets — that can take a while. I'll tell you, though. If you don't want your head blown off first thing, I'll tell 'em to wait while I teach Mrs. Pope all the ropes for having a helluva good time. I'll let you watch."

"That's never going to happen," Harper said.

"No? The odds are all against you. You can't stop it."

"I already did, John. General Norgan, the Inspector, Donald Rogers, and all their guns are locked inside the storage vault. You saw the room. Concrete walls, one steel door."

"Yeah? Who locked 'em, a ghost? Until now, you were staying all nice and cozy in your middle evil fireplace."

"It was a simple trap," Harper said. "After I gathered all the evidence I needed, I just removed the door's two-sided handle and replaced it with a one-sided dummy. Then I set the hinges off-level; so the door would swing shut from its own weight. It's a steel door and frame. They won't be able to break out the way you escaped from the closet, John."

Baker stared at Harper. Finally, he shrugged. "I get the setup, but... What made you think they'd fall for it?"

"It's the old classic mouse trap, John. You rig a trap and toss in some bait. Even though Norgan and Rogers were a surprise to us, our trap was able to accommodate them all. And that's because we decided the bait would be a hidden treasure. We counted on just you and the other guy in Salt Lake City — Inspector Carlisle. But that didn't matter, because greed is universal. Isn't that right, John?"

Baker said, "I think you're crazy. I still don't know, again, what the hell you're talking about. What treasure?"

"Oh that's right! They didn't tell you they were hunting *treasure*, did they?"

Baker frowned. He cracked his knuckles. "No, they didn't. What *kind* of treasure?"

"Never mind. There isn't any. I'll explain it all for you:

"Last night at Lake Tahoe, Elissa and I agreed she would hire a taxi to the Reno airport and check flights to San Jose and Chicago. Then she'd phone me in Carmel. If I failed to answer after two separate attempts, or answered with the wrong greeting, she'd fly to Chicago and get a lawyer. But if I gave her the okay, she'd fly to San Jose to meet with me...

"...Or, if you guys got to her first, she'd play along and slowly feed you a story about a pile of cash in my storage room. She'd describe it as a *vault*. You'd go in, and the trap would keep you in. Even if you brought Elissa in with you, you couldn't harm her — because you'd be *found* with her."

"Oh, yeah? Found by who?"

"By me and the cops I'd call. With you guys and a whole sack of evidence in my possession, I'd call them right away."

"Why aren't you calling them now?"

"I'll get to it. Everything's secure, and I want to relax."

Baker smirked. "Fine. But what if we dumped her and came here alone? *Then* how could you get us into the vault?"

"It could take longer, but eventually one of you would wander into that room to search it. Whoever got trapped would pound and shout for help. During the distraction, I could slip out the same way I came in and get help from my neighbor's house. Of course, I couldn't plan for every kind of scenario, just the most likely."

At that point, Harper stood up.

"And by the way" — he made a theatrical bow and a wave toward Elissa — "don't you agree, John, that Elissa is one terrific actress? All the while you guys thought you were fooling her, she was fooling *you!*"

Burned by that, Baker suddenly lunged at Elissa. Harper immediately fired a shot across his path and shouted, *"Not one more step! Sit down, John and stay sat!* And be glad I'm not yet through with you. The next shot won't be a warning."

Harper glanced at Elissa. "Are you all right?"

She made a helpless gesture. "I guess... I'm fine. But I'd be better if you had shot him instead of the wall."

Baker slowly sat and cooled down. "You assholes. You think you're tough, Harper, because you can shoot a gun? I knew some smart guys like you. They all lived to regret it. And you're next, pal. You can count on it. Both of you."

Harper said, "I see that you really enjoy violence, John. Did you find great pleasure killing a rat? Or was it more fun killing Keith Munro?"

"Hell, I didn't do Munro. General Norgan did. And the Rogers guy. They did it. I was busy keeping my eyes on you."

"How about the *Tribune* reporter? The real one?"

"Not me, neither. This hot Japanese babe comes roaring in aboard a Gulfstream jet, blows her assignment, and then blows town! So the Inspector's all upset. He pops the Chan babe right afterwards. Hell, I didn't care for either of them."

"Why did he kill Rita Chan? Just because he was upset?"

"He didn't like her nosy questions. Besides, he could put the rap on you and turn the heat way up. Yeah, it was the same gun from the Munro hit. Mrs. Pope guessed right about that. But *I* never killed nobody over this — not yet."

"About the Inspector," Harper said. "What's his stake?"

"They all go way back. To Vietnam. Who the hell cares?"

Harper said, "Not that it matters much, where they met, or why they're working together now. It seems obvious that Inspector Carlisle kept other FBI colleagues at a distance. That suggests he was not acting on behalf of the Bureau. In fact, why don't we call the FBI right now and let them fill in the blanks? They're the real pros. Right, John?"

"Hell," Baker said. "The General and the Inspector — they didn't need no other stinking pros. They had *me*."

Harper smiled. "I won't argue that, John. Anyway, I'm sure the Bureau will figure it out after hearing the tapes."

"Tapes? Honest?" Baker twitched. "Let me tell you all about tapes. Your standard household recorders are no good for eavesdropping. They pick up too much ambient noise. If I was you, I wouldn't put any faith in your setup. Why don't you show me? I can tell you if it's good, or good for crap."

Harper said, "Nice try. But architects sometimes pay attention to what goes *into* their structures. Several years ago, I worked with a team of sound and acoustics engineers, converting a San Francisco warehouse into a media production studio on Union Street. It was a good education, John."

"But your house ain't no studio," Baker said. "Then you got the ocean out there. It makes the kind of low noise you barely notice, but it ruins playback. Same with wind noise."

"Yes, and Union Street is just off the Embarcadero, with shipping docks, boat horns, the freeway, and flights departing north from SFO. By comparison, this house was easy.

"After picking up my car in San Jose, I drove through the heart of Silicon Valley today. It's the electronics mecca of the world, John, and I have an account at a store that offers expert help. They provided wireless microphones, a receiver set to frequencies and levels for the environment I described, and a compact recorder. I used the recorder to play my voice in various locations, adjusted the receiver antennas, then connected the recorder to the receiver. There's even a remote mic in the ceiling above the storage room, John. Right now I'll bet the talk down there is dynamite!"

***

IN THE VAULT, the General took charge of the escape plan. "Let me show you." He knocked over two empty file cabinets and motioned Rogers to grab the opposite end of one. "Let's set it lengthwise atop the first one... There! These cabinets are all the standard fifteen-inch width. We can roughly measure everything we need from that."

In minutes, they had knocked over four more cabinets and arranged them into a crude platform. "Plenty of room for all of us to stand right up close to the ceiling," Norgan said. "Thirty inches high and wide, almost nine feet long."

The General knocked down one more cabinet and shoved it with his foot alongside his platform. "And there's our step. I'm sure you men can lift your feet fifteen inches."

Rogers tried it. "No problem."

"Good. Now let's step up and take down some ceiling tiles. That's going to be our way out."

***

Before long, Inspector Carlisle was oozing sweat, squatting atop the cabinets, pulling down ceiling tiles and stuffing bundles of paper into the bridging between the joists. "More," he grunted. "Hand me more paper."

The floor held a huge repository of scattered papers.

"You know, I don't like this," Rogers complained. "We could get burned to death or die of smoke inhalation."

"Stop whimpering," the Inspector said. "Just hand up another bunch of paper! We gotta burn a hole you can climb through. What's your weight, Donald — about one-forty?"

"One forty-five," Rogers said, handing up a sheaf of documents. "Fifteen inches between joists is a snug fit even for me. It's going to take *lots* of burning and chipping, and I just don't like it. Fires have a way of getting out of hand."

The General grew impatient with Rogers. "Heat rises, Donald. Fire burns *upwards*. You see it's just wood planks up there. The rooms we passed through had ceramic tiles over that, and we can shatter the tiles with a few pistol shots."

"Which can blow sparks everywhere!" Rogers said.

"Now look! We're on safe concrete down here. Thanks to Harper's safeguards for his precious blueprints, we've got a fire extinguisher. If there's fire, I'll promptly put it out."

"What about Baker? Have you given up on him?"

"You heard the shot, Donald. If Baker shot Harper, he'd be down here now. Since he's not, we can assume Harper fired that shot. That means Harper's in this house, and he's loose! And we can't stop him. So get out your Zippo, Donald, so we can mount a breakthrough and a counter-attack!"

Above them, the Inspector shouted, *"Damnit!"* and held out a small object. "Look what I found! Know what this is?"

The General said, "Is that a microphone?"

"It sure as hell is! A wireless! Harper must have planted it. I don't see any way to turn it off. God-damn him! Do you remember all the stuff we talked about down here?"

Rogers said, "We talked way too much. Shit!"

"Hell, too late now," the General said. "Son of a bitch!"

The Inspector snapped his fingers. "Now we've really got to get the hell out of here and damn quick! Give me your god-damn *Zippo*, Rogers. Right now!"

Chapter 47

THE CLANGING, banging, and pounding in the storage room carried upstairs.

"They're working to get out," Baker said. "Knowing the General like I do, he wouldn't try all that stuff if he didn't have a *plan*. They're gonna shoot your *head* off, Harper!"

"I don't think so," Harper said. "That door is solid, and they have no power tools. They'll only hurt themselves."

Harper went to the table beside Elissa and lifted Baker's long-barreled revolver. He compared its load and balance to the Beretta in his other hand. "I guess I've become attached to your old gun, John." He held out the revolver to Elissa.

"I don't want that," she said. "That's a cannon."

"Please, take it away and hide it. I don't like having *two heavily loaded* guns in one room." He stared at her.

Elissa caught the hint... and took the weapon away.

Baker snorted. "Harper, I don't need either gun to take you down. I can do that with these." He waved his fingers.

"Here's a better idea," Harper said. "Use the fingers to hand over your wallet, credentials, and handcuffs. Do it with care, using one hand, and slide everything across the floor."

"Ha! You've been watching too many movies," Baker said.

"I don't watch any movies," Harper said.

"You don't? Not *Basic Instinct?* From next door? Is it because they scare you? Does violence give you bad dreams?"

"Your *stuff*, John. Right now!" Harper fired a shot into the couch.

"Jeez, you *are* scared!" Baker shoved the items forward.

Harper scooped up the wallet and examined the cards. "Quite a collection. I'll be fascinated to see how the police react to all this when they arrive."

"Seriously? You want to call the cops? Now?"

"Do you mind?"

"The worst thing you can do. They all received faxes and photos describing you as an armed lunatic. The minute they see you with a gun, they'll blow your head off."

Elissa rushed breathless into the room. She looked at Harper. She looked at Baker. "I just heard a shot. What the hell's going on?"

"Only another warning shot," Harper said. "We were talking about calling the police. I think we have plenty of evidence. Would you agree?"

"Well, yes, but..."

"But... ?"

"Won't it be dangerous if you're holding a gun when the police arrive?"

Harper sighed. "Oddly, John just voiced that same concern. He fantasizes about everyone blowing my head off."

Harper paced, reflected. "Let's do something about this. John — get spread out on the floor, face down, hands behind you. Take your time and be very slow and very careful."

Baker judged Harper's steadiness, calculated his own catalog of tricks. Satisfied, he lowered himself to the floor.

Crouching, Harper jabbed the gun behind Baker's ear. "Elissa," he said, "please bring the cuffs and fasten them to John's wrists. Also be careful doing that, or he might move a fraction and I'd have to shoot him."

***

INSIDE THE VAULT, smoke tumbled from the ceiling.

"*Douse* it, General!" The Inspector coughed hard. "*Auk-Huck!* Something's wrong... not burning right... *Auk-Huck!*"

"*I told you this would happen!*" Rogers yelled.

With fiery paper scraps falling around him, the General aimed the extinguisher and pulled the safety pin. A fog whooshed from the nozzle and smudged out some flames. Eyes watering, stepping onto cabinets like a battle-hardened infantryman, he intensely sprayed fog across the embers.

At the same time, Rogers and Carlisle were kicking and stamping the sparkling debris on the floor.

The extinguisher sputtered out with the flames. Norgan hoisted the bottle and knocked it around the hole in the ceiling, breaking off charred fragments of wood. He poked the cylinder higher and felt it clang against some metallic obstacle. "Damn!" he said. "No wonder — there's something on top the floor. It was blocking the fire. No wonder the smoke came pouring down here." He stepped down.

"What the hell is it?" Rogers asked.

"Hell, I don't know." The General strutted across the room, hands on his hips. He jerked open a file drawer and searched the interior. "These drawers — they have steel file rods inside. Pull 'em all out. Give me some help, damn it!"

They all got busy extracting rods.

"That second shot worries me," the Inspector said. "It could mean Harper killed Baker, because Baker's not here. If Harper's at large, we can't waste any time down here."

"Agreed," Norgan said. Climbing onto the platform, he shoved a bundle of rods through the ceiling hole. Exerting his strength, he pushed until he felt the obstacle slide a bit. "Yah! We can move it! Grab some rods and give me a hand!"

The Attorney and Inspector climbed next to him and rammed more rods against the underside of the obstacle. "It feels like... like another steel cabinet of some kind," grunted the General. His face was lobster red, his cheeks puffing. "All together, men... One, two, *Heave!*... One, two, *Heave!*"

As they struggled mightily, they heard and felt the object scraping ponderously across the floor above their heads.

"It's a damned stubborn *whatsit*," the General rasped.

They stopped for a minute, huffed, wiped sweat from their faces, stared at each other. The General said, "All right, men, that's enough slacking off. Back at it. Harder now!"

They were making progress when a corner of the object, with a short leg, crashed through the burnt hole, producing a sharp snap (!) and a thunk on the floor above their heads.

They all stared at it.

"What the hell is that thing?" the Inspector asked.

"Some other kind of cabinet," the General said. "Who cares? We'll need *all* our strength to move it. The hell with Harper. Let's get down for a minute and catch our breath."

They stepped down, sank among the debris on the floor, and wiped their sweat. "If Harper does show, don't shoot to kill," Norgan said. "Not until I stick these rods up his ass."

Moments passed.

Rogers sniffed. He gazed around suspiciously. "What's that strange smell? Anyone notice it? Not just all the smoke and burned wood — something else mixed with all that."

The Inspector rubbed his fingers across the base of his nose. "I'm catching a whiff, too — kind of like a skunk?"

The General scrambled upright. "So, maybe some skunk managed to sneak inside while the house was vacant. Forget it. Let's get back into action!" He waved his arms, urging Rogers and the Inspector to remount the cabinets. "Let's get working as a real team now," he demanded. "Get a good strong grip on your rods, and let's move that damn thing!"

Rogers and Carlisle fumbled earnestly with the rods and brought them into compliance with the General's orders. As they did so, the spreading smell reminded Rogers of the skunks that roamed the Wisconsin woods — near his summer cabin up there; the log cabin with its propane cooking stove; a large professional stove; one that stood on corner legs similar to the leg he was staring at now.

He had heard somewhere that propane gas also smelled like skunks...

"One, two, Heave!" the General ordered. "Everyone heave again... one, two, *heave!"*

A skunk? Propane?

The rods were scraping and chipping the burnt edges of the ceiling hole. *Holy shit,* Rogers realized, *there might be live embers up there...*

"NO!" the Attorney shouted. *"No! DON'T heave!"*

The sudden blast of wind and fire from Harper's terrace kitchen was enormous.

Chapter 48

CROUCHING beside Baker, Elissa had one cuff firmly on his left wrist and had started latching the second when the floor bounced. A huge thud sent her swaying, and she snapped at Harper, "You shot him!"

With his finger at rest on the trigger, Harper said, "I did not. I almost did... But I didn't."

"Shit!" Baker yelped at them. "What in hell *was* that?"

Harper nodded in the direction of the blast. "It came from the summer kitchen that serves the terrace. It has a propane stove. They must've ignited the propane somehow. That kitchen is directly above the storage room."

"I'll get help," Elissa said, dashing for the phone. She jabbed buttons, listened, and then quit. "The phone's dead."

Half the lights were out. Harper stood. "The utilities are going. Let's get out of here. I smell smoke and I feel heat."

Indicating Baker, Elissa said, "What about..."

"I'll bring him. You get out."

"But... your files! The *tapes* ..."

"Yes, yes..." Harper set Baker's gun on a table, went directly to the fireplace and reached into the smoke chamber. He pulled at something, bringing more soot onto his face, then pulled at something else. A thick manila envelope fell into his hands, followed by a plastic bag containing a bundle of batteries, clips, and a still running compact recorder.

Rising from the hearth, Harper quickly transferred the cache to Elissa. "Take all this and get out. I'll bring Baker."

"Please — be careful..." she said. "And hurry!"

"I will. *Go!*"

While Harper watched Elissa, Baker's right wrist found enough slack in the cuffs for his fingers to get into his sock.

Elissa ran up the steps to the entry hall, opened the door, then stepped back to grab her luggage where the Inspector had left it. Harper yelled, "Elissa, get out now!"

"You too!" She hauled out the door. Harper swerved to the table where he had left the gun, and Baker had it aimed at Harper's chest. Baker pulled the trigger twice.

Harper heard the double clicks with relief. And he said, "Forgot to tell you. We fired a lot of practice bullets. They're all used up, John. But hey! You've still got all your fingers."

***

THE FIRE RAGED through Grey Harper's home, attacking everything combustible — draperies and furnishings, wooden cabinets and framework, potted trees and ferns. The fire became uglier, gaining strength to devour redwood posts and beams. Glass windows and doors shattered, admitting winds that nourished the blaze. Steel columns fell over. Flames leaped into an intricate network of roof members and slithered across the entire length of the house.

In the living room, Baker's gun sailed through the air past Harper's head and clattered off a glass wall.

Then two bodies, locked together, crashed through the glass and scudded across the rough stones of the terrace.

Baker wrapped his wiry arms like cables around Harper's midsection and hoisted the architect, bending his back over the stone wall. He poured sour breath onto Harper's face and said: "Told you I don't need a gun!" But his exertion in the cold fog was straining his voice. "You...think you're cool, calling me *John*... like I'm still fourteen years old! But I'm no kid, you asshole! I'm the *Baker*... and you're toast!"

Above and behind Baker, flames scorched through the mists; and Harper's muscles were tiring; his thoughts were drifting... But he managed enough determination to say: "I'm not thinking of any *kid* by calling you *John*. I'm using the name prostitutes call you for always pestering them!"

Baker's face shimmered with red-eyed rage — but his voice cranked out nothing but a throaty gargle: *"Fughayooo!!!"*

Harper aggravated that rage by yelling: *"I didn't catch that, John! It sounds like you have a frog in your throat!"*

Now Baker's face morphed into an animalistic snarl — teeth bared, nose crinkled, eyes bulging.

Harper felt all the hard pressure. Below them, the ocean roared, driven by a rising wind. With the wind came other odd sounds... a *whispering* that sounded like *Heather,* lurking within the blowing curtains of fog, watching the murderous scene, *wanting* it, wanting Harper to experience for himself the absolute terror she had suffered in her fall to the rocks...

Not long ago, Harper might have accepted that. But something had happened in recent days, and this new Grey Harper no longer felt a mystical responsibility for Heather.

What Harper felt instead was an intense craving to crush Baker's head. His hands found familiar locations in the rock wall — a wall created by those very same hands...

Harper's resistance was more than Baker expected. He wished he had spent less time on push-ups and had worked more on lifts, which involved different muscles. His veins bulged in purple madness, and his throat throbbed.

A stone in Harper's grip loosened. The mortar cracked.

Baker sensed this weakening and widened his stance for a huge push to send Harper tumbling down to the rocks.

The move exposed Baker's groin to a sharp thrust from Harper's knee — a jolt that allowed Harper to writhe downward and break out the loose stone. He was arcing the stone upward when Baker's left shoulder got slammed sideways from a bullet.

A second shot dropped Baker at Harper's feet.

Elissa stood behind the man's heap, the big S&W 686 swaying in her hands. "God," she breathed. "Did I kill him?"

Stepping away from Baker's feeble grasp, Grey Harper dropped the rock and watched his assailant squirming on the flagstones. "No, you didn't kill him, but you put him out of action. I think he's had all of you he can stand tonight."

***

SOMEHOW they had scrambled through the burning house, dragging Baker with them, to a cool and misty space where Elissa had dropped her luggage and Grey's evidence. They sat among cypress trees and watched as Harper's brilliant creation collapsed piece by piece into the flames.

All around they heard sirens and sensed flashing lights.

But they saw only the flames.

Author's Note: The life-threatening danger was over. But Grey Harper was still a mystery to Elissa in many crucial areas. She needed a long and deep talk with him, for better or worse. Here's that fateful exchange in its entirety:

Chapter 49: Revelations

GREY HARPER AND ELISSA POPE returned to the Carmel cliffs and sat on a massive boulder above the ocean.

It was a sunny morning. The sea glittered like diamonds.

Harper had cleaned up in the police locker room, changing into fresh clothes from the luggage in his car trunk. Those clothes (laundered by Elissa in Salt Lake City), plus the car and his bank accounts, were all he had left.

Among the ruins of Harper's home were strange odors and mists. Nothing seemed familiar except the ocean, and even that smelled of foreign molecules.

Elissa said, "I called my secretary this morning. She said American Express suspended my Gold Card after getting billed for stupendous gunshot damages to the house at Lake Tahoe." She grimaced. "So much for *no preset spending limits.*"

Harper chuckled. "Okay. So what are your plans now?"

"I have no idea," she said. "What about you?"

"I don't know, either. Look at those ruins. It's incredible, that I can protect a house from wind, lightning, floods, and even earthquakes... But there's no defense against fools."

Elissa inhaled. They were exhausted from hours of late-night interrogations, and a full investigation was pending. But they were free for now, and they were alone. Together.

He continued, "Do you realize, I had them in a room with a concrete floor and walls. The ceiling tiles were fire-rated. All my papers were inside steel drawers. Even so, as the tapes revealed, those three men dumped paper everywhere, knocked cabinets over, pulled down ceiling tiles, used a Zippo to start fires, moved a heavy stove until its gas coupling broke, then waited in complete ignorance as gas filled the area... and then they ignited the whole works!"

Harper laughed once more. "None of that is the product of any *genius*. It's the reincarnation of The Three Stooges!"

Elissa rolled her eyes. "Here I am, on the verge of tears, and you're laughing! What the hell is the matter with you?"

"As I've said before — sometimes I can't help myself."

"Well, sometimes *I can't help myself from crying*," she said. "The last time I came to the sudden end of a terrible ordeal, I cried for weeks over *nothing!* So be prepared for showers."

She looked around. "And where is everyone? I thought they'd all be here. Nobody has even put up any crime tape."

Harper said, "A duty officer told me they're squabbling over jurisdiction. The Carmel police, Carmel Highlands Fire Department, Monterey County DA, the U.S. Army Criminal Investigation Command — and, of course, the FBI and the Department of Justice. It's one hell of a mess."

"You know what's most startling in what you just said?"

"What?"

"You actually used the word 'hell' as an expletive. It's the first time I've ever heard you swear!"

He grinned. "I should try to leave that habit with you."

"Oh? Is that snide? Are you trying to start an argument?"

"I don't think so," he said. "But... are you? If so, why?"

"Why not? Didn't we start like that?" She smiled. "I kind of miss it. It's fun to argue with a man and not get slugged."

He said, "That smile of yours will immediately stop any argument from me."

"I know," Elissa said. "I just ran another test with it."

Harper began studying elements of the house that were intact: its solid bearing walls, sturdiest beams, its fireplace and chimney. He said, "While I was in that fireplace, I could hear all the talk in the living room. But when those men dragged you onto the terrace, I had no idea what they did to you, until I heard your scream on the tapes. Had I known..."

"Had you known," Elissa said, "you would have charged to the rescue and they'd have shot us both." She shivered. "God! Seeing my own body hit those rocks was the shock of my life. But I didn't faint — and *that* to me is a miracle... *Oh, and speaking of danger, why did you use your last bullets as warning shots? What kept you from shooting Baker?*"

"The risks," Harper said. "I might've killed him, and we needed Baker alive. I thought warning shots would control him. Of course, you had plenty of reason to shoot, because he was out of control at that point, and dead set on murder."

"And I was in total panic," Elissa said. "Later, a cop told me that bullets wearing *jackets* — which I can't imagine — would have gone right through Baker into you. *Oh my God!*"

Harper said, "Have no regrets. We were all lucky. Those hollow-point slugs dislocated Baker's shoulder, fractured his hip, and produced mild shock. But no permanent damage. Even so, do you know he wants you arrested? He said he rigged his gun for his self-defense. He never imagined any *woman* would take advantage of its light recoil and accuracy, and then turn his own gun against *him* — on offense yet."

Elissa rolled her eyes. "The irony of that is staggering."

"Especially as a third strike against him. Of course, the tapes proved we were the ones acting in defense," he said.

Gazing at Harper, Elissa said, "I'm still curious, though. Why did you want me to hide that gun? And then you fired your own last bullet at the couch?"

"Yes. I was reasonably certain I could hit that."

She gave him a puzzled look.

Harper explained, "Unlike you, I don't have a knack for instinctive shooting. If I had shot that bullet and missed, he could have charged right into me. So I needed to bluff him into believing I had enough ammo and skill to put him away.

"Also, when I compared both weapons, I saw his hollow-point rounds in the cylinder. And I realized that load, with long-barrel accuracy, would make his revolver a much better weapon for you. Just in case. And that's why I sent you to hide it, where only you could find it."

Elissa widened her eyes at him. "You are amazing — how you process so many contingencies in the middle of a crisis."

"I'm not half as amazing as you are," he said.

"Me? What did I do?"

"Starting with your ex-husband, then Baker and Carlisle, Norgan and Rogers, the Colorado Highway Patrolman and those three Desert Rats, I count nine guys who thought they were tough as railroad spikes. Then you came along, and they never even knew what hit them."

Elissa's jaw dropped. "Oh, wow! Do you realize what it means to me — hearing you say that? You'll make me *cry*."

"And that's another thing. With all your strengths, you are by far the most compassionate and affectionate woman I have ever heard of. How does Heaven manage without you?"

"Good Lord, now I *am* crying! And of course I'm *deeply* compassionate about the loss of your beloved home!"

"Please, don't feel awful about that — I don't."

She turned her head to see if he was remotely serious. His face looked calm. She said, "But it was such a distinctive and beautiful home. How can you *not* be devastated?"

He shrugged, leaned an elbow on the boulder and stared at the ruins. "That house didn't offer any happy memories after Heather died there. I lost interest after that."

Elissa turned away. She felt ocean breezes streaming through her hair and the sunlight warmth on her back. She said, "Can you tell me, someday — how it happened?"

"I'll tell you right now, if you wish."

She hesitated, then whispered, "Yes, if you don't mind — that is, if you're really *okay* with it."

Harper nodded, still staring at the ruins. "Donald Rogers told you most of everything that happened. However, he neglected to tell you how, and why..."

Elissa tilted her head, watching him closely, anxiously...

"It's true Heather came back one night to settle our dispute over this house. Half of it was hers, but I had no desire to sell it merely to divide the proceeds — not after spending years building it mostly with my own hands. She didn't want the house for herself, you see, and she didn't need the money. I couldn't understand why she was trying to force me out — so I invited her over here to talk about it."

Elissa nodded unhappily. She wasn't sure whether this was really any of her business. But Harper went on:

"That night, it was dark — like last night — and foggy. It was intensely quiet, and we talked quietly, and I told her I would be glad to buy her share of the house if she could just wait a few months. I had a large project bid underway, a sports arena in Santa Clara — and I had nearly finished constructing a display model of it. I brought her into the study and showed her the model — proof, I suppose, that I would earn a large enough commission to buy her share."

Harper lowered his head, scratched the silver-speckled hair at his temple.

"None of this satisfied her. Heather sometimes had a violent temper, tantrums that seemed to leap from nowhere. That night, she had been wavering between lightness and anger. When she realized I had meant what I had said, that I would buy her share of the house, she became... desperate. She said she didn't really care about the house or the money — she had wanted *me*. She had wanted me back with her in San Francisco, on her terms. She said Ed Kiening had met with her — that ABK also had wanted me to return and were prepared to offer a partnership."

Squinting at the bright sea, Harper picked up a small stone and tossed it from hand to hand.

"Heather had played games with me before, but this one seemed unreal. It was she who had instigated the divorce, while I had been contented. But what she had proposed was impossible. I told her I had absolutely no interest in returning to ABK — and if that was a condition for reconciliation, I had no interest in that, either." He tossed the stone.

"That was the moment she went out of control. She started smashing the model of the arena with her fists..."

Elissa leaned against him, imagining that violent scene with stark clarity — like so many ugly scenes with Patrick.

He said, "I had been landscaping the model with miniature trees — trees fashioned with bits of ground green foam attached to wire armatures. As she swept her hand through them, the wire must have cut her. I don't know if she thought I had hurt her while trying to stop her destruction, but she grabbed a scissors and stabbed me in the shoulder."

Elissa stiffened. "Oh, God — the scar on your shoulder."

"That's the one. A stubborn memento of that night. Of course, her blow wasn't strong enough for serious damage, but it dropped me to my knees. She went into a rage, throwing something that shattered the terrace door. She lifted the model, it weighed about forty pounds, and ran with it onto the terrace. I had just managed getting to my feet when I heard the scream, and then — much worse — the silence."

Elissa gazed into his eyes, saw them shining like the sea.

He said, "I stumbled outside. And the blood on the terrace, the blood Rogers told you about, was from her hand and from my shoulder. She was gone. I saw a few pieces of the model scattered near an outdoor lamppost. Then I realized what had happened."

Elissa drew a breath, waiting.

"During our separation, I installed a lamppost on the terrace. She hadn't known it was there. In darkness and fog, intent on throwing the model over the cliff, she bumped into that lamppost and was startled. She spun around, and with the heavy model in her arms... she went over the wall. There's no other conceivable way it could have happened."

"Dear God."

Harper said, "It was the kind of insane accident that could not have happened without a peculiar combination of circumstances — Heather's state of mind, her furious distraction with the model... The lamppost was new — I hadn't even wired it yet. There was the fog, and it was so dark...

"Even so, she had to career against the wall in a certain way, so that her momentum and the weight of the model would carry her over — too suddenly to drop the model and grab something. The whole thing was — from any point of common sense or understanding — ridiculously tragic."

Elissa recalled the liquor in Harper's cabinet, wondered if he had kept it for Heather and if she had an addiction. Had he also sensed a similar need in Elissa? The thought caused her to tremble. She resolved to erase the question.

"There was an autopsy," Harper said. "A detailed one, because police were investigating. In the process, the pathologists discovered an aneurysm in Heather's brain. She had been prone to migraines, and neither of us had a hint that anything more serious was going on. I had thought her tantrums were from her upbringing — spoiled by her father, that sort of thing. The possibility that her mental state was linked to a medical catastrophe had never occurred to me."

After a long moment, he said, "But it created more than enough reasonable doubt — among the investigators and the district attorney's office — to preclude them from filing any official charges against me. "

"That should have given you immense relief," Elissa said.

"Nonetheless, I remained haunted by a fear that I had indeed caused her death — with inexcusable negligence."

"Oh, Grey — don't say that. Don't even *think* that."

He faced Elissa squarely. "It's another reason I avoided shooting Baker. I've been bothered for years over a death, for which I felt marginally responsible. So how could I live with anyone else's death — if I had deliberately caused it?"

"Grey, you must not let yourself feel that way!"

"Well... I don't, Elissa. Not anymore. While Baker was trying to throw me over that wall, I discovered there was a big difference between my self-inflicted concept of murder and his. He literally scared Heather's ghost out of me."

Elissa, hearing this, felt her lungs fill with air. *Thank God!*

Then after a long silence, broken only by the whoosh of the surf, she said, "Grey, I have a confession. After Baker shut me in your bedroom, I... went exploring... and I peeked into Heather's closet."

Harper nodded. "All her things are still there. Or were. That's another problem the fire eradicated."

"But... why, Grey? Why did you keep them?"

"I didn't know what to do with them. I dreaded going through everything, recalling her scent and how the clothes had looked on her — in contrast to what she had looked and smelled like when I had to identify her body..." He flipped a hand. "So I left it all. And I focused entirely on my work. As you know, I didn't even allow time to see a movie."

"Oh my God!" Elissa grabbed his hands. "And I mocked you for that! I am so sorry! I didn't realize! You poor man!"

He gave her a complaisant smile. "Well, that's all in the past. Now you're here, and it's... well, like your sunshine has broken through my overcast." He looked at her sheepishly.

She rolled her eyes mockingly, then tilted her face to the sky and smiled from all the sunshine she felt inside.

He touched her cheek. "Seriously, no other woman like you has ever existed, not in my universe. When you say words of love to me, it's with a tenderness that radiates from your core. I can't believe how lucky I am to know you. It's more than luck, in fact. It's a miracle."

"Darling, you're sending me to heaven before I'm ready for it! Don't. I'm not an angel and cannot ever be."

"You're not giving yourself enough credit. Remember the orange swivel chair in the living room, where you sat last night? It doesn't fit the overall house, but it was Heather's choice. It set off her blonde hair, and she used it as a throne whenever we entertained, swiveling from guest to guest."

He looked vaguely at the ocean. "There were times after her death when I crossed the room in stormy weather to shut the terrace doors. In the darkness, I sensed something and turned — and there she was, in her chair, staring at me."

A frightful look swept Elissa's eyes. "Oh, no."

"Those were illusions, of course, but then I watched you settle into that chair last night. And later, as we fled the fire, I looked back. The chair was empty. And the lasting image I will have for that chair is all you, with those wonderful legs."

Elissa turned away. "I don't know what to say. I can't fault you for admiring my legs in that context, can I?"

"We're well past mere flirtation, I think," Harper said.

"I agree. Isn't it marvelous?" Elissa sighed.

After a moment of contemplation, she said, "Then allow me one more troubling question... Are you afraid of me?"

Harper drew back a bit. "*Awed*, absolutely. But *afraid?* What prompts that question?"

She crossed her arms. "When we made love, you were rather passive. You allowed me on top; you let me lead. And before that, when I asked you for a razor and asked you not to ask about it, you didn't ask. And there are other things. Considering how bold you are about everything else, I keep wondering... *why* are you so, well, considerate with me?"

"Timid, you mean. On the razor, I simply surmised the purpose. The brevity of your bikini bottom confirmed it."

Her brows lifted. "Really! Well, Patrick would have made some slimy deal over it. He would have wanted to watch, or supervise, or shoot video. But you, the perfect gentleman, demonstrated your complete respect for my privacy, and you always have. It's those little things that count for so much but are so rare. How do you happen to be so different?"

"I suppose there's a reason, but it might disturb you."

"Disturb me? But how?"

He shrugged. "It goes back to when I was a boy, eight or ten years old, on my grandfather's farm in Wisconsin."

"Hmm. This sounds deep. But.. I'm sorry, go ahead."

"There was a little rabbit, wounded somehow and bleeding. I went after it, but Granddad called out to stop me. He said I'd scare the rabbit and cause it further injury. 'Never chase a wounded animal,' he said. 'Let it come to you.'"

"You mean... you've been thinking of me, all along, as... *Good heavens!* A wounded little *bunny rabbit?*"

He nodded. "I had been so deeply moved by your story, Elissa. Especially your need for a courage ring. You wear it day and night." He tapped her ring and smiled. "Then, one night, you proved yourself entirely capable — Miss *Lioness.*"

"Ah." She peered at him. "And this transformation from a little bunny to a horny lioness caught you by surprise?"

"Not really. Your courage was never a doubt in my mind — although perhaps it was in yours, judging by that ring."

"I never thought of it that way." She hesitated. "But I had been aware of how I was falling in love with you — and I was *stymied* by your stubborn restraint in our relationship!"

"The restraint seemed proper at the time," Harper said.

"Proper is one thing. Being stubborn about it is another. I had not even a *hint* of how you felt about me!"

"What did you expect? You firmly *resisted* all my hints!"

"No, I resisted *flirting*, which I had associated with pain."

"I could never have known that, from that *look* of yours."

"What *look?* What in the world are you talking about?"

Harper sighed. "The first time I ever saw you, your eyes drilled mine with such *intensity*, you nearly set me on fire."

"I *did?* I can't imagine... unless... as I think back... there was a moment when our eyes first met, and I started fantasizing about you in my bed! *Oh God*, that is so embarrassing!"

Harper said, "Despite all your marital hardships, your allure tends to be overpowering. Perhaps unconsciously?"

"I generally know when I'm using allure and when not."

"Ah — for example, your Estes Park shopping spree?"

"God yes! That was like putting up a billboard! I couldn't help it. You and I were sharing that honeymoon-style lodge, you drew that *beautiful* sketch, you were telling me about your career, even your *philosophy*... and I destroyed that beautiful day with some ghastly remark concerning Heather. Well, I had to recover. And the debutante response to stress is to dress. I wasn't only parading a drop-dead wardrobe in front of you, Grey. I was putting my whole *self* on display."

He said, "I very much appreciated both exhibits."

"It was totally shameless. I wanted to get a rise out of you that I could then pretend to dismiss. Strategically, it would put us back on equal footing, you see. It's just one of those little schemes women deploy as a first line of defense in a world where men call the shots... as my ex-husband had so literally pounded into my head." She knuckled her brow.

"Of course, I botched it further by getting giddy and then morose in that lovely Estes Park restaurant. Even now... am I not embarrassing you with all these revelations?"

"Not at all," Harper said. "Elissa, that restaurant scene was the first time you exposed your complete trust in me — and I realized I could trust you in return. As I told you then, you botched nothing. Instead, you gave me immense relief."

She smiled. "I did trust you. In fact I gushed all over you and thought it was the wine." Elissa placed a hand on his thigh. "But Grey, was your *relief* as big as I gave you in bed?"

And she gave him *that look*.

"Whoa! Stop *doing* that! I haven't even had breakfast."

"Aha! You *are* afraid of me. Do you suspect... witchcraft?"

"Just like the song," he said. "Am I getting a message that you wouldn't mind if I were more aggressive in bed?"

"I... no. I wondered why you weren't, but because of my history, I might've had a flashback and fainted." She gave him an engaging smile, and added, "But now I do trust you, and I love you, and it's probably okay to play rough — as long as it's play. I do enjoy acting, you know."

"And I admire your performances," he said.

"And don't overlook rehearsals," she said. "That's when actors try everything."

Harper watched with interest as her eyes wandered out to sea, and he wondered what next was on her mind...

And then she said, "Did the bunny rabbit come to you?"

He winced. "It started to. But it was too late."

"Oh, that's so sad!"

He flipped a hand. "Now I'm sorry I told you."

"Don't be sorry. Your grandfather was a wise man, a true gentleman. Perhaps that's why you're a gentle man, and you make me feel safer than I've ever felt. It's like... escaping a dungeon to soar in the clouds! Now, how's that metaphor?"

"Probably better than mine." He pulled her against him, and with her breasts, in that cashmere, making soft contact with his arm, she stroked the speckled hair at the side of his head. "And here you are, Grey, suddenly facing a whole new beginning. Have you even considered where you will live?"

He said, "Where do *you* want to live?"

She sat upright. "Is that a *factor* for you?"

His slapped his forehead. It *most certainly is, Mrs. Pope*. It is a *considerable* factor!"

"Oh, Lord! There we go with Mrs. Pope again." She gazed longingly at him. "Grey, how long have we actually known each other? How many days have we been together?"

"I don't know; I've lost count. Nearly a week, I guess."

She said, "In that ridiculously brief time, what are you thinking? Are you suggesting that I share a place with you?"

"We've sort of formed that habit, haven't we? I was starting to feel like we were married."

"You, *too?* Wow." She was entranced, her eyes distant. "All those miles beside you in the car, the togetherness... I sometimes dreamed of us as an old married couple." She clutched her hands in her lap and lifted her shoulders. She faced him. "But Grey — you haven't said... that word."

"Elissa, I have... *loved* you from the moment we met."

Eyes wide with gladness, she said, "You *have?* You clown! Why in heck did you never say so! I'd been dying to hear it!"

"As I've said, it was tough just giving you a compliment."

"Oh, pooh! That's no excuse! If a man *loves* a woman, he must tell her immediately, before another man grabs her."

"I did offer to marry you."

"Yeah, in Iowa. I thought you were kidding."

"I said I wasn't kidding."

"I didn't know you well enough to know that."

"It's a few days later. *Now* do you know me well enough?"

"Oh, I do, I really, really do," she said, her body shaking. "But don't you ever stop teaching me."

She shifted to a soulful posture and said, "Please realize, I'd been engaged to Patrick more than a year, had known him years before that, and our marriage was a *disaster*. I've known you since last Tuesday. And I've got to wonder. Is *this* a dream? Am I a fool? A freak? A lost lamb? How can I be sure another marriage won't be another disaster?"

Harper hesitated; then he said, "We've done disasters. I think we're ready for something else."

Her gaze went out to sea. Her eyes began glistening.

He said, "I pledge not to hound you with compliments."

"Oh Jeez!" She tossed her hands. "My aversion... my *fear* of compliments... that was all Patrick's doing. Thank *God* that's over! From now on, my darling, compliments are okay. In fact they're required. Plus hugs and kisses" — she smacked a kiss to his lips — "and of course, regular sexy shenanigans."

"I can't imagine any difficulty over that," he said.

"Excellent, because... I cannot help *loving* you! I love you with all my mind, all my heart! My *soul!*" She embraced his shoulders, went nose to nose and stared into his eyes. "And what is the word you say to all that?"

He said, "Elissa, I love you." He kissed her nose.

She sighed. "That's so tender. God, I am so happy."

Breathing deeply, feeling fresh and exuberant, she said, "Okay. Let's turn to business, my love. What comes next?"

"Well. The Fort Sheridan project is dead. This morning, the corporation and the lawyers and government and law enforcement and military have decided none of them know anything, and the men who did know, are all dead. Baker will be hospitalized and charged with vandalism until they figure him out. As a result, except for alerting soldiers who may be harmed, nothing can be done until there's a thorough study or two or more, for which there's no available funding in the foreseeable future. And I'm out of a house and out of a job."

"Oh, hell. I think that's awful," Elissa said.

"Why? I'm free. I surely won't have trouble selling this property for enough to satisfy all obligations, including your American Express account. As a matter of fact, since I can travel freely again, it might be a terrific time to reunite you with your mother in Florida, her new husband, and your father in Italy. We could all travel together. I'd ask your father for his blessing on our marriage, and he'd walk you down the aisle. We might even arrange a romantic church wedding, Italian style. And this time it would be for all time."

Suddenly emotional, Elissa felt tears pouring from her eyes. Her hand went to her heart, feeling it pounding, her breath in gasps. "Oh, Lord, Grey! You can really knock a girl off her feet! That's how I feel, like *a girl* again!" She sobbed.

Concerned, he said, "What have I said or done wrong?"

Her head came up. "I told you earlier, how I'm apt to cry over anything. But *this* isn't *that*. This is *real!* It's a *beautiful* gesture — way past anything that's ever been said to me. It is just like when I was a little girl and the whole world was so bright and shiny and safe. You just brought it all back to me! I can't believe it! Can you really make it all come true?"

"Sure I can. Are you ready for it?"

Elissa wrapped her arms around herself and shook. "I'll have to adjust to the idea — but *yes*. I will muster up more courage. Despite our differences, I never wanted my parents to live without my love. I am so grateful to you! I'm excited!"

She stopped hugging herself and hugged Harper. "Grey," she said, gazing into his eyes, "what planet are you from?"

"I beg your pardon?"

"You really are a good *listener* to everything I ever told you. Men like that are not native to this earth."

He laughed. "Then come with me to *explore* this earth."

"But that's going to be awfully expensive, and I wasted so much money on clothes! I could kick myself in the ass."

Harper said, "*I* didn't consider those clothes a waste!"

"But you won't collect fire insurance, if ever, or sell the land, for months — or years! Can we *afford* your suggestion?"

"Yes. Actually, I can and you can."

Elissa was puzzled. "I... well, maybe if I sold my Volvo..."

"Keep the Volvo. Buy two if you like."

"Are you crazy?" She plopped her fists on her knees. "Why are you talking to me like that?"

He gathered her fists in his hands. "Listen. Heather was the sole heir to a substantial portfolio, which by law became mine after she died. The problem is, I didn't want it. Like her closet, I didn't know what to do with it. Now I do know. I'm giving it to you. All of it."

Elissa pulled both hands from his grasp and stood. "Oh, no, Grey! You mustn't do that!"

"I already have. It won't make you *royally* rich, but it will provide the kind of life you thought you achieved in Lake Forest, before it went sour. By the same token, under the circumstances of Heather's death, I need her money to go to someone who really deserves it. And that's you. I also know Heather had the kind of sensibility to approve."

"But it's way too much... for so little..."

"Elissa. You financed our entire escapade with your Gold Card! You said yourself, four eyes were better than two. You risked your own life to save mine! You *earned* the portfolio."

"I didn't save either of us. We both did. But you say you've already arranged everything? When? How? Where?"

"In Estes Park. I made the decision after our dinner. The next morning, when I went to the lobby for your breakfast, I used the lodge's stationery and mailed instructions to Abe Jacobs, Heather's lawyer. I had your business card in my wallet — not a good place for it then; so I enclosed the card with the letter. Abe has all the information about Heather and me on file, including my signature, from finalizing our divorce. He's one of the *great* lawyers. I liked him better than my own lawyer. Anyway, I verified with him this morning. With no one to object, it's a done deal."

Elissa wiped more tears away. "You once said you were going to name me in your will. Is that why you did this?"

"No. This comes from Heather. As I've explained."

"Then I don't know what to say," she said.

"Say yes to the portfolio. Yes to the marriage. Yes to the Italian wedding and the reuniting of your family. Yes to life with me. Keep in mind, none of it is a prenup. The portfolio is yours regardless."

"But I can't ever have you wondering if I married you for money. I hate it when money is involved."

"I know that, Elissa. That's exactly why matrimony is not even a contingent. You threw away a larger fortune than this because you couldn't stand being married to it. This one has no strings at all."

"Except my love?" she said.

"Except *my* love for *you*. And my devotion."

"Devotion," she said. "That is the kindest love of all."

"That's why I said it. And I mean it."

"Dear Lord. And you arranged all this one morning from Estes Park. Wasn't it the same morning when you doctored those license plates and repaired the heel of my pump?"

"Yes, it was."

"For God's sakes, Grey! Whatever time did you get up?"

"I never went to bed. To avoid waking you, I hammered the plates inside the car under interior lights. I didn't care if it was late. It was mostly your turn to drive that next day."

Elissa said nothing. She appeared lost in thought.

Harper said, "If something else bothers you, I'm here."

Elissa wiped her wrist across her cheeks. She said, "I've kept no secrets from you. Not one. I would prefer the same trust from you, our mutual trust always, on everything, or..."

He stood and touched a finger to her lips. "Or how could you trust *me* if I'm not completely open with you? I understand, and I fully agree, Elissa."

"You do? That's all I ask, Grey. It means a lot."

"I know. But all week, I strived to avoid implicating you in my affairs, as I would by confiding in you. If the FBI were to arrest you, they could interpret your intimate knowledge of me as evidence you were my accomplice. I behaved like a lone wolf to protect you from that... until Lake Tahoe."

She stared at him. "Wow. How did I fail to see all that? It explains it all! But from now on? Please don't hold back. I am your most *dedicated* accomplice. Do you understand?"

He gathered her in his arms. "I most certainly do."

Pulling back, Elissa fluttered her fingers and said, "Now, with all your planning, all these revelations, have you had even one minute to consider, finally, where we might live?"

"In fact — yes," he said. "How about Estes Park, where those rocks resemble sleeping elephants?"

She sat down on the boulder. "You've got to be kidding! That's *whopper number three!* You do mean that truly elegant house you sketched for me? That house I fell *totally* in love with? Do you actually want to build it? *For us?*"

He sat beside her. "We don't know if the land's available. But you know real estate. You'll arrange something. Of course, you'd also want to know if Estes Park has room for another broker, and if they have a summer theatre..."

"They do! I know they do! If they don't, I'll start one! And by the way, can you dance? Like at a wedding?"

"The last time was at my wedding with Heather."

"Oh." She slowly closed her eyes. "Wow."

He said, "That means I'm rusty. But if you teach me, I'll try my best to dance properly with you for our wedding."

"Gosh, yes! But forget 'properly.' I want passionately."

"Any way you wish."

She gathered his hands in hers. "Can you believe it's less than thirty-six hours since we made love for the first time? So much has happened. And we're on the brink of a whole new beginning... as the *two of us*. I'm floating!"

"One problem," he said.

"Now what?"

"There is a small problem about building the house."

"Oh no. Really?"

He said, "I don't know if I remember everything in that sketch. Maybe... if we sat in the same place, recalling the same moments, I might have a similar vision. I don't know."

Elissa twisted around and capped her hands over her knees and gazed urgently into his eyes. "Don't you recall at least some of your sketch?"

"Too much has happened since then. And it's unlikely we'll find the sketch in those ruins. I'm sorry."

She said, "Darling. Stick your hand inside my bra."

"Umm... Does this have something to do with... what?"

"Just do it!"

He diligently obeyed... and slowly, carefully felt between her warm breasts and gently extracted — *his sketch*, folded meticulously and richly scented with her fragrance.

Elissa's New Home.

"You've become *very* closely attached to this," he said.

"During Baker's attack, I fought to protect that sketch more than myself. It's a precious piece of your creativity! And you're more than a fine architect, a terrific friend and lover, even more than a future husband! And I'd *love* to make more little guys like you, because... Grey, you are a *Godsend!*"

Smiling, he asked, "Are you serious about children?"

"I am serious. If that's even possible. But is it? I..."

He said, "Do you know, Doris Day lives here in Carmel? Long ago, she sang a hit song called *Que Sera, Sera*."

Elissa smiled. "Italian: *Whatever will be, will be*. I agree."

She tugged the onyx courage ring from her finger, gazed out to sea. "With such faith and trust, who needs this?" She *vigorously* threw the ring far beyond the cliff. "And there goes my obsession. I just hope a seagull doesn't choke on it."

His eyes glowed with admiration. "I'm so proud of you!"

With a shy smile, she gazed at her bare hand and said, "Oh look, Darling! I now have enough space on my fingers for a truly grand engagement set. Don't you think so?"

He said, "Yes, I see that. Would you like to go shopping together right now? We have many fine stores in Carmel."

"That is such a lovely thought, Darling... But only after I take care of some more important business!"

"Oh? And what could be more important now?"

"First, you have already replaced that courage ring many times over. So before anything takes its place, I *must* have at least fifteen minutes to offer you... my deepest gratitude!"

"Oh, well, if you must..." he said. "And second?"

"Don't forget what I once said about your Rolex."

For at least fifteen minutes, the Pacific Ocean heaved up great slabs of surf and threw them against the rocks, while on the cliff high above, two earnest people also made waves.

Beneath nearby cypress trees, a silver Mercedes waited for them to come.

(!)

THE AUTHOR:

DAVID EMIL HENDERSON began his journalism career in 1960s magazines, when he wrote exclusive interviews with Henry Fonda, Barbra Streisand, Robert Preston, Charlton Heston, and other stars, along with a range of news and features. As editor for a Chicago suburban newspaper chain owned by Time, Inc., he directed the news content of *The Evanston Review*, chosen by the American Newspaper Publishers Association (Newspaper Association of America) as First in the Nation for General Excellence. Later, as editor and publisher of a Montana newspaper, he won that press association's top statewide awards for editorial writing, column writing, feature stories, and news reports. In California, he created national print and video marketing programs for nine San Francisco Bay Area daily newspapers, including those owned by Gannett, The Tribune Company, Media News Group, and The New York Times. He now owns a long-established publishing enterprise in Northern California, where he is partnered with his wife.

During his journalism career, Henderson also practiced residential and commercial Architectural Design, designing and building new and remodeled structures in Illinois, Montana, Wyoming, and California.

His first novel, *Montana Midnight*, captures the humor and strife of a town caught between environmental militants and corporate kingpins.

Are you interested in sequels to this book?

Send an email to David Emil Henderson at pinetreearts@gmail.com
Your input will help decide any future exploits of Elissa and Grey Harper.

Author Footnotes

Radon's health hazards are not widely reported, but the U.S. Environmental Protection Agency estimates radon exposure in American homes is responsible for 20,000 lung cancer deaths each year. A simple radon test kit as used by Grey Harper in this story would reduce those fatalities considerably.

•

The Chicago Tribune deadline mentioned in Chapter 11 is not applicable to current news cycles.

Made in the USA
Lexington, KY
01 August 2014